CHANGING SEASONS FOR THE COUNTRY NURSE

KATE EASTHAM

B
Boldwood

First published in Great Britain in 2025 by Boldwood Books Ltd.

Copyright © Kate Eastham, 2025

Cover Design by Colin Thomas

Cover Images: Colin Thomas and iStock

The moral right of Kate Eastham to be identified as the author of this work has been asserted in accordance with the Copyright, Designs and Patents Act 1988.

All rights reserved. No part of this book may be reproduced in any form or by any electronic or mechanical means, including information storage and retrieval systems, without written permission from the author, except for the use of brief quotations in a book review. This book is a work of fiction and, except in the case of historical fact, any resemblance to actual persons, living or dead, is purely coincidental.

Every effort has been made to obtain the necessary permissions with reference to copyright material, both illustrative and quoted. We apologise for any omissions in this respect and will be pleased to make the appropriate acknowledgements in any future edition.

A CIP catalogue record for this book is available from the British Library.

Paperback ISBN 978-1-83656-216-0

Large Print ISBN 978-1-83656-217-7

Hardback ISBN 978-1-83656-215-3

Ebook ISBN 978-1-83656-218-4

Kindle ISBN 978-1-83656-219-1

Audio CD ISBN 978-1-83656-210-8

MP3 CD ISBN 978-1-83656-214-6

Digital audio download ISBN 978-1-83656-212-2

This book is printed on certified sustainable paper. Boldwood Books is dedicated to putting sustainability at the heart of our business. For more information please visit https://www.boldwoodbooks.com/about-us/sustainability/

Boldwood Books Ltd, 23 Bowerdean Street, London, SW6 3TN

www.boldwoodbooks.com

For Ann Hall (1936-2023)

'Live life when you have it. Life is a splendid gift – there is nothing small about it.'

— FLORENCE NIGHTINGALE

1

INGLESIDE SURGERY, LANCASHIRE, LATE SEPTEMBER 1936

A high-pitched voice holding the edge of a scream woke Lara instantly and she shot bolt-upright in bed. Not knowing if someone had just yelled her name or she'd woken from a nightmare, she strained her ears above the pounding of her heart. Instantly she recalled the ghost story her nurse colleague Marion had told her when they'd felt that first nip of autumn air. Her skin prickled at the thought of the cloaked figure – a tragic young woman who'd lived in this house before it had become a doctor's surgery. Fully aware she wasn't usually prone to imaginings, right now, she sensed a charged atmosphere in the room, and a shiver flashed through her. Instantly she pulled the bedclothes tightly around her body.

But, when a bloodcurdling cry of 'Nurse Flynn!' came from downstairs, she knew right away that whatever had woken her was firmly rooted in this world. It was Mrs Hewitt; the village practice housekeeper and she sounded very agitated. Fearing a horrible incident with a carving knife or an armed robber in the house, Lara jumped out of bed, ran full pelt to her door then down the broad, red-carpeted staircase with her white cotton nightdress clinging to her legs. Gasping as she felt the cold tiles of the corridor under her bare feet, she hurtled towards the kitchen. Her heart lurched at the thought of what she might find. But she was a trained nurse, so, in an emergency, she ran straight towards it.

In through the door, she paused for a second, rapidly assessing the situation. Mrs Hewitt stood on the opposite side of the clean-scrubbed kitchen table, her breath coming quick. She glanced sharply to Lara and, in the early morning light, she appeared white-faced, frozen between the kitchen table and the Aga with a heavy frying pan raised in one hand.

'Mrs H?' Lara called gently.

The housekeeper shot her a wide-eyed glance then pressed a finger to her lips. Then, almost immediately, she screamed, dropped the pan with a loud clatter, dragged a wooden chair out from the kitchen table and jumped up onto it. Standing aloft as she scanned the stone-flagged floor, she glanced back to Lara and croaked, 'It's a mouse. A big fat mouse.'

Lara blew out a breath, relief flooding through her – there were no intruders, no ghosts. And she'd never been afraid of mice or rats, a good thing since they'd been regular visitors to the nurses' home where she'd lived in Liverpool. For her, it hadn't been a problem, in fact she'd been intrigued by the tiny grey-brown creatures. But many of the other nurses, including her friends Fiona and Maeve, had been terrified of the mice with their nibbling and nest-building.

'Don't worry, Mrs H, I can deal with this,' Lara called to her.

'I hope so,' the housekeeper groaned, wobbling slightly on the chair. Then she pointed to a place between a wooden cupboard and the Aga and whispered, 'It ran down there.'

'Alright, that's good,' Lara breathed as she walked slowly,

silently, on bare feet across the kitchen. 'I'll see if I can locate it then I'll shoosh it towards the back door.'

'I'd rather you kill the thing,' the housekeeper gulped. 'I can't stand the thought of it scurrying about, nibbling the food.'

Lara knew instantly she wasn't a person who could kill a tiny mouse, but she didn't want to further unsettle Mrs Hewitt by telling her so.

'So, where exactly did you last see it?'

'Right there, near your left foot.'

The moment she glanced down she saw the tiny creature with its pointy nose and little ears and instantly it ran over her bare foot. As Mrs Hewitt screamed and wobbled on her kitchen chair, Lara grabbed a long-handled brush and chased after it towards the open back door. Out it went and relief surged through her.

'Are you sure it's gone?' the housekeeper asked tentatively, as she pressed the flat of her hand to her chest.

'Most definitely,' Lara replied, holding out a hand to steady the older woman as she clambered down. But the chair slipped and tipped, clattering to the stone-flagged floor.

She had the housekeeper firmly held, so no damage done.

Mrs Hewitt's expression softened to relief, then she straightened her apron, brushed a strand of black hair from her cheek. 'Thank you, Nurse Flynn. I knew you'd be the right person for the job. I'd have been hard-pressed waking your colleague Nurse Wright because she sleeps like a log, and I'd never even consider trying to wake Angus – young doctors like him who spend too much time in the pub are notoriously hard to rouse. And it goes without saying Dr Bingham would not have appreciated his strict morning routine being disrupted.'

'That's fine, I'm happy to help.' She smiled, suddenly aware of her flimsy cotton nightgown and bare feet.

'Strewth!' shouted the housekeeper, two spots of bright pink flushing her pale cheeks. 'What time is it? I need to get Henry's—I mean Dr Bingham's—breakfast ready.'

Lara glanced to the clock. 'It's 7 a.m. Do you have enough time? Do you need me to—'

'What the blazes is going on? I heard a loud bang,' a gruff voice called from the doorway.

Horrified, realising she was still in her nightdress, Lara turned to see Henry Bingham, the senior doctor, his greying hair fluffed up and messy from sleep. But, worst of all, he too was still in his nightclothes. It made him seem taller and even more daunting, and the sight of his thin legs poking from his blue-striped nightshirt felt very unsettling. But he was blocking the door so there was absolutely nothing she could do but stay exactly where she was and hold a conversation. So, as Mrs Hewitt hurried off to continue her breakfast preparations, Lara rapidly explained the situation with the mouse. Bingham nodded his head as he listened, and it didn't seem to concern him at all that they were holding this conversation in their nightclothes. When she'd finished her description of events, he muttered, 'They're a blasted nuisance those mice but at least it's not rats this time... Then again, where there's one mouse there's usually more, so I'll have a word with Septimus Finch, the ratcatcher. He'll come and sort it for us.'

'I'd be very glad of that,' Mrs Hewitt called as she walked briskly from the pantry carrying a side of bacon and a tray of eggs. Then, once she had the items set down, she gestured with her bread knife to Lara. 'I appreciate you coming to my aid this morning, Nurse Flynn. But you get yourself back upstairs and, as soon as you're down, I'll have your favourite porridge with a swirl of cream and a sprinkle of sugar ready and waiting for you.'

'Thank you, Mrs H,' Lara replied, already feeling a giggle rising from her belly as she passed by Dr Bingham in his bare feet and nightshirt. She swallowed hard to contain it and swore to herself that she wouldn't tell her colleague Marion about the senior doctor in his nightclothes because she'd take the story and tell it so loudly to Angus that Bingham would be bound to hear. No, she'd keep it to herself.

But, even before she was halfway up the red-carpeted stairs, she felt that tickle of amusement building and knew she had no choice but to tap on Marion's door and spill the whole lot.

'No way,' Marion hissed as she stood bleary-eyed in her pink polka-dot pyjamas, her dark curly hair lopsided as it grew out from the head injury she'd sustained in a motorcycle accident during the summer.

Marion began to chuckle, then she clapped a hand over her mouth, grabbed Lara and pulled her into the room. Instantly, Lara felt a bubble of laughter rising in her chest, quickly turning to guffaws, unstoppable. They were clinging to each other, and Lara felt as if she couldn't breathe as she fought to contain it.

Still giggling, Marion said, 'All the years I've worked here, I've never seen Bingham in his nightshirt. And you've only been here a few months.'

'Exactly, why did it have to be me?'

It set them both off with another fit of giggles and Marion was sitting at the side of her bed now, doubled over. 'I swear this place, this job... you'd think it'd be all serene working out here in this grand house in the countryside but it's just ridiculous. I mean, how many times when you were in the hospital did you see one of the senior doctors in his nightclothes?'

'I know.' Lara chuckled. 'Especially a nightshirt with his thin legs...'

Marion clamped a hand over her mouth again and reached

to grab her hand. 'It's a good job this surgery was built with thick stone walls so none of our patients can hear what's going on.'

'True,' Lara breathed, and that was probably why, despite the opposition she'd faced as a city girl out here in a country practice, she'd felt secure inside this solid stone building right from the start. Yes, she could hear noise from the village in the early mornings as workers set out in their clogs for Ingleside sawmill or the cotton mills in Ridgetown. And the church bell sounded on the hour every hour. But, when she lay in her bed listening to the night-time hooting of owls or the early morning chorus of the swallows waking from their roosting to swoop outside her window, it made her feel part of the fabric of this place, even though she was still viewed by some locals as very much an outsider.

'I'll see you in the kitchen before you go out on your visits,' she called gently to Marion who sat quietly now at the side of her bed.

'Righto.' Her colleague smiled, with that certain faraway look in her eyes that alerted Lara to what felt like Marion's buried thoughts and feelings. Not just since the motorcycle accident, this was something she'd noted in the summer during her first few weeks at the surgery. So Lara asked gently, 'Are you doing alright back out on your visits? It's good to see you riding your motorcycle again but maybe you should have taken a bit more time to recover?'

Marion seemed to force a smile. 'No, honestly, I am absolutely fine.' Then she rubbed her tousled head in the place where her hair was growing back. 'My cracked skull is all healed up now... And the fractured wrist still aches a bit, but it feels stronger than ever.'

'Well, I wasn't thinking so much about your physical healing, but what's going on up here.' Lara tapped her forehead as she gently scrutinised her friend's face for a reaction.

Quickly, too quickly, Marion was standing up from the bed. 'My head's always been a bit of a mess, so nothing new there,' she said, seeming to force a laugh, then she reached out to give Lara a hug. 'Now off you pop to your early morning rituals while I get on with having another half hour in bed.'

It felt as if the door had been closed yet again on Lara finding out exactly what was troubling Marion, so there was no choice but to withdraw. 'OK, I'll see you downstairs,' she said. 'But please, Marion, if you ever need to talk about anything… I'm a good listener and I can keep a confidence.'

'I know you are, and thank you for that.' Marion sighed, and there it was again, that niggling flash of pain in her friend's eyes.

As Lara walked back along the corridor to her room, she wondered if she should tell Marion her own story and explain the reasons why she'd chosen to leave behind all she knew in the city to come out here. Maybe it would help her colleague to know that she'd also had an accident while she'd been out on visits, and she'd spent many weeks in the Liverpool Royal Infirmary as a result. She'd confided in Mrs Hewitt, but she hadn't told anyone else here because the telling of it brought it back. And she still felt annoyed with herself because it was all tied up with an ill-fated relationship with Patrick – a man she should have realised much earlier was a fake and a cheat. The truth had come at her abruptly the day she'd spotted him leaving the Adelphi hotel with another woman. She'd confronted him then and dealt with the situation, but, as she'd cycled back into heavy traffic, she'd collided with a van and sustained a head injury. After she'd recovered, she'd needed to get away from the busy Liverpool streets and that's why she'd applied for a position as a country nurse.

She had no regrets about Patrick, she didn't even think of him, her only niggle was that she hadn't returned the emerald and diamond necklace he'd gifted her. But when she'd heard that he'd turned up at the hospital as she lay unconscious and tried to persuade her friend Fiona to find the necklace and give it back to him, she'd felt justified in holding on to it for a while longer. But, now, she needed it gone. So, before the darker, colder weather came, she'd take a trip back to Liverpool to return the necklace and draw a strong line under that episode of her life.

Lara wasn't fully settled here; it would take more time to adjust to the different style of working, especially in such a tight-knit community where her every move was scrutinised. And she'd learned the hard way in the summer that, if a patient or a relative had an issue with a nurse, it spread like wildfire. Things had come to a head when Vic Taylor, the father of a child she'd been attending, had wrongly accused her of neglectful practice, and it had riled some of the locals until the truth came out. But that didn't mean things were now plain sailing; she was still snubbed by some and, even if it wasn't outright, she sensed whispers of underlying opposition. She wasn't sure she'd stay out here long term, but she'd promised herself she'd give it at least one full year before even considering going back to Liverpool or heading off to New York to join Maeve at the Belle Vue hospital.

And now, as the nights grew darker and the colder, wetter weather came at her, she knew her work would be even more challenging. But this place had got under her skin from the first day, when she'd been required to attend an emergency call. As she'd cycled along the country lanes with the dramatic sweep of the fells in the distance, and the seemingly endless countryside with its wildflowers and trees, she'd fallen in love.

She drew a sharp breath then, recognising there was another reason she *had* to stay on. There was absolutely no way she could miss the upcoming Harvest Ball hosted by Lord and Lady Harrington at Ingleside Hall. Marion had been beside herself with joy for weeks and a big part of that was the fact that Lara would be accompanying her. She couldn't even contemplate letting Marion down; they'd clicked from her first proper day, when Lara had ridden pillion on the back of Gloria, her colleague's Norton motorcycle.

Lara smiled to herself when she recalled how she'd had to hoick up her uniform to get on the motorbike and she'd clamped a hand over her district nurse's hat to stop it blowing off. She'd been petrified at first as they'd sped along the narrow country lanes, with hedges and drystone walls whizzing by. But, even before they'd arrived at their first visit to a farm at the foot of the fells, she'd begun to enjoy the warm breeze on her face and the reassuring solidity of Marion in the driving seat.

2

Even though Lara's morning had been disrupted by that mouse, she was still first down to breakfast. And, as she sat alone quietly eating her sugar-sprinkled porridge, Mrs Hewitt mixed a spicy fruit cake in her earthenware baking bowl. Beyond her reply to the housekeeper's initial greeting, no words had been spoken because, even in her first week, she'd established an easy rapport with Mrs Hewitt. Maybe it had something to do with the chats around the kitchen table with a glass of sherry the women had after Dr Bingham had retreated to his quarters and Angus had dodged out for a pint to the Fleece across the road or the Old Oak down the hill. Again, even though it was still early days for her here, she felt a real closeness with the housekeeper and Marion, and even sometimes with Angus. But Dr Bingham was tricky, his moods could switch and change like the squally weather that descended out of nowhere to swirl around the fells.

When Tiddles the brown-and-orange striped tabby strolled by and brushed his silken back against her leg, she reached down to give him a stroke. In the next second, she heard the hammering of feet on the stairs and the cat shot off. Marion was on the move, a little earlier than usual, but that was good because maybe they'd have time for a quick chat before they set out on their visits.

'Morning,' Marion called as she rushed by the table. 'Sorry I can't stop, I've just remembered my first call is to a patient up near the fells and I'm not sure I've got enough petrol. So, I need to nip down to Stan Smith's garage and get Gloria topped up so I can set off in double quick time.'

'Here, just take a breath, will you, and have a drink of tea,' Mrs Hewitt urged, and Marion grabbed for the cup that was held out to her, slurped a good mouthful then wiped her lips with the back of her hand. Then the housekeeper handed Marion a list of visits in one hand and a slice of toast with strawberry jam in the other. In seconds, her colleague was running towards the door, calling over her shoulder, 'See you later.'

Mrs H was shaking her head. 'Always the same that one. I've tried every which way of dealing with her... But, even though she's forever in a rush and never seems well prepared, she gets the job done and all her patients love her.'

'I know, she's a whirlwind,' Lara replied. She felt like a quiet mouse in comparison, but, with the adjustment she'd needed to make to work out here in the wilds, she knew she had her own strengths.

Next in was Angus, bleary-eyed and yawning as he came through the door, running a hand through his dark blond hair so it stood up in tufts. It was a good job he was always a neat dresser with his pristine shirts and expensive ties because otherwise he wouldn't have looked anything like a man who'd had professional training and now held a position of responsibility. Lara smiled to herself then when she thought of Bingham's dishevelled hair poking out from beneath his ancient-looking checked trilby. It still struck her, that difference to how things were at the Liverpool Royal where all the doctors wore smart suits and white coats.

'Morning, Lara, I see you're up bright and early as always,' Angus called as he slumped onto his chair next to hers and reached for his first slice of strawberry-jammed toast. Often, like Marion, he was just passing through and he didn't sit at the table, so this was nice in a way, but it made her feel a bit on edge. No need, though, because the young doctor just sat and munched contentedly through his toast. Then, with a final slurp of his tea, he was jumping up and calling, 'Once more unto the breach,' then quietly adding, 'I'll see you both later... that's if I survive the morning clinic with Dr Bingham.'

Once he was gone, the housekeeper leaned in to speak in hushed tones. 'He'll want to make sure he's properly set up and he's gone through the patients' notes.'

'Always good practice,' Lara replied as she tidied her plate, cup and cutlery away. Then she scraped back her chair and walked to wash the pots at the sink.

'Leave them there, I'll see to them,' Mrs Hewitt called but Lara already had them in the warm soapy water and out onto the draining board.

The sky was slate grey as she wheeled and bumped her black bicycle with its white mudguards down the side of the stone-built double-fronted surgery. And she felt encumbered by the waterproof mac and rain hood that covered her brimmed district nurse's hat. As she freewheeled down the cobbled street running through the centre of the village, she passed the stone steps that led up to the spired church, then raised a hand to Sam Collins the butcher as he unloaded his van outside his shop. It heartened her to see the warm smile he offered but the moment felt instantly undercut by the deep frown and pursed lips of the postmistress, Miss Shaw, as she turned from opening her shop door. Leaving the rows of quaint stone cottages behind, Lara deftly manoeuvred over the hump-backed bridge spanning Ingleside brook and pushed on towards the country lanes.

Even as she ran through her list of morning visits in her head, she felt the first heavy spats of rain on her waterproof hood. She pushed hard with her legs to pick up speed, glad she'd been able to get used to the narrow country lanes in the brighter days of summer. Her first call was to young Peter Valentine, a farmer's son who had sustained a nasty leg injury from a protruding nail when he'd fallen from a hayloft.

The Valentines' farm was along the road leading out of the village towards Ridgetown, so not too far. But, when she felt gusts of wind pick up and drive the increasingly heavy rain straight at her, she needed to push hard against the pedals to make sure she got there before the worst of it hit. Arriving in the nick of time, she dismounted, then quickly wheeled her bicycle to park in the shelter of an oak tree already dropping its leaves. As she sploshed through the cobbled yard, avoiding patches of cow muck, she felt grateful for the wellington boots Mrs Hewitt had issued her with as the colder, wetter weather began to bite.

Catching sight of an unoccupied kennel, she felt relieved there was no vicious farm dog to contend with here. But, just as she thought it, she heard a low growl and a white and tan mongrel came at her from a ramshackle barn, baring its teeth as it moved low on its belly. She knew to stay calm and just keep walking but all the while her heart was thudding. Then, catching a glimpse of the snarling creature as it crept closer, she thought she might not make it safely to the door of the brick-built farmhouse. Right then, even though she knew that rule number one was not to run, she felt like taking her chances and legging it.

'Get here, Fly,' a man's voice shouted, and she heard the creature scurry back. Turning, she saw a rosy-cheeked farmer offer a good-natured raise of his cap. 'Sorry about that, I usually have him tied up when you nurses come.'

'That's alright. I've still got both legs.' She laughed. 'But please make sure he's secure in future.'

'Will do,' the fella called as he stooped down to snap a chain to the dog's collar. Lara couldn't help but feel sorry for the creature then as he stood and gazed at her with his big, dark eyes.

After wiping her boots on the bristled mat, she knocked and waited, shifting the position of her leather bag in her hand. In moments, a startled-looking woman with short-cropped red hair opened the door and beckoned her in. 'I'm so sorry to bring you out here, nurse. I know you're still quite new to the surgery. But Nurse Marion says these dressings need to be changed daily.'

'That's perfectly fine, Mrs Valentine. It's all part of the service,' she offered, following the woman as she bustled through the kitchen and down a darkened hallway.

A timid-looking girl of around ten years with the same red hair as her mother peeped out of the room Mrs Valentine was heading towards. 'Come on, Izzy, it's alright. Just the new district nurse come to check on Peter's leg.'

The girl pressed her lips together, her face flushing scarlet as she shyly bowed her head.

'Hello, Izzy. Nice to meet you,' Lara offered gently as she slipped by the child and followed Mrs Valentine into a sitting room with a single bed by the window.

'We put him down here so we can have the fire lit to keep him warm and I can sleep right beside him on the couch.'

The room was clean and bright with flower-patterned curtains at the window. 'It's a good room to nurse a patient in.' Lara smiled as she approached the bed. 'Hello, Peter, I'm Nurse Flynn, I've come to change your dressing.' The lad had the same brown hair and round cheery face as the man in the yard, so she assumed they had to be father and son. And, as he propped himself up on one elbow, he offered a broad smile. Instantly noting his pink cheeks, Lara placed the back of her hand against his forehead to check for fever. Thankfully, he didn't feel overly hot.

'So, I'll just check your temperature with my thermometer and then I'll have a look at the wound. Is that alright?'

'Yep.' He grinned and already she liked this cheery matter-of-fact young man.

Peter's temperature was in a normal range so that was good and, as she began to unravel the bandage securing the dressing pad, Mrs Valentine came to stand beside her. 'I always like to check on the progress of the wound. Young Dr Fitzwilliam made an excellent job of putting the stitches in and he's been back a few times to check on Peter.'

'All part of the service,' Lara said, feeling a glow of pride at the mention of her colleague. Angus could appear slapdash at times, and he didn't help himself by drinking too much in the village pubs. But, even though he was regularly in trouble with Dr Bingham or Mrs Hewitt, she was increasingly aware of his potential.

As she gently removed the dressing pad, she noted the precision of the deep cut running almost the full length of his inside leg. It looked almost surgical so the nail must have been sharp to inflict it. But Mrs Valentine was right – the silk sutures had been expertly applied and currently there was no redness or purulent exudate. 'It's looking good,' she told Peter as she prepared to clean the wound. Then gently, 'As you know, this will sting, but I'll be as quick as I can. Are you ready?'

The young lad nodded, sucked in a breath and held it as she swabbed down the length of the wound with carbolic solution, then soaked some squares of gauze with eusol and liquid paraffin solution before applying them.

He grimaced, then gritted his teeth.

'Almost done,' she said gently. 'And I know this might not help right now, but the ward sisters I worked with at the Liverpool Royal Infirmary always used to say that the stinging was a good sign.'

He nodded, forced a smile as she prepared to rebandage. Then he asked, 'So is that where you're from, Liverpool?'

'Yes, I was born and raised there, and it's where I trained as a nurse.'

'One day I want to visit Liverpool,' he said. 'I can't imagine how big it must be, and they have ships that sail across to America.'

'They do indeed.' She smiled.

'Don't you miss it, nurse? It's so quiet here, it must drive you mad.'

'Well, as you probably know, I'm quite new here and I'm enjoying the peace and quiet of the country lanes so far. But maybe later I'll start pining for the hustle and bustle of the city.'

He was gazing into the distance now, his eyes shining, and she could almost hear his brain ticking over the prospect of visiting Liverpool. She hoped he'd get there one day – just so he could see how different life was. It worried her, though; the thought of a young country lad being met by the chaos and potential shortfalls of city life. She'd heard Preston being jokingly referred to by some Inglesiders as the 'big city', so something on the scale of Liverpool would be incredibly daunting.

With a final turn of the bandage, she secured it with the safety pin. 'Right, so there you go... all done for another day. You can take some aspirin for the pain if you want.'

He swallowed hard. 'No, that's alright. It'll settle down. But, in those few days just after...' He blew out a slow breath. 'I've never felt anything like it... not since I had a bad toothache and the local fella... not a proper dentist but somebody who works with horses... he came with his pliers and whipped it out.'

'Ouch.' Lara grimaced.

Mrs Valentine chuckled. 'You've been through a lot for a youngster, Peter. So, I think you've had your share now. Let's get you better and one day you might make that trip to Liverpool.'

He grinned then as he propped himself up on one elbow to wave goodbye.

As Lara walked back through the house, Mrs Valentine thanked her and the Ingleside team for the scrupulous way they were caring for her son.

'It's a pleasure,' she smiled, 'and, depending on our schedules, it'll be me or Nurse Wright tomorrow. In the meantime, if you have any worries, ring the surgery.'

'Will do,' the woman replied. 'And it's lovely to meet you at last, Nurse Flynn.' She paused then, twisted her mouth for a second before she spoke again. 'And I hope you don't mind me mentioning this. But it's a relief to see you in the flesh, so I can ignore all the gossip that's been going round about the city nurse who's out of her depth. Those folk don't know what they're talking about. And now I'll be able to set them straight.'

'I'd be grateful for that.' Lara smiled, hiding her frustration at still being the subject of rumour. But one good thing that had come out of the violent incident with Vic Taylor all those weeks ago was that it had helped many of the locals move on more quickly. She wasn't far enough through the whole thing yet to feel secure, and she still sometimes had a creeping feeling at the back of her neck, as if Vic were watching her. But it was much easier now to win more of the local folk around.

'I'm not sure of my visits tomorrow, but I'll probably be back to see Peter at some stage,' she called as she raised a hand in farewell. And, as she picked her way back across the mucky yard, the farm dog, Fly, sent her on her way with a menacing growl.

Once her other morning visits to an aged villager with chronic bronchitis and a farmer's wife recovering from a stroke were done, she was back to the surgery for lunch. And, even as she opened the back door, she sensed an unusual quiet. Then Mrs Hewitt walked out of the kitchen with tears shining in her eyes and Lara knew something was up.

'What is it, Mrs H?'

'I'm so sorry, Nurse Flynn. We've had news of James Alston... he died this morning.'

'Oh,' she said, swallowing hard. It had happened sooner than she'd expected. And she'd been heavily involved with James Alston and his family through the final harrowing stage of his Parkinson's disease. He'd been one of the first patients she'd attended as a country nurse, so the news hit that bit harder. Instantly she wondered how his daughter Grace was doing. They'd clicked from her first visit to Manor House Farm for the removal of stitches from a head wound Mr Alston had sustained during a fall. Grace had an irresistible lightness of being and they were now friends.

'I'm sorry to hear that, I hope Grace is alright... I mean, given he was so poorly, it's not unexpected but, even so, it's often still a shock for the family.' Lara's voice sounded a little forlorn even to her own ears. 'Did Doctor Bingham say how the family were coping?'

Mrs Hewitt sighed heavily. 'He said Grace and her Aunt Agnes were managing but they were wrung-out, devastated. And my goodness did Jim Alston suffer with that condition.'

Mrs Hewitt dabbed at her eyes then and Lara made to reach out to her, but the housekeeper immediately lifted her chin. 'I'm alright... and it's no bad thing to shed a few tears. It shows that we care... And no wonder given I remember Jim from years back when he was fit and well. He was always a caring, generous man. Someone who looked out for others, helped where he could. He led a good life.'

'Yes, I can imagine that. In fact, that's how I think of Grace.'

And then, as Lara slipped into her seat at the kitchen table, Mrs Hewitt brought a cup of tea for them both, then topped her own up with a dash of brandy, motioning to Lara with the bottle. Lara shook her head. 'No thank you, I don't want to be wobbling on my bicycle when I go out on my afternoon visits.'

'Now that would really give the locals something to gossip about,' Mrs Hewitt smiled, then she reached out to Lara across the table. 'I know you nurses are trained to manage these losses. But your predecessor, Nurse Beecham, always shed a few tears when she got back to the surgery after a patient had died.'

Lara gulped, nodding. 'Yes, the crying thing is taboo at a patient's bedside, it's trained out of us. But that doesn't mean we can't vent our sadness in private.'

'Exactly, and that's what I do. Even though I'm just the person at the end of the telephone.'

Seeing the housekeeper upset, Lara felt her throat tighten and tears pricked her eyes. 'Ours is a funny old business,' she tried to say but her voice snagged.

Mrs Hewitt dabbed at her eyes and walked to put an arm around Lara's shoulders. 'Well, we're thinking, feeling human beings, just like the rest of them out there... It's just that we need to be strong for our patients and their families. I mean, when I answer that telephone to a family in distress, sometimes I need to grip the table just to steady myself. But I make sure my voice never falters.'

Lara nodded. 'It's hard, isn't it? But it was always drummed into us during training that the patients and their families are the absolute priority. And our own feelings come way down the list.'

Mrs Hewitt offered a wobbly smile. 'Sounds like you were trained by women like my mother. She grew up in the time of Queen Victoria… when it was tight stays and very stiff upper lips. A good thing maybe… with what came at us later, with the war. So many young men killed or maimed for life…'

The housekeeper's voice thickened with emotion and Lara thought she wasn't going to continue, but she cleared her throat. 'I don't think I've told you about my own son, Ben. He lied about his age so he could join up straight away, but then he got gassed in the trenches and blown up by a shell, spent ages in a French hospital. And, when he came back, he was changed forever.'

Lara felt shocked, not so much by the revelation, she'd heard many similar stories, but the fact that Mrs Hewitt had spoken openly about her private life.

'I'm so sorry to hear that,' she breathed, reaching for the housekeeper's hand. 'What happened to Ben?'

Mrs Hewitt pressed her lips together, dropped her gaze.

'It's alright if you can't talk about it right now, I do understand.'

The housekeeper lifted her head. 'The truth is, and this sounds awful for a mother to say about her only child… But I don't even know if he's dead or alive. He came back briefly after armistice in a terrible state – still recovering from his injuries and hooked on those morphia injections he'd been given in the army hospital. He stole all the money I had in the house – this was when I still lived in Preston; he took a gold brooch my mother had given me… and since then I haven't seen or heard of him.'

'I'm so sorry,' Lara said, with heartfelt sympathy.

Mrs Hewitt shrugged. 'I wasn't the only mother to be abandoned by the generation of young men who came back changed forever… and Ben's father had died from a nasty influenza bug when the lad wasn't much more than a baby. So, he grew up thinking there was something he had to prove, or that's how it felt. Anyway, I've told myself he most likely died years ago from morphia poisoning…'

Mrs Hewitt offered a wry smile then, not much more than a twist of her mouth. 'But, even so, when I moved out here from Preston, I left the surgery address with my best friend growing up. She calls me sometimes on the telephone and each time I hear her voice…'

The housekeeper cleared her throat again, took a big swig of her brandy-laced tea and, with tears shining in her eyes, she croaked, 'Is there any limit to a mother's love?'

'I don't know the answer to that question because I never knew my own mother. But her sister, the aunt who raised me, she tried not to show it – stiff upper lip and all that – but I know she would have done anything for me.'

Mrs Hewitt was nodding, pulling a handkerchief from her apron pocket and dabbing at her eyes. Then she drew a slow breath, pulled back her shoulders and said, 'Well, all this talk of our troubles isn't going to get the ham and pickle sandwiches made.'

'Do you want me to help?' Lara asked.

The housekeeper cleared her throat. 'No, thank you, Nurse Flynn. As you well know, I have my own system… But thank you for listening… I've never told anyone about my past life except Nurse Beecham. Oh, and Dr Bingham – he served as well, as an army doctor, and when I first started working here, he was still suffering from shell shock and having terrible nightmares. One night he woke up screaming and I had no choice but to go in there and sort him out. He talked to me then, told me some of the things he'd had to do.'

'I can relate to that,' Lara breathed. 'During my work in Liverpool, I nursed many veterans still dealing with physical and mental injury.'

Mrs Hewitt cleared her throat then. 'Well, all we can hope is that what they're saying in the papers about another war coming is just scaremongering.'

The housekeeper went about her household duties then and soon had a plate of sandwiches on the table. 'We might as well make a start on these... Dr Bingham will take his time at the Alstons' because he and Jim were always good pals, Angus is at the cottage hospital with a full list of patients and Matron Sharples on the rampage. And, as we know, our Nurse Wright is always running late.'

Mrs Hewitt reached for the teapot and topped up both their cups. 'So, going back to Grace. When you do get up there to see her, please tell her she's always welcome to bob in here for a cup of tea and a slice of cake.'

'Will do,' Lara breathed, feeling an ache of sadness for her friend.

Lara and Mrs Hewitt sat quietly for a few moments enjoying their easy companionship. Then, just as Lara reached for another sandwich, she sucked a sharp breath as a mouse scurried gamely along the back of Mrs Hewitt's chair. Knowing how terrified of the creatures the housekeeper was, she froze. The mouse stopped dead in its tracks and looked straight at her.

'Are you alright, Nurse Flynn?' Mrs Hewitt asked, her eyes full of concern.

'Yes, sorry... I...'

Distracted, knowing she had to hold the housekeeper's attention, she asked, 'It's just that I was wondering if you've ever been to the Harvest Ball.'

The housekeeper blurted a laugh, which startled the mouse into moving along.

'Oh no. Not my thing. And somebody needs to be here at the surgery to take any emergency calls.'

'Yes, of course,' she said, sighing with relief as the mouse ran down the side of the chair and away.

'Phew,' she said, 'I mean that you can be here. To answer the calls.'

'Are you sure you're alright? You seem a bit flustered,' Mrs Hewitt said, scrunching her brow, leaning forward in her chair.

'Yes, sorry,' she breathed, midway through wondering when Septimus Finch the ratcatcher would be laying his poison. Then she said abruptly, 'I was thinking about what I'm going to wear for the ball on Saturday night.'

'You could wear a sack if you wanted, Nurse Flynn. With your blonde hair and bright blue eyes, you're as bonny as a flower and you're bound to be the belle of the ball.'

Lara was already shaking her head. 'Oh no, not really... And all that going to balls and stuff...' She was about to say it wasn't her thing, but, in fact, after leading a cloistered, quiet life at boarding school, she'd always enjoyed dressing up and going out into the city with her nurse friends. It was the thought of that night at the Adelphi in Liverpool with Patrick that had made her think otherwise. So maybe now she was free from all that had happened, she could start enjoying herself again. She began to relax then and found herself actively looking forward to putting on her make-up, slipping into her silk evening gown, all of it.

3

It was Saturday morning; the day of the Harvest Ball and Lara was agitated because she'd switched off her alarm in her sleep, then woken with a jolt. Already she felt behind time for the morning clinic she attended with Dr Bingham. As she pulled on her navy-blue uniform with its white starched collar then shoved her black-stockinged feet into her low-heeled lace-up shoes, she felt on edge and tutted to herself as she straightened the patchwork quilt over her hastily made bed. As she ran down the red-carpeted stairs, she noted a gleam of autumn sunlight through the tall, arched window and it gave her enough of a boost to calm down.

Every Saturday morning, she was the sole attendee at breakfast because Marion was their senior district nurse, so she'd handed the clinic for weekend emergencies to her. And, of course, Angus always had a long lie-in on a Saturday after being out in the village pubs. She tried not to be judgemental regarding the young doctor but, when he turned up bleary-eyed and looking miserable, she felt concern for him and his patients. Mrs Hewitt ran a tight ship here at the surgery and she'd had many urgent conversations with the young doctor but, so far, he hadn't amended his behaviour one bit. It didn't help that his favourite pub – the Fleece, also playfully known as the 'Dorchester' – was just across the road. And, as she'd sat in the sitting room last night sipping a glass of sherry with Mrs Hewitt, she'd heard Angus and his drinking buddy, Leo Sullivan the vet, laughing and shouting as they'd come out of the pub. 'I know these young fellas need to blow off steam... but it's a good job Angus isn't on call over the weekend,' Mrs H had said with a twist of her mouth.

Lara hadn't been able to form a ready response because, from her first week at the surgery when Angus had tearfully confided how upset he was because Ada the barmaid at the Fleece didn't reciprocate his devotion, she'd felt oddly protective of the young doctor. And, given that working with Dr Bingham could be tricky because of his fickle temperament, she often felt much more at ease with Angus. He and Marion were her allies and, even though she was now more comfortable with Bingham, she always had to be alert to his moods, which could switch and change like the light and shade rolling across the fells.

'Morning, Mrs H,' Lara called, slipping into her place at the table.

'Ah, there you are, Nurse Flynn,' the housekeeper replied good-naturedly as she glanced up from her mixing bowl and wiped her hands on a tea towel.

Seeing Mrs Hewitt busy, she offered to get her own breakfast.

'Oh, dear me, no. We can't have that,' the housekeeper tutted in mock horror. 'If I let you nurses start serving yourselves, it'll throw my whole system into disarray.'

It made Lara smile and, as she poured her first cuppa from a brown teapot swaddled in a red crocheted tea cosy, she felt well cared for. Then, as she sat quietly at the table, Mrs Hewitt placed her bowl of sugar-sprinkled porridge and her toast with homemade strawberry jam in front of her before going straight back to her mixing bowl.

'What are you making?' Lara asked.

'Oh, just a quick batch of sultana scones for afternoon tea... the recipe was handed down from my grandmother. It's one of my favourites.'

'What's the secret then, to the scones?'

'Well, they need just the right amount of sugar. And, of course, they're always best eaten fresh with butter.'

'Mmm... delicious. I hope I don't get called out to an emergency so I can properly enjoy them.'

Mrs Hewitt glanced up from her bowl. 'And it's the Harvest Ball tonight so you need to be back in time to get ready.'

'Yes,' she smiled, 'Marion has told me... many times.'

The housekeeper chuckled. 'Oh, Nurse Wright loves the ball and she's even more excited this year because she's going with you. Your predecessor Nurse Beecham was never interested in attending anything like that, so it's good you two youngsters can go together.'

'Yes, it is.' She smiled, glancing to the clock. 'But I need to get straight into clinic or I'll end up in trouble with his lordshi—'

Lara gasped, almost choked, as Bingham strode abruptly into the kitchen, walked to his place at the head of the table and noisily scraped back his chair. It felt odd to even see him at this time of day because he always breakfasted in his room on the ground floor. He flopped down with a heavy sigh and pushed a hand through his dishevelled fluffy grey-brown hair, and it took no effort at all to see he was agitated. All of it enhanced by the jut of his angular unshaven jaw.

'Morning, Doctor Bingham,' she called politely up the table, but he muttered incoherently in reply.

Mrs Hewitt exchanged a knowing glance with her and then piped up, 'Cup of tea, Dr Bingham?'

'No, I don't think so,' he grizzled, running a hand through his hair again, leaving it standing up on end this time.

It made Lara feel like giggling, but she swallowed it right down when she saw Mrs Hewitt flash a narrow-eyed glance in his direction. And, when the housekeeper spoke, her voice had an almost indiscernible edge to it. 'Is everything alright, Doctor Bingham?'

'Yes, yes,' he grumbled impatiently. Then, glancing down the table, 'Where the hell is Doctor Fitzwilliam? Late again I suppose.'

'Well, it is a Saturday morning, so he isn't scheduled for duty.'

'Damn and blast it, woman. Of course I know what day it is.'

Clearly, he didn't know or else he wouldn't have asked the question and, as Lara exchanged another glance with the housekeeper, they shared a fleeting smile.

'Well, that's it, you've hit the nail on the head, Mrs H,' he growled. 'Today is Saturday so that means it's the blasted Harvest Ball at Ingleside Hall this evening.'

'It is indeed,' Mrs Hewitt offered. 'But if you don't want to attend, you could send your apologies and that would be that. After all, you'll be "on call" anyway, so I'm sure Lord and Lady Harrington would understand.'

He heaved a sigh, slumped his shoulders.

Mrs Hewitt shrugged and turned back to rolling out her scone mixture.

Lara took another bite of her toast but, even as she strove to ignore Bingham's bad humour, she felt his glowering presence at the head of the table and her throat felt tight as she swallowed.

'Oh, for goodness' sake, Henry. Whatever is the matter with you?' Mrs Hewitt called.

'You know exactly what the matter is, Mrs H. And it's the same every year on the day of the Harvest Ball.'

The housekeeper drew a slow breath then walked to the table, wiping her hands on a blue-striped tea towel. She halted beside her own chair, which was to Bingham's left. 'So, yet again, you don't want to attend?'

He heaved a sigh, shot her a glance. 'Correct.'

'Well, why don't you make your excuses?'

'You know damned well why not... I can't not go because Arthur Sullivan, that blasted vet, he'll plague the life out of me and won't let me live it down if I don't attend the elegant country home of Lord and Lady Harrington.'

'Exactly,' Mrs Hewitt said. 'And correct me if I'm wrong but there is also another important consideration... we lease the surgery building from Sir Charles Harrington, so he is our landlord.'

'Yes, of course. And that makes it worse because it all feels like going cap in hand to him and his family.'

'But there's no getting around it, is there, because, like many of the folks in the village, including your supposed arch enemy Arthur Sullivan, we have no choice but to lease from his lordship.'

'Hmph,' he grunted.

Mrs Hewitt smiled then. 'I'm sorry, Doctor Bingham, but don't we have this same conversation every year on the morning of the Harvest Ball? And am I not right in thinking that, by the evening, you always end up going?'

Bingham emitted a low groan and slowly shook his head. 'Am I that predictable, Mrs H?'

'Yes,' she said simply. Then walked back to her earthenware bowl.

He heaved a sigh, glanced down the length of the table to Lara. 'So, Nurse Flynn, what do you think about the issue?'

'I don't think I can offer an opinion either way because I've only been here a few months, I've never attended a Harvest Ball before, and I have no clue about leasehold buildings.'

'Hmph, sitting on the fence are you, Nurse Flynn?'

Lara looked directly at him then. 'Not at all, as I've just said, I have no experience of these matters.'

He pressed his lips together, glanced to Mrs Hewitt, who had her head down as she deftly cut the scones and slipped them onto a baking tray. Then abruptly he stood up from the table and shouted, 'Damn and blast. It looks like I've no choice but to pull that dusty dress suit out of my wardrobe and bloody well go.'

Mrs Hewitt glanced to him, didn't make any comment, then went straight back to her scones.

After he'd tutted and sighed, then stomped out of the kitchen, the housekeeper glanced over with a smile and began to shake her head. 'Every year it's the same, he comes in here in the morning all het up about attending the ball. He says his piece, does his morning clinic, huffs and puffs a bit more in the afternoon. Then he gets into his suit, downs a glass of whisky and off he goes. I've never attended the ball myself but, from what I've been told, he's all pally with Arthur Sullivan as soon he arrives and the pair of them seem to have a fine time together. But, then, by the next morning they've fallen out again.'

Lara chuckled. 'How odd... and they were like that at the village show in summer. Drinking in the beer tent, side by side at the bar as if they were the best of friends.'

'Exactly,' Mrs Hewitt offered, shaking her head. 'They

behave like children sometimes... but, then again, they were both together in France during the war so maybe that has something to do with it.'

'But Arthur Sullivan is a vet so—'

'There were horses and dogs who served out there with the men, that's why they needed the vets. And they took lots of horses from the farms round here as well.'

'Yes, of course, I hadn't thought about that... so Dr Bingham attended the soldiers, and Mr Sullivan saw to the livestock?'

Mrs Hewitt nodded. 'I think it was mostly putting the poor injured creatures out of their misery with a pistol. And once, when Dr Bingham had had a few too many whiskies, he told me they'd even had to destroy good horses to stop the Germans making use of them.'

'Oh, that's awful,' Lara said, feeling the impact of the information alongside the previous discussion they'd had about Dr Bingham's shell shock.

Mrs Hewitt let out a ragged sigh. 'And he was another one, Arthur Sullivan, who came back messed up after what he'd been through. He was here at the surgery once for some medical appointment – his heart, I think. But it was coming up to Remembrance Day and he looked shocking. So I brought him into the kitchen for a cup of tea and he sat down there, where you are now, and he poured out some of the stories. Then he began to sob.'

Lara drew a slow breath. 'It probably did him good. I know my bicycle accident was tiny in comparison, but it helped to talk to you about it.'

Mrs Hewitt paused from her baking. 'I just wish your colleague Nurse Wright would open up about what's been eating her since she came back to us from Scotland.'

'I'm glad you've mentioned that because I wasn't exactly

sure, and I've only been here a few months anyway... but I've been sensing that too.'

'I've tried all ways to get her to loosen up but, unless she's telling one of her entertaining stories about riding her motorbike up a mountain to see a patient or dealing with some eccentric laird of the manor, she clams right up.'

'I know, that's exactly what I've found,' Lara said.

The housekeeper sighed. 'All I can think is that she'll talk when she's ready but I'm beginning to wonder if that time will ever come.'

'I don't think we can do more right now,' Lara replied as Mrs Hewitt slid her tray of scones into the Aga. 'Shoosh, Tiddles,' the housekeeper called to the striped tabby cat who lay stretched out in front of the stove. Lara saw him stretch his legs, lift his head, but he didn't move an inch and Mrs H began to chuckle. 'My goodness, Nurse Flynn, no wonder this creature can't catch any of those mice that've invaded the house. Have you ever in your whole life seen such a lazy animal?'

'Most definitely not,' she offered, 'but if I walked over there now and tried to stroke him, he'd soon shift.'

'Yes, he's like that with everyone, especially Dr Bingham. But no wonder given how often he comes in here shouting and causing a kerfuffle... And just look at this cat, even at the mention of our senior doctor, he's unsettled.'

Tiddles jumped up then and sidled towards the back door.

When the housekeeper straightened up from the oven, she dropped her voice a notch. 'I know Marion isn't ever bad-tempered, not like his lordship... But they are similar in that they're both making so much effort to hold things in. So, if there's anything you can do, Lara, to loosen her up, I'm ready and willing to give you backup.'

'I'll do my best, Mrs H.'

Suddenly realising the time, Lara jumped up from the table with the remains of her toast and jam in her hand. 'Wish me luck in clinic,' she called over her shoulder as she ran from the kitchen, down the green-tiled corridor past the waiting area that was thankfully empty, then straight to the door of the clinic room. Wiping the last few crumbs of toast from her lower lip, she straightened her uniform, lifted her chin, then tapped at the door.

4

Thankfully the Saturday morning clinic was busy, so Dr Bingham had no choice but to click back to his affable country doctor mode. And, as he attended to his patients, Lara's faith in him felt restored. Feeling the synchrony of their practice was a positive thing but, given his earlier outburst in the kitchen, she still felt slightly on edge. So, she was relieved when an urgent call came in and she was out through the door to see young Peter Valentine. He was already first on her list for a Saturday morning visit anyway, but his mother had telephoned anxious because he felt hot and his face was flushed.

All too aware of the risks of sepsis, she swiftly retrieved her bicycle from the shed and, as the cold, damp air met her, she was glad to be free from the confines of the surgery. But, as she pedalled by the village school and out towards the Valentines' farm, the sky darkened with slate grey clouds and a sense of foreboding crept in with the autumn air.

Arriving at the farm, she was relieved to find the white and tan yard dog securely tethered on his chain. And, as she parked her bicycle then swiftly picked her away across the mucky yard, strangely the dog didn't bark, he just sat and gazed at her with his dark eyes. One of his ears was ragged and it made her feel sorry for him. 'You're a strange one, aren't you, Fly?' she told him. He whimpered then and lay down with his head resting on his paws. It made her smile and, even as she knocked at the door, she glanced back to him and he lifted his head.

'Hello there, Nurse Flynn,' Mrs Valentine called as she opened the door, her shoulders held square, her bright red hair almost on end. 'Sorry to call you in early but Nurse Marion drilled the importance of reporting any changes in Peter's condition immediately.'

'Yes, of course. You've done the right thing,' she soothed as she followed Mrs Valentine through the kitchen.

Halting just before they entered Peter's room, Mrs Valentine turned to her. 'I don't know if you'll see any difference in him, maybe I'm overreacting. But he had a very restless night and he's all flushed in the face.'

Lara placed a gentle hand on her arm. 'You've done exactly the right thing by making the call. And once I've checked his temperature and inspected the wound, I'll let you know exactly what I'm thinking.'

Mrs Valentine offered a single nod, then led the way into Peter's room. As Lara followed, she noted the warmth of the room with the open fire stacked with wood. And, when the young lad raised himself on one elbow and called out a greeting, it felt reassuring.

'Let's have a look at you, Peter.' She smiled, placing her leather bag at the side of his bed, then using the back of her hand to feel his forehead. He did seem hot, and his cheeks were flushed. And when she checked with her thermometer, his temperature was raised above his usual baseline, but he didn't have a fever. So maybe it was the heat from the fire that had caused the increase.

Next, she unravelled the bandage and removed the dressing pad to check the leg wound for exudate. It was just as clean as it had been previously.

'All seems to be fine.' She smiled, first to Peter, then turning her head she acknowledged Mrs Valentine who blew out a breath in relief.

'Well, I'm sorry to have brought you out here early for something and nothing.'

'No, you did the right thing. He does have a slightly raised temperature and it's always best to be cautious.'

Once the bandage had been reapplied and Peter had taken a good drink of cool water, Lara said her goodbyes and followed Mrs Valentine out to the hallway. Peter's little sister, Izzy, was there and she offered a shy smile then turned her body away.

'Hello again, Izzy,' Lara called gently, wishing she had one of the caramel toffees she often carried in her coat pocket.

'I'm worried about Peter,' Izzy said quietly as she twisted a lock of her bright red hair.

'That's alright, it's OK to be worried. But I've checked everything, and he seems to be fine.'

The child scrunched her brow. 'But I've got a bad feeling right here,' she whispered, placing her small hand in the centre of her chest.

'Well, that's probably because Peter is poorly right now, and when he gets better it will go away. But if it doesn't, you tell your mummy. Alright?'

'Yes,' she breathed, maintaining a serious expression.

'Come on, Isobel,' Mrs Valentine called to her then, 'don't be holding Nurse Flynn up.'

Then she glanced to Lara. 'She really seems to have taken to you. Mostly she won't say boo to a goose, I've never known her like this with anyone apart from close family.'

'We get on, don't we, Izzy?' Lara smiled.

The little girl offered a decisive nod.

Then, after she'd said her goodbyes and reminded Mrs Valentine to telephone straight away if there was further change in Peter's condition, she picked her way back across the muddy yard as Fly emerged from his kennel and watched her go with his coal-black eyes. She gave him a nod, which strangely he seemed to acknowledge. Then, as she retrieved her bicycle, she set her sights on her second call – a bereavement visit to Grace at Manor House Farm.

She felt free as she cycled back to the village and, as she passed the Fleece, she waved to Ada as she bobbed out of the door at the top of the pub steps and called a cheery good morning. Then, as she turned right at Sam Collins' butcher's shop, he stepped out carrying a tray of sausages.

'No rest for the wicked,' he shouted jovially to her as he pushed the tray into the back of his van. For a second, Lara thought he was referring to her, the new district nurse. And it seemed that Miss Frobisher, the elderly retired schoolmistress, who was at the opposite side of the street thought so too because she called out to the butcher and waved her stick at him. Clearly, she'd taken exception to what he'd just said, and in seconds he was calling after her, 'I mean me, not you, Nurse Flynn.'

Lara raised a hand and shouted back to reassure him as she freewheeled down the cobbled street, passing by ancient stone cottages with their low doorways and small windows. Then, hearing Miss Frobisher still berating the butcher, she glanced over her shoulder to see him flushed in the face. She smiled to herself because, when she'd first arrived in Ingleside, Miss Frobisher had been the first to show her disapproval of a city girl taking up the position of rural district nurse.

If only I *was* wicked, Lara mused, and even as she thought it, she saw Leo Sullivan, the young vet, emerge from the surgery he ran with his father midway down the street. Instantly, he smiled and shouted a greeting as she rumbled by over the cobbles. 'Good morning,' she called in return, feeling the annoying catch of her breath she'd fought hard to manage since she'd kissed him on the cheek that day Marion had come home from hospital. As she negotiated the bridge, she felt Leo gazing after her and she pushed hard against the pedals to be beyond the bounds of the village. Once she was out on the country lane heading to Manor House Farm, she felt free again, with the big sky above and just the sheep and wild creatures for company.

Spotting the roof and chimneys of Ingleside Hall up ahead, she knew she'd soon be arriving at Grace's. And after negotiating the five-barred gate she was wheeling her bicycle over the potholed track that led up to the farm as the black-faced sheep cropped the thin autumnal grass. There were still some scrappy yellow buttercups, but the taller stems of grass were brown and the turning leaves on the trees had begun to show the first hues of orange, brown and gold. Feeling a nip in the air even through her raincoat, a shiver ran down her spine that felt like a foreshadowing. But then a scraggy sheep lifted its head from its meagre grazing and continued to stare at her as she laboured her way up the rough track and for some reason it made her smile.

At the angry bark of the black and white farm dog that leapt up and down on its chain in the yard, she expected to see Grace emerging from one of the outbuildings. But there was no sign of her friend, and it made her feel a little forlorn as she parked up her bicycle. She walked across the yard and knocked firmly at the door of the slate-roofed farmhouse. No sound of life inside, but she knocked again, waited, before opening the door. 'Grace?' she called gently, pushing the door fully open. 'Are you there?'

The low-ceilinged, beamed kitchen was neat and tidy as always but it was empty and silent bar the tick of a clock. And it was cold with no Aga lit, no kettle on the hob. Instantly, she felt perturbed. Without doubt this was a trying time for Grace, but the deserted kitchen sent a shiver of concern through her.

It made sense to try the outbuildings – so, closing the door behind her, she crossed the clean-scrubbed cobbled yard to the barn – no sign of life. And even the farm dog sat quietly, then he whined and retreated to his kennel. Her ears pricked then at the low moan of a cow from the shippon, triggering thoughts of the calf she'd helped deliver on the day she'd arrived from Liverpool. Even before she entered the low, stone building she heard another louder, almost unearthly bellow of pain. Then Grace's voice shouted, 'Go on, Winny, that's it, your calf's coming!'

As Lara stepped into the pungent-smelling interior, she heard the first snufflings of a newborn calf and the lowing of the mother cow. 'Grace,' she called, but all that came back was the rustling of straw. She walked further into the shippon, past more empty stalls. Then called again, louder this time, 'Hello, Grace, it's me, Lara.'

A voice came from the far end. 'Ah hello, Lara. You're too late to assist with the delivery of this little one.'

In the low light, her friend's face appeared ashen and instantly Lara noted the dark smudges beneath her too bright eyes. But Grace offered a wobbly smile as she pushed back her unruly strands of wavy brown hair.

'Hello, Grace, it's good to see you busy and so nice to see a newborn,' Lara crooned, delighting in the sight of the mother cow licking her offspring as it struggled up on its big-kneed legs.

As the calf wobbled to standing then bleated for its mother, the cow snorted and sniffed, then continued to lick.

'I love this moment, I truly do.' Grace sighed, still gazing at the cow and newborn calf. Then she turned to Lara. 'I'm so sorry, I knew we had this appointment, and I meant to leave a note on the door of the house, but I forgot.'

'That's alright, I found you.'

'Yes, you did, and this beautiful calf, this new life has given me a boost this morning,' she said, grabbing another handful of straw to rub the newborn down. 'The mother, Winny, she was always my dad's favourite Jersey cow... That's when he could still get out to the shippon.'

Lara noted the instant sheen of tears in Grace's eyes as she sped up her drying of the calf. And when she spoke again her voice quavered. 'It's strange but, as soon as I came out here to see to the calving, I felt as if Dad was with me. I'm sure I heard his voice at one stage... Is that normal?'

'Well, I don't think there is a normal, each bereavement is unique. But that feeling of a presence is often mentioned. It feels as if the spirit stays around to make sure their loved ones are alright.'

Grace twisted her mouth in the semblance of a smile. 'Well, knowing Dad, he was just checking I delivered the calf right.'

'Maybe there is that too,' Lara replied with a gentle smile.

When Grace spoke again, there was a catch in her voice. 'Aunt Agnes has been telling me over and over that it'll take time, this grieving. But it's bloody awful being without him, even with the state he was in, we still had our laughs together. I was overworked, even with Agnes's help, but I'd have carried on just so...'

She stopped speaking, gazed into space for a few moments,

then she said, 'But I'm glad I've got the farm and the livestock to keep me going.'

'Are you sleeping alright, Grace?'

'Sleep, what's sleep?' She tried to smile but the gesture didn't reach her eyes. 'I nod off in the chair, wake up hearing him call for me, nod off again, same thing wakes me. Then dawn's breaking and he's there with me as I go out to the yard.'

'That feeling of him being with you is what you might call normal but, if better sleep doesn't come back, ring the surgery and I'll ask Dr Bingham to prescribe a sleeping draught.'

Grace sighed. 'That's good of you but I probably won't take it. Not when I need to keep up with my work on the farm... Speaking of which, I'm running behind right now. I need to finish up with Winny and the calf then get on with the mucking out.'

Lara reached out, placed a gentle hand on her arm. 'Stay with me for a few moments... take a breath.'

Grace nodded, covered Lara's hand with her own, sticky with calf mucus. As they stood together in the shippon, Lara smelled the warm, sweet breath of the mother cow and she sensed Grace steadying up.

Then, when her friend shifted and sighed, the spell was broken, and Lara knew it was time to leave. 'I'm planning to attend the funeral, so I'll see you there. But don't hesitate to call the surgery if you need anything before then.'

'I will, I promise,' Grace replied, nodding her head as she picked up another handful of straw and got back to rubbing the calf's fluffy coat.

As Lara exited the shippon into brighter light and walked across the cobbled yard to collect her bicycle, the farm dog nosed out of his kennel and, with a whine, he slumped to the ground. It felt strange but she knew it to be true that animals pick up on emotion, and this dog was also grieving. Then, as she wheeled her bicycle back down the farm track, she was surrounded by the mournful bleating of one sheep and then another and she felt salt tears sting her eyes. Glad it was Saturday, and she didn't have any more planned visits, she took her time to cycle back to the surgery and, as she pushed against the pedals, she breathed her sorrow at James Alston's passing out into the damp autumn air.

5

It felt good to arrive back at the surgery and, as Lara stashed her bicycle in the shed and entered through the back door, she was shrugging off her damp macintosh, removing her district nurse's hat, and hanging them together on one of the brass hooks in the green-tiled corridor. Then, as she caught a waft of those freshly baked scones from the kitchen, she felt the thick stone walls of the surgery close protectively around her. Climbing the red-carpeted stairs to her room, she heard the first heavy patter of rain against the arched window and felt glad she'd made it back before the worst of the weather hit.

As soon as she reached the landing, Marion stuck her tousled head out of her room down the corridor and shouted, 'Lara, I need you right now! I don't have a thing to wear for the ball tonight.'

'I'm coming,' she called, knowing that helping Marion with her 'what to wear' issue might be challenging. But it would serve as a wedge between her work and the forthcoming Harvest Ball.

Once she'd crossed the threshold into Marion's room, her

fellow nurse confronted her with a dramatic, sorrowful expression and pointed to a dishevelled pile of dresses on the bed.

'It's alright, we'll get it sorted,' Lara said confidently, even though she knew this was probably going to take much longer than expected.

Instantly, Marion offered a lopsided grin, then she gushed, 'Thank you so much, Lara... You're an absolute angel.'

'Mmm, I think I might be too domineering to be an angel... But come on, let's get started with creating a pile of "definitely nots". And, given we're attending a posh ball, we can probably rule out a few items immediately.'

Marion narrowed her eyes. 'Well, maybe... and yes, there is a dress code, but last year I saw a woman in culottes and a silk blouse, and she looked absolutely stunning.'

'Well, we could consider that as an option...' Lara's voice tailing off as she held up a deep pink dress that looked like a strong contender.

After an hour of going through the many dresses Marion had stuffed and pushed into an untidy pile on her bed, a decision was made, and it was time for Lara to retreat. Her own choice of what to wear had been made ages ago, but it niggled her now because the turquoise silk gown that was her only possible choice was the dress she'd worn for that special night out in Liverpool with Patrick a week or so before her accident. She wished now she had something else because, despite her bravado at wanting to reclaim the gown, seeing it hung on the wardrobe door as she entered her room, for the first time in ages the scar on her hairline began to throb. Instantly, she felt annoyed, and the scar throbbed some more. 'I'm not having this,' she muttered to herself, dousing a flannel with cold water and pressing it to the healed wound. Gazing at her reflection in the mirror above the sink once the prickling sensation had settled, she pressed her mouth into a firm line and knew she could wear the turquoise silk dress. Not only that, she'd take the emerald and diamond necklace that Patrick had gifted her out of the trunk beneath her bed and she'd wear that as well.

Right away, she heaved out the trunk and, after wiping a fine layer of dust from the lid, she clicked it open. It was empty bar the red leather case containing the necklace and an unopened letter from Patrick she'd received in the summer. She went to the letter first and tore open the envelope to find no more than a brief note. As expected, it demanded the return of the jewellery, and it was signed off with a brief reference to the good times they'd had in Liverpool. It made her frown at the brass neck of the fella, but she'd gone way beyond mustering any emotion for Patrick. So, she clicked open the box, pulled out the necklace and placed it ready on her dressing table for when she got dressed later.

Over a lengthy lunch, with Marion across the table chatting on about the ball and Angus quietly eating his way through a pile of ham sandwiches and at least three scones with butter and jam, Lara began to relax. She laughed when the young doctor began to tease Marion about last year's ball. 'I can't believe you don't remember... I mean you'd had many glasses of champagne. But you insisted on dancing with Lord Harrington at least three times.'

'Don't remind me,' she groaned.

Angus emitted a low laugh. 'Well, I don't remember much either, it was Leo who told me the detail.'

'Cheers for that, Leo,' she said, but good-naturedly. Then, reaching out to Lara across the table, 'Don't worry, I'm going to moderate my drinking tonight – so I can pay you back for when you looked after me after I'd had more than one too many at the village dance.'

'Oh, that's alright,' Lara began to say but Marion cut her off. 'No, it's my turn to be the responsible one... and you need to loosen up and let your hair down a bit.'

'Please don't let her stay sober, Lara,' Angus sighed theatrically. 'She's such good fun when she's tipsy.'

Mrs Hewitt emerged from the pantry then. 'It's up to Marion what she does on her night out, Dr Fitzwilliam. And, as we know, you tend to do your own thing and there are plenty of stories I could tell...'

'See!' Marion grinned, pointing a finger at Angus. 'Anyway, I want to enjoy the ball and be able to remember it.'

'Goody two shoes.' Angus laughed, then he pushed back his chair, stood up and yawned loudly. 'I'm just going to have a nap in my room, then I'll be up and out to the Dorchester early doors.'

'No, you will not,' Mrs Hewitt called after him. 'I need you dressed and ready to board the charabanc with everyone else.'

'Roger that, Mrs H,' he called, but Lara knew by the glint in his eye he wouldn't be obeying that order.

As he left the kitchen, he glanced back and winked at Lara and Marion. And, as if she knew exactly what he was up to, Mrs Hewitt glanced sharply at him from the Aga. As soon as he'd gone, she was shaking her head. 'It's a good thing he's a decent doctor because he pushes me to the limit sometimes with all his going out to the pubs.'

'He'll probably grow out of it,' Marion said.

'Hmph,' was all that the housekeeper had to offer in reply.

Later, once Lara had applied her make-up and was fully dressed in the turquoise silk evening gown, she stood in front of the mirror to fasten the emerald and diamond necklace. It looked good. Patrick had been right when he'd told her it suited her, but that was it now – she'd make sure it was returned to him as soon as possible after tonight. Picking up her beaded evening bag, she headed out to join the rest of the party downstairs. Even as she clicked shut her door, she caught the sounds of Marion bumping about in her room, then the noise of shouting voices from downstairs made it seem as if the whole surgery had fallen into chaos. As she walked down the stairs in her heeled shoes and new silk stockings, she realised she didn't feel remotely awkward in her evening gown, but she wasn't quite sure about the necklace any longer. But that was it, she'd made her decision and there was no going back.

To keep out of everyone's way as they completed their own preparations, she slipped into the small sitting room at the front of the surgery and settled herself in one of the red brocade armchairs. She felt comfortable in this room where she sometimes spent her evenings sipping sherry and listening to the radiogram with Mrs Hewitt. But, when she heard gusting wind and a heavy patter of rain against the window, a shiver ran through her.

As she rested back to wait for the rest of the party, she started to relax in the cosy room. But, at the bang of a door and the tramp of shoes in the tiled corridor, she began to feel twitchy. And when Dr Bingham called to Mrs Hewitt, and she heard the stamp of his leather-soled shoes right outside the door, she felt glad to be tucked away in here.

'Mrs Hewitt!' Bingham yelled. 'Damn and blast those mice, they've gone and chewed all the way through the collar of my dress shirt.'

She clapped a hand over her mouth to stop herself from making a sound.

Instantly, she heard the confident tap of Mrs Hewitt's shoes on the tiled corridor and, when she spoke, her tone was brisk. 'Whatever is it, Dr Bingham?'

Bingham spat and swore again and seemed barely able to get his words out, then she heard him say, 'Look, the mice have chewed it all. It's ruined.'

'Well, it's a good job I've got a brand-new freshly starched one ready and waiting in the kitchen for you, isn't it?'

He muttered and grumbled some more about the blasted mice and Septimus Finch, the damned ratcatcher who should be on top of all this by now. But, as his footsteps retreated towards the kitchen, Lara smiled at Mrs Hewitt's deft handling of the situation. As ever, the housekeeper was vital to the smooth running of the surgery.

There were a few quiet moments, then came the sound of running feet and the sitting room door burst open.

'Cripes, you scared the living daylights out of me,' Angus cried as he clicked the door shut behind him and threw himself down into the armchair opposite. With his eyes shining, his fluffy blond hair dishevelled, his suit jacket unbuttoned and bow tie skew-whiff, it didn't take a genius to work out he'd just run back from the pub.

'Angus,' Lara hissed, 'I heard Mrs H telling you very firmly that under no circumstances were you allowed out to the Fleece this evening. We need to be assembled and ready to board the charabanc.'

He grinned. 'Well, I'm here now, aren't I, so no harm done.'

'I suppose not,' she said, feeling him drawing her into the role of co-conspirator. She'd witnessed him do it with Marion too and of course that charm of his was how he managed to get away with so many things.

When Mrs Hewitt's voice shouted his name down the corridor, he offered a mischievous grin and whispered, 'Let her think I've bunked off to the pub, just for a few more moments.'

Lara was shaking her head, but she was also enjoying his playfulness.

'I know you're in there, Angus,' the housekeeper said as she pushed open the door.

'What the heck, Mrs H,' he beamed.

'I can smell that fancy expensive cologne of yours from miles away.'

He laughed then and shrugged his shoulders.

'Honestly, it's like herding cats in here tonight, but at least I know where you two are. Please can one of you go up to pull Marion out of her room right now. I've got Dr Bingham in the kitchen complaining his new collar is too damned tight and I'm right on the edge of wanting to throttle him... And then he'll know what tight is.'

Lara and Angus were both giggling, then Lara held up her hand. 'I'll get Marion.'

As she stood up, she saw Angus's eyes widen and he glanced her up and down. 'My goodness, Nurse Flynn, you look very different out of your uniform.'

'It's just a frock and a necklace, Dr Fitzwilliam. Don't start getting ideas that I might be a changed woman.'

'No, no. I was just thinking that...' He cleared his throat then and, clearly not knowing what else to say, he grinned. 'But, all the same, that style, that colour, it really suits you.'

'Thank you.' She smiled. 'And you look very smart too... but you'd look even better if you straightened your tie, brushed your hair and buttoned that jacket.'

'Not much, then, hey.' He laughed.

In moments, she was up the stairs and, as she tapped on Marion's door, she felt concerned by the silence in the room. She was just about to push the door open when her friend came out of the bathroom.

'Sorry, Marion,' she smiled, 'Mrs H sent me to check if you were ready.'

'That's alright,' Marion beamed as she stood resplendent in the deep pink gown with its plunging neckline, and with her dark curly hair pinned up, her red lipstick and black eyeliner perfectly applied. She was ready to go.

'You look amazing,' Lara breathed as she linked her arm and walked with her down the stairs towards the increasingly heightened chatter between the two doctors and Mrs Hewitt.

When she appeared with Marion on her arm, they all stopped dead, immediately, and Angus's mouth dropped open.

'Well, I must say, nurses, I mean...' Bingham stumbled.

'You all look smashing,' Mrs Hewitt called, then added with a mischievous smile, 'Especially you, Dr Bingham, with that new shirt collar... But please will you all go out through the door, right now, because I can't stand a single second longer of this kerfuffle.'

'Right you are, Mrs H,' Angus called, linking Lara's arm at one side and Marion's at the other.

Dr Bingham pulled a silver hip flask from his pocket and took a swig before he stepped forward to lead the way.

'Damn and blast, it's pouring with rain,' he shouted back as he opened the door. 'Ah, but I can see the charabanc right there waiting outside the Fleece so it's not far to run.'

Lara pulled a black umbrella from the stand in the hall and opened it over her and Marion's heads as they ran out first, with Bingham holding the door. Laughing as they splashed through puddles, they then clambered up the steep steps onto the bus. Bingham and Angus were wet with rainwater when they scrambled on board. But as Bingham took another swig from his flask and offered it to Angus, he began to call out a greeting to the other folks on board and it made Lara smile to think how agitated he'd been about attending the ball. She could see he was putting a brave face on it but, even so, there was a genuine warmth in his exchanges with the other passengers. And as Lara glanced around, she spotted the Ingleside vicar, Reverend Hartley, next to the retired schoolteacher Miss Frobisher, the next seat behind held a sole occupant – Miss Shaw, the postmistress who Lara had never seen smile once inside or outside of the village Post Office. She recognised Ted, the landlord from the Old Oak down the hill, sitting next to an older man who she thought was probably Sid Lightfoot, the landlord of the Fleece. The other passengers towards the back she'd seen around and about the village but didn't know who they were. Then, of course, right behind Dr Bingham and Angus were the vets – Arthur Sullivan and Leo. Seeing her glance in his direction, Leo offered a bright smile and raised his hand. She returned the gesture, but then quickly turned back to Marion because sometimes the way Leo looked at her seemed a little bit too intense.

'All on board,' shouted the elderly driver as he glanced over his shoulder and offered a broad, toothless grin.

'I think so, Mr Smith,' Bingham called.

Angus leaned across from his seat to murmur, 'The driver is Percy Smith from the garage, he's Stan Smith's dad – the one who repaired Marion's motorcycle. Do you remember, from the summer?'

'Yes,' she said, 'of course I remember… and, as we both know, that gesture to welcome her home from hospital could have gone very badly wrong if she'd had a funny turn after seeing the motorbike she'd crashed on.'

Angus turned down the corners of his mouth and nodded.

As the aged driver crunched the gears of the coach, alarmingly they rolled backwards. 'Sorry about that,' he called over his shoulder, 'forgot to put the handbrake on.'

'This isn't inspiring confidence,' Marion hissed in Lara's ear, 'not after what happened to me in the summer.'

'It's alright, Percy's a good driver when he gets going,' Angus advised.

Bingham leaned in with, 'His eyesight's not what it used to be though.'

Lara heard Marion groan, and it helped her manage her own anxiety when she had to be strong for her friend. 'It'll be fine, and the roads will be quiet.'

'Not necessarily,' Marion said through gritted teeth, 'the folks who attend the ball, many of them have their own cars.'

'Right, so, let's just hold fast then,' she said as Marion clutched her arm.

'Tally-ho,' the elderly driver shouted as he finally got the bus in gear, and it lurched violently forward.

A collective gasp of concern rippled through the passengers as Lara gulped in a breath.

They chugged and jumped then steadied up as the driver swung the bus around.

Angus leaned across the aisle to say, 'We'll be going the long way round to the hall because the bus won't fit over the hump-backed bridge.'

She was glad of the information but hoped the vehicle would be able to manage the very narrow lanes they were heading for. At least Percy seemed steady at the wheel now, even though he was slumped quite far forward in his seat. The rain was easing off and, when she glanced out of the window, she saw a tall man pass by with his hat pulled low over his face and his shoulders hunched against the weather. For a split second, she felt a glimmer of recognition, then realised she couldn't know him because, by the expensive cut of his overcoat, she knew he wasn't one of the villagers or local farmers. Must be here for the ball, she thought, immediately distracted as the charabanc began to pick up speed and Marion pulled her close to tell a story of Harvest Balls past.

6

The rain persisted as the bus lurched in and out of potholes and frequently brushed against hedges bordering the narrow lanes. Marion squealed and clung to Lara, who found herself sitting ramrod straight on the prickly moquette seat, gazing tensely out of the window. And, as the evening began to darken further, she prayed there'd be no rain on their return journey because she knew from experience that headlights even on the more modern of motor vehicles never gave enough light to fully see the road. She heard her friend Maeve's voice in her head then. *You need to relax and stop mithering about that. You're barely travelling above a crawl anyway and it'll be a soft landing in the bushes.* She drew a slow breath at the memory of her fellow nurse's straightforward approach to life.

'We're nearly there,' Angus called, his voice already a little slurry.

She furrowed her brow, glanced in his direction to see Leo Sullivan raise a half bottle of whisky, and she knew where the alcohol was coming from.

Arriving at Ingleside Hall in a slow scrunch of gravel, she felt relief flood through her. 'Come on.' She smiled to Marion, taking her hand, pulling her up from the seat so they could be first off. They were forced to wait, though, as Percy Smith struggled out of his driver's seat and moved slowly to the bus door to release the catch. 'I hope you have a good time.' He smiled.

'We will, Percy,' the young vet called over Lara's shoulder.

She felt cooped up and mildly agitated with Leo breathing down her neck as she waited for Mr Smith to free the lock on the door, which seemed to be jammed. Then, as soon as the driver had the door open, the dank air swirled in to meet her, and she felt as if she could breathe again. As soon as she stepped down onto the gravel, she thrilled at the sight of the stately building all lit up, the heavy wooden door standing wide open and the sound of an orchestra drifting out to the autumn air.

'Come on, let's get in there first.' Marion giggled, taking the lead now as she pulled Lara across the drive to the doorway graced by those tall stone pillars she'd noted in the summer when she'd been here with Grace for the village show.

The inside of the hall felt much more sumptuous than the Adelphi Hotel in Liverpool and, as she walked beneath a huge crystal chandelier towards a liveried footman holding a silver tray of champagne in fluted glasses, she glanced to her silk frock and raised a hand to feel the emeralds and diamonds, and knew she'd done the right thing by wearing the necklace this final time.

The footman smiled and offered a single nod as she selected a glass of champagne, and she was sure he'd called her milady. Marion was grinning broadly but, when Angus stumbled alongside and knocked into her, she linked Lara's arm and walked briskly away to shake the hands of Lord and Lady Harrington, who were waiting to greet their visitors.

Lord Harrington barely smiled but he gave a firm handshake, and she appreciated that. But his wife was very effusive and spoke at length to Marion about the motorcycle accident and hoped she'd taken enough time to recover. 'Ah, so you must be Lara Flynn, the new district nurse.' She smiled then offered a gloved hand. Instantly Lara noted the resemblance to the daughter she'd seen riding her horse and chatting to Leo at the agricultural show. The same black hair, sharp cheekbones and elegant tilt of the chin. 'Please feel free to wander anywhere on the ground floor and I do hope you have a lovely time this evening,' Lady Harrington said with a smile that didn't quite reach her eyes.

As Lara linked Marion's arm and they walked away together, she felt a little catch in her breath when she heard Leo behind her responding to a noisy greeting from a woman who was undoubtedly Phillipa Harrington.

Marion glanced over her shoulder. 'Look at our young vet with his highbrow connections. Rumour has it that, since he fixed her horse's sprained fetlock in the spring, they've been getting quite cosy those two.'

'Good for them,' she quipped, not knowing why the information irritated her. Then, finishing the remains of her champagne, she was instantly glancing around for another footman with a tray of full glasses.

After two more glasses of bubbly, she felt starry-eyed and had a sensation of gliding through the evening with everyone around her smiling. She'd been asked to dance by many partners, including Leo and even Dr Bingham. And at some point as she waltzed and tripped her way around the dance floor, she began to feel like a character in a Jane Austen novel. *Elizabeth Bennet for sure.* It made her smile even more. Then, seeing Marion at an ornate gold-painted table on the other side of the ballroom, she wove her way through to her.

Marion had an array of canapés and two more glasses of champagne ready and waiting on the table. 'Thought you might need a bite to eat after all the dancing you've been doing.' She grinned. And, as Lara slipped into the chair opposite, she was already picking up a delicate square of pastry topped with buttered shrimp and popping it into her mouth. Marion snorted with laughter then and pointed to the dance floor. 'Look, there's Doctor Bingham.' And, as Lara gazed in that direction, she saw him taking a turn of the dance floor with a portly middle-aged woman with henna-dyed hair.

'Who is that woman?' Lara giggled, reaching for another morsel of food.

'I have no idea, probably some wealthy landowner's wife.'

'Well, she looks like she's enjoying herself, but look at Dr Bingham's face.'

Marion snorted with laughter, and it set Lara off with a fit of giggles. Then, as they continued to watch the frown line between Dr Bingham's eyes deepen with every turn of the dance floor, Lara knew it had been worth coming to the ball just to see that.

'Uh oh,' Marion whispered, 'looks like you have another young gentleman coming to ask for a dance.'

'Oh no, I'm on a break,' she breathed, fanning herself with her napkin.

And, as the shy-looking young man came right up to the table and asked Lara for a dance, she explained her need to rest and told him politely, 'Maybe later.'

Once he'd retreated, Marion grinned. 'You're very popular tonight.'

'Well, you were on the floor every dance earlier on, so I could say the same for you.'

'I suppose so... but, you know what, I'm just not looking for that kind of thing right now. Since Scotland, I can't be bothered.'

'Did you have anyone there, in Scotland?'

Marion sat up straighter, furrowed her brow, and she was just about to say something when Angus staggered towards their table.

'Oh dear, he looks more than a bit worse for wear,' Marion murmured and, protective as always, she rose from her seat to steer the young doctor towards one of the open French windows. 'I'll get him out into the fresh air, might make him feel better.'

'Do you want me to help?'

'No, that's alright, I'm used to handling him when he's like this.'

She felt comfortable to sit alone at the edge of the dance floor sipping her drink and nibbling on cucumber sandwiches and cocktail sausages and, when she saw Leo dancing with Philippa Harrington, she noted a softening of the young woman's haughtiness as she danced with the vet. And when, on the next turn of the dance floor, Leo nodded in her direction, she smiled and raised her glass. However, his dance partner didn't look at all pleased if the pursing of her lips and narrowed eyes were anything to go by. It didn't bother her, she was a nurse, she'd seen humans in all states of joy and despair, so she knew all this here, right now, was mostly window dressing.

But, to avoid being a target for Miss Harrington's stern glances on her next turn of the dance floor, she stood up from the table and gazed out to the terrace to locate Marion and Angus. She saw them through the open French window and was just about to walk towards them when Marion saw her, waved and mouthed, 'We're coming back in. Wait there.'

She nodded, turned to go back to her table and that's when

she saw a man striding briskly in her direction. He looked just like... Wait. It was...

'Patrick,' she gasped as he stood before her in a wet overcoat, with his sodden hat clutched in his hand.

His face was set with rage and his eyes blazed as he glanced her up and down.

She was so stunned, she couldn't speak; she couldn't move.

'So glad you're making full use of that necklace,' he spat nastily, reaching for her then, trying to grab it from around her neck.

Quickly, she sidestepped him.

A hard ball of fury swelled in her throat and, knowing there was about to be a confrontation, she turned and walked towards one of the open French windows. Hearing the shouts of people from behind as Patrick bumped his way through to get to her, she felt her jaw tighten with aggravation. She wasn't having this. She wouldn't stand for it. For him to come here to the new life she was making for herself and accost her, it was outrageous.

Once outside, she turned to face him and stood her ground.

His eyes were burning into her, he seemed lost for words. And, when he put his soggy hat back on his head, she realised he'd been the stranger in the expensive overcoat she'd seen from the bus.

'How could you come here, like this, to my new home?' she demanded of him, her voice clipped as anger rose, bubbling inside her.

He smirked and she felt her stomach twist with fury at how she could have been taken in by this man.

'Well, Nurse Lara,' he spat, 'if you'd answered my letters and returned the necklace as requested, I wouldn't have needed to come all the way out here.'

'I don't want the necklace, I never wanted it. I was about to come back to Liverpool to return it to you.'

'Ha! Didn't stop you from wearing it tonight, though, did it?' he snarled.

'Well, given it was a gift, I've done nothing wrong.'

He grabbed her arm, pulled her roughly towards him. 'Well, what about giving me a kiss for old times' sake, given you're wearing my family jewels.'

'Let go of me,' she shouted, twisting her body away.

'Let go of me,' he mimicked, then nastily said, 'Come on, Lara. I had to pay through the nose to get some fella to bring me up here in his butcher's van. So, the least you can do is be a bit nicer to me.'

It was satisfying to know Mr Collins had made a good profit from his taxi service and she relaxed a little at the thought of it. Sensing a moment of weakness, he tightened his grip on her arm, and she pushed then thumped at his chest with a balled fist, but he managed to pull her even closer. She could hardly breathe now, crushed against his chest, and the once familiar smell of his expensive cologne was making her nauseous. Her mind was whirring with what to do next, she lashed out with her foot, tried to kick his shin, but he laughed and tightened his grip. Her heart contracted painfully as if it was being squeezed by an unseen hand. She tried to shout out, but her voice wouldn't come.

Suddenly he fell back, dragging her part way with him. He let go then crashed violently into a cane garden table. She was struggling to breathe, her vision felt blurred but, when she straightened up, she saw Marion standing with a balled fist, her eyes blazing with fury. She was standing over Patrick's prostrate form, threatening to punch him again if he didn't leave right now.

Others were arriving as he lay on the ground groaning – Bingham stormed through, shouting, 'What the hell are you doing to my nurses?' Angus was swaying and swearing and trying to threaten Patrick as he struggled up from the ground. Then Leo came running out through the French window, shouting, 'Lara, are you alright?'

'Yes, I'm fine.' She gulped, glancing down to her crumpled evening gown, still feeling the impression of Patrick's hands on her body.

Patrick was gasping for air, holding his ribs where he'd whacked himself against the table.

'I'm a doctor,' Bingham said. 'Do you want me to check you over for any injuries?'

'Bugger off,' Patrick growled.

'Alright,' Dr Bingham called, holding up both hands, then announcing to the group, 'It looks like he's refusing treatment, so there's nothing more we can do.'

Lara reached for Marion. 'Are you alright? Did you hurt yourself?'

Marion turned down the corners of her mouth, waggled her head as she opened and closed her right hand. 'Don't worry about that, I grew up fighting two brothers, so I know how to land a punch. It'll probably bruise up a bit, but I'm glad I whacked him good and hard before he got even rougher...' Then, with a wry twist to her mouth, 'So I'm thinking this fella is your ex?'

'Oh, yes. Most definitely *ex*.'

As Patrick straightened up, still groaning in pain, Lara walked to stand in front of him and she unfastened the necklace. Then, she dangled it in front of him. 'Like I said, I don't want it, I never wanted it. And I was going to bring it back to you in Liverpool anyway.'

He gulped a breath, swiped at his swollen, bleeding lip and, without a word, grabbed the emerald necklace from her hand and staggered away.

'Hmph,' Marion offered. 'Let's hope that's the last you ever see of him.'

Lara felt grateful for the solid presence of her friend because she was already beginning to feel a little shaky in the aftermath of Patrick's crass intrusion into her new life. And it made her annoyed to realise she'd been having a lovely time here at the ball before Patrick stomped in and ruined it.

'OK, team,' Dr Bingham called, 'I'm just going to have a word with Lord Harrington about organising some transport home for us. So, I suggest you sit here at these tables, then I can easily locate you.'

'Righto.' Marion nodded, already leading Lara to a seat, then grabbing hold of Angus and helping him down onto another. 'Keep an eye on each other, will you? I'm going to the ladies' cloakroom to soak my hand in some cold water, then we'll be ready to leave.'

Leo was still standing by and, even though he appeared more than a little tipsy, he was glancing around protectively like some kind of lookout. 'You can go back in now if you want,' Lara called to him, 'Patrick won't be back, not after that.'

The young vet was shaking his head. 'Well, I'm waiting here anyway. Just in case.'

'That's up to you,' she breathed, feeling a prickle of hairs at the back of her neck at the determined tone of his voice.

As soon as Bingham came back with Marion following behind, he gestured for them to follow. 'We've struck lucky, Lord Harrington has loaned us his big car and his chauffeur to take us back to the surgery.'

'Hurrah,' Angus cheered as he staggered up from his chair –

his ruffled hair and unbuttoned shirt collar adding to his disarray.

And as they straggled around to the gravelled drive at the front of the stately home to squash into a shiny cream and black Rolls Royce with an impressive chrome radiator grill, Lara smiled at the ridiculousness of their situation.

'No more bloody charabancs for me,' Angus slurred, 'I'm being chauffeur driven I am...'

Leo helped load his friend into the back while Marion and Lara clambered in at the other side, with Bingham sitting up front with the driver. 'You come too,' Angus slurred, reaching out to him.

'No, that's alright, I'll get on the chara with the rest of them.'

Angus chuckled then, tried to wink, but his eyes wouldn't work properly so he tapped his nose. 'I know what you're saying, old man... wouldn't do to leave the lovely Miss Harrington all alone at the ball.'

'No, no, it's not—'

'Your secret's safe with me,' Angus tried to whisper.

Leo laughed and shook his head. Then once more he glanced to Lara, his eyes piercing as he raised a hand in farewell before carefully closing the car door.

A tall, quietly spoken chauffeur in navy-blue livery soon had the engine ticking over and called over his shoulder, 'All back to Ingleside surgery?'

They muttered blearily, 'Yes please.'

And, as the car lurched forward then scrunched across the gravel, Lara snuggled against Marion and whispered a thank you.

'It's all part of our nurses' pact. You look after me and I look after me. No, that's not right. You, I mean, I look after you.'

Lara was giggling and she felt light-headed, but, even in her tipsy state, she sensed something shift inside of her. She reached up to where the emerald necklace had rested heavy against the base of her throat and, even though it was gone, she still felt the weight of it. But, as she stroked the skin where it had been, she realised she'd been searching for something even before she'd met Patrick, and right now it felt as if she were waking up to realise that. She'd see what the autumn and winter brought in Ingleside, but what had happened tonight had felt like a much stronger line being drawn under her previous life in Liverpool. And, even if she didn't stay on at the surgery, she knew now that she had the confidence to strike out even further. Maybe she would move to nurse somewhere else in the British Isles or America, Australia even. She heard the whisper of her Aunt Matilda's voice – *when you get your nursing qualification, the world will be your oyster*. And maybe it was just the champagne talking but, in the back of this posh car with her new colleagues from the surgery, she felt as if all manner of things might be possible.

7

Waking the next morning with a thumping headache, Lara groaned then turned over in bed. Hoping she wouldn't need to do anything other than rest and that for once her Sunday would be free from emergency calls, she closed her eyes and tried to drift back to sleep. But flashes of twinkling chandeliers and the chink of champagne glasses drifted back to her. Then her heart jumped at a flashback of Patrick's angry, snarling face. She groaned, buried her face in the pillow, forcing herself to picture him sprawled on the ground with Marion standing over him. The image eased her and, as she rolled onto her back, she tried to clear her head by gazing up to the whitewashed ceiling with its one simple light in a tasselled ivory white shade. Hopefully that would be it now, she would never need to see or hear from Patrick ever again. And, with that thought, she dozed off back to sleep, only waking when someone tapped gently at her door.

'Come in,' she called groggily, only realising when she'd pushed herself up on one elbow that she had no idea who was there.

It was Marion, and she tiptoed in, speaking quietly. 'I've come to check you're alright,' she said, standing over the bed like the kindly nurse she actually was.

'I'm fine. Just a bit of a headache, that's all.'

Marion perched on the edge of the bed. 'It's just, with that ex of yours turning up like that out of the blue... and how aggressive he was towards you, I was just wondering if you needed to talk things through.'

She felt her stomach tighten and, given the choice, she'd have pushed all her history with Patrick right down and not breathed another word. But, as Marion tipped her head to one side and offered a gentle smile, she knew this was her opportunity to spill the beans. So, once she'd settled her throbbing head back down on the pillow, she told Marion everything. The woman she'd seen him with in Liverpool, her collision with the van as she rode away from the scene, her head injury and hospital admission. And, when she spoke of Patrick turning up on the ward when she still lay unconscious to try and take back the necklace, Marion emitted an exasperated groan. Then she said, 'Given everything you've just told me, Lara, I wish I'd thumped him so much harder.'

Lara began to laugh, but it made her head hurt and she groaned with pain. And as Marion handed her the two aspirin and drink of water Mrs Hewitt had left on the bedside table, she felt cared for. As soon as she was settled, she reached for Marion's hand. 'Seriously though, I am so grateful for what you did last night.'

'All part of the service.' Marion smiled. 'Just glad I kept a check on my glasses of champagne, or I might have throttled him good and proper.'

'You did enough to deter him, that's for sure. He certainly

wouldn't have been expecting that from a woman in an evening gown.'

'I suppose not.' Marion chuckled.

'How's your hand, is it alright?'

'Yes, just a bit stiff, but no bruising.'

'That's good… and I'm so glad the confrontation took place outside, just imagine if we'd disrupted the dancing and been seen scrapping in the midst of such a lovely ball.'

Marion began to giggle and, when she could get her words out, she said, 'We wouldn't have wanted to get in the way of Dr Bingham dancing with that lady friend of his. I mean, he looked like he was enjoying it *so* much.'

Lara laughed out loud, then she was clutching her sore head. 'Maybe it's a good job the Harringtons only have a ball once a year. It might take me that long to recover.'

'Oh, well. They do have other balls at their London residence. Angus knows where it is and he says it's very grand.'

Lara blew out a breath. 'What a life, hey? We don't know how the other half live.'

Marion began to shake her head theatrically. 'Well, I don't think it would work for me… I mean, how the heck would I be able to ride my motorcycle in a fur coat and tiara? It'd draw way too much attention.'

Instantly, Lara was laughing again and, when Marion joined in, neither of them could stop.

'Everything alright in there?' Mrs Hewitt's voice called from the other side of the door.

'Yes. Please come in,' Lara called.

Mrs Hewitt clicked open the door and poked her head through. 'Oh, thank goodness, you're both laughing and not crying. It's hard to tell sometimes.'

'Oh, we're fine, we were just having a laugh about Marion riding her motorcycle in a fur coat and—' Lara stopped speaking abruptly as the housekeeper walked fully into the room with a perplexed expression.

'You alright, Mrs H?' Marion asked.

'Yes,' she said too briskly, clearly trying to shrug it off. 'It's just that I had a young man at the door last evening. He was a stranger – well-dressed, polite and he was asking for you, Nurse Flynn. I didn't tell him a thing, but it's been niggling at me because, although he was very handsome, I didn't like the look of him one bit.'

Lara felt her stomach tighten. 'Oh, I know exactly who that was, Mrs H. And you did absolutely the right thing by keeping quiet. That was Patrick, my ex, the one I told you about in the summer.'

She saw the housekeeper glance to Marion.

'It's alright, I've told Marion all there is to know about him. Because he caught up with me last night at the ball and gave me a bit of a shock.'

'We sent him packing though,' Marion purred.

The housekeeper emitted a low growl. 'If I'd known who he was, I'd have given him a piece of my mind. He didn't hurt either of you, did he?'

'Oh no,' Marion blurted. 'In fact, he was the injured party.'

'Well, that's all I needed to know,' Mrs Hewitt said firmly. 'Now, I'm just making some tea and toast. So, you two get yourselves down to the kitchen.'

'Right you are, Mrs H,' Marion called as the housekeeper clicked the door shut behind her. Then she leaned in to say, 'For an older woman, she's fearsome, isn't she, Mrs H?'

'She is indeed,' Lara replied. 'But she's also got that soft spot... I mean, look at the way she is with Angus and his behaviour at times would try the patience of a saint. Not to mention Bingham and his shenanigans. She deals with everything and everybody and I've no idea how she does it.'

'It's her life I suppose. I know she has a son out there somewhere but, beyond that, our Mrs H is a mystery.'

'I suppose we're all a mystery in our own way,' Lara offered, gazing to Marion then, hoping she'd use the hint to spill her own secrets.

Marion swallowed hard, dropped her head, but when she glanced up, she had that cheeky smile she often used. 'Come on, lazy bones, get yourself out of bed. I'm absolutely starving. Let's get down to the kitchen for that jammy toast.'

By the time Lara was downstairs at the table in her nightie and dressing gown, she felt boosted by a mug of sweet tea and a slice of toast. And as Marion chattered on, she began to feel very relaxed. 'Right, so I think it's my turn to make some more toast,' Marion called just as the telephone in the hallway began to ring loudly.

'Aaargh,' Lara groaned, clutching her still sensitive head as Mrs Hewitt went to answer.

In moments, she was back in the kitchen, her eyes wide. 'It's Sally Valentine about her son – he's spiked a high fever, he's delirious and he's having painful spasms through his body, especially the jaw.'

Marion gasped and leapt up from her seat. 'Tell her we're on our way. Then ring for an ambulance. This is almost certainly a case of lockjaw due to tetanus; it's a dire emergency. Is Dr Bingham still out?'

'Yes. And Angus went off earlier somewhere or other.'

'So, get straight back on the phone, tell her we'll be there as quick as we can.'

As Mrs Hewitt ran from the room, Marion called, 'It's me and you, Lara, let's get going.'

Lara was already on her feet, hurtling up the stairs behind Marion, all awareness of her sore head thrust aside. In minutes, she'd changed into her uniform, picked up her medical bag and was running back down.

'You alright on the back of the motorcycle, Lara?'

'Yes, absolutely. The quicker we can get there the better.'

Marion ran to the shed, pulled out the motorbike and jumped on with Lara straight there scrambling onto the back with her gaberdine mac hoisted up her legs. Clinging to Marion as she set off at speed, Lara snatched a breath as the back wheel skidded. Marion had it righted in seconds and, as Lara clung to her colleague, her brain ticked over the visit she'd made yesterday. Peter had been hotter than usual, but he hadn't spiked a fever, the wound had been clean with no signs of infection, so she'd put it down to heat from the open fire stacked with logs. She hadn't even considered the possibility of tetanus… But, if that's what it was, he would have picked it up from bacteria on the nail that caused the injury and there would have been no way of knowing until it showed itself fully. She felt her heart clutch with dread, tetanus was a very serious complication. The couple of cases she'd known in Liverpool had both died. Her whole body tightened as she silently urged Marion to go faster. Skidding around a corner, they both nearly came off, but Marion deftly righted the Norton and pushed ahead.

As soon as they arrived at the farm, they leapt off and ran across the yard, sploshing through mud with the dog barking madly and jumping up and down on his chain. The door was already open, and a distraught Mrs Valentine ran out to urge them in. 'Please, come quick. He's in a terrible state. My husband Harry's having to hold him down, he's having such strong spasms.'

They heard the lad even before they reached the room, he was grunting, thrashing in his bed. 'The nurses are here now, they're going to help,' Harry called, tears streaming down his cheeks.

He stood back from the bed and Marion instantly took charge. 'Right, the ambulance is on its way, but we need to bring his temperature down. So, please, Sally, can we have a bowl of tepid water and some cloths.' Already Lara could see Peter's jaw tightly clenched, so there'd be no chance of getting aspirin into him to bring down the fever.

She was right there beside Marion now, holding on to the lad to stop him injuring himself. Mrs Valentine ran back with the bowl of water and Lara felt the hairs at the back of her neck prickle when she heard Harry sob. 'Peter, stay *with* us. You have to fight.'

As Lara took the bowl, she saw little Izzy in the doorway, her eyes round as saucers, her face blanched. She glanced to Mr Valentine. 'We can manage him now, if you want to take Izzy and go outside to listen for the ambulance.'

Harry nodded, gave Sally a quick hug, then he was leading Izzy away.

Lara was already dipping cloths in the water, wringing them out, sponging the lad down. 'You've got a fever, Peter,' she murmured. 'That's why you're feeling so bad. But we'll cool you down and it will help.'

She didn't know if he'd taken it in or not, his eyes were glazed over, but she kept sponging as Marion checked his pulse and placed the thermometer under his arm to record his temperature. As they worked on the lad, Lara fought to stop him injuring himself with his full body spasms. Then, at the first urgent sound of the ambulance bell, her heart squeezed painfully tight at the sharp awareness of this desperate case. She knew there was every chance, given the severity of Peter's condition, that he would not return home.

The ambulance men moved quickly with their stretcher and, as Harry walked by the side to hold the lad in place, they got him safely loaded into the back. 'It'll be a struggle for one person to manage him with the strength of the spasms he's having, so I'll go in the ambulance,' Marion called, her voice clear-cut, decisive.

Sally shouted after her. 'Can I come with you? Please let me.'

The ambulance driver nodded. 'You'll have to come up front with me, lass. There's not much room in the back and that's where we need the medically trained.'

'That's alright,' Sally called, removing her apron, pushing it at Harry before running to the ambulance.

Just before the back doors closed, Lara shouted to Marion. 'Call with news as soon as you can.'

'Will do... Oh and you can ride Gloria back to the surgery when you're ready?'

'But I—'

'You've seen what to do. Go slow. You'll be fine.'

As the back doors closed, and the ambulance skidded away with its bell clanging, Lara felt her body begin to tremble. Then, when she saw Izzy white-faced and clinging to a stunned, shocked Harry, she held out an arm to the little girl. 'Come on, let's go back inside and have a cup of tea. It'll be a while before there's any news.'

Izzy nodded, broke free of her dad and walked silently beside Lara towards the house.

'Will Peter die?' Izzy asked, stopping as they were about to go in through the door.

'I don't know the answer to that question. But what I do know is that he's strong, and he'll fight hard to get home.'

The little girl gulped, nodded. 'I know he will... and I dreamt about him going away in an ambulance. But I woke up before the ending.'

'Well, let's hope it's a happy one.'

The little girl took a slow, shaky breath. And then the dog in the yard began to howl pitifully.

'It's alright, Fly,' Izzy called, 'Peter will be back soon.'

Almost as if the animal had fully understood what she'd said he emitted a heavy, desperate whine, then slipped down to the ground with his head resting on his paws.

'Fly and Peter are best friends,' Izzy said matter-of-factly as she grasped Lara's hand and led her through the door and into the kitchen.

The kettle was steaming on the stove so, as Lara reached for the teapot and the caddy, Izzy brought cups, sugar and milk. Harry walked in and slumped down onto a kitchen chair. He began to groan and put his head in his hands. Izzy went straight to him and placed her small hand on his arm. 'It's going to be alright, Dada,' she said softly, 'Peter will get better.'

'I hope you're right, lass,' Harry said, his voice strangled back in his throat.

Izzy nodded decisively. 'Peter is strong, just like you, Dada. We need to stay hopeful for him.'

Harry sat up straighter and wiped a hand around his face.

Then, as they sat quietly sipping their tea, Lara felt a part of the family closeness in the kitchen. After a while, Harry glanced across the table. 'So, all of us out here in the country know about the lockjaw and how dangerous it is. But I'm not sure where it comes from, how it's picked up. I mean, could me or Izzy start with it as well?'

'No, it's not like scarlet fever or measles or flu. It's an infection that comes from soil or manure... So, it's most likely Peter picked it up from the shippon or the farmyard via the sharp nail that caused his injury.'

Harry visibly slumped in his seat. 'I just wish I'd kept everything cleaner,' he croaked.

'It's impossible. These bacteria are so tiny you can only see them through a microscope. And, even if you scrubbed and cleaned spotlessly, they'd still be there. It's just potluck whether they're picked up from a nail or a muck fork or anything sharp.'

Harry nodded, but she could see by his anguished expression he wasn't convinced.

'Your Peter is young and fit, so he stands a good chance of coming through this. But I'll be straight with you, he'll need to fight very hard.'

Harry pressed his mouth into a firm line, nodded. 'I know. And our lad will be up for that.'

Izzy piped up then. 'He's going to get better, Dada, I saw it in my dream.'

Lara knew instantly that the little girl had given her dream a happy ending to comfort Harry and for someone so young it felt exceptional.

Harry pulled Izzy close. 'Well, that's good to hear, but sometimes dreams are just dreams.'

'Yes, I know that. But I think this one will come true.'

After a while, when Harry had finished his cup of tea, he rose from the table and pulled on his cap. 'I need to get on with the milking – it's a curse and a blessing when something like this happens, but the livestock need to be looked after come what may. Izzy, can you come and help me like you've been doing since Peter got sick.'

'Yes, Dada,' the little girl chirruped, 'I'll just get my welly boots.'

Lara got up from the table, picked up her medical bag, and told Harry that someone would telephone with news of Peter when it came. Harry offered a nod, then headed out to the yard with Izzy in tow.

Then, as Lara clicked shut the farmhouse door behind her, she remembered she'd have to ride the motorcycle back to the surgery. As she walked across the yard, she glanced to where they'd hastily left Gloria parked up and tried not to feel daunted. A few weeks ago, Marion had explained all the functions of the motorcycle. She'd got Lara to sit on it, kick start it, rev it... but then they'd been called out to an urgent case, so she hadn't had a chance to ride the thing. She blew out a breath as she walked, then muttered, 'It can't be much different from riding a bicycle.' But still she stood for a moment, then swallowed hard before she secured her medical bag above the rear mudguard. Without Marion, the machine felt bigger, more metallic and daunting. She did wonder if she should just push it back to the surgery but, no, she'd bite the bullet, she'd ride it.

So, first, she made sure the fuel was turned on, then she grabbed the right-hand lever to give some choke and attempted a kick start. Her foot slipped off clumsily and it riled her, especially on top of the exhaustion from her late night. She tried more keenly, aggressively this time and the engine caught. It sounded loud, so loud, and urgent. So, hoisting up her mac and uniform she slipped her leg over and sat astride. She twisted the throttle, it was lively, maybe a bit too lively.

'Blow it,' she said out loud, revving the engine, lurching out onto the lane.

Fly emitted a piercing howl, and it made her want to glance back to see what the dog was doing, but she was going too fast and veering wildly. She eased off in the way Marion had instructed her and managed to slow, but she was still riding through a brisk breeze with damp leaves fluttering in her face.

It felt miraculous to arrive back unscathed and, as she wheeled Gloria down the side of the surgery, she felt her body fizzing. Once she had the motorcycle in the shed, she was about to step in through the back door when it opened, and Dr Bingham emerged, looking tense.

'Ah, Nurse Flynn, how did it go? I was just about to set off to the Valentines'. What's the news on young Peter?'

'Not good,' she sighed, 'it's definitely tetanus with lockjaw and he's in a very poorly state. Marion went with him in the back of the ambulance and Mrs Valentine was up front with the driver – she just wanted to stay with him.'

Bingham blew out a breath. 'Probably a good decision. As you will be aware, the prognosis for tetanus is poor. I've only had one case that survived.'

She nodded. 'Let's hope his youth will be on his side.'

He pressed his lips together, nodded. 'So, Nurse Flynn, if you can hold the fort here, I'll nip down to the Infirmary and see what's what. If nothing else, I'll be there to support Sally.'

Lara offered a nod. 'That's good. And as soon as you have an update, please ring it through.'

'Will do,' he called as he made to move past her, but then he turned back with the beginnings of a twinkle in his eye. 'Nurse Flynn, I'm so sorry, but I can't help but comment on the smudges of dust you have on your nose and cheeks.'

'Oh, have I?' she replied, wiping at her face with the flat of her hand. 'It's just that I rode Marion's motorcycle back from the Valentines'.'

Bingham began to chuckle, and he was shaking his head as he walked towards the garage. Then he called back to her, 'It's good, it's so good you can ride that motorcycle. And I just want to say how proud I am of what you and Nurse Wright get up to on behalf of our patients.'

Lara felt a jolt at his words, he'd never offered any outright praise like this before and it threw her for a moment.

'Thank you,' she called after him, but he was already distracted as he opened the garage door.

8

By the next morning, it was business as usual, and Lara was first down to breakfast and anxious for more news of Peter Valentine. Dr Bingham and Marion had arrived back late after dropping Sally at the farm and the news had been stark. Although the lad had settled with sedation, it was still touch and go whether he'd survive. Lara's heart went out to the whole family, but she couldn't help but think especially of Izzy. If she had time after her morning visits, she'd call by the farm to check on the little girl.

As Mrs Hewitt handed her the list of visits, she noted how tired the housekeeper looked this morning. 'Are you alright?' she asked gently.

'Yes, I'm fine. I just couldn't sleep last night thinking about that poor young lad in hospital. I got to know Peter when his dad had a nasty cut to the hand with a scythe one hay time and he needed to come to the surgery for dressings. The lad had such a lovely smile and a lightness about him. I found it refreshing and...' she glanced down then, cleared her throat. 'And, well, he looked so like my son Ben at that age, it felt uncanny. It's hard to even think about it now but, as a child, Ben was bright and smiley, my little ray of sunshine.'

'Oh, Mrs Hewitt. I feel for you, I truly do,' Lara offered gently.

The housekeeper sighed, and shook her head. 'Thank you, Lara... I don't know what I'd do without you and Marion.'

Mrs Hewitt visibly straightened her back then reached into her apron pocket for the lists of visits, passing Lara hers. As she scanned through, she noted Daniel Makepeace first on the list. He was an elderly patient with heart failure who she'd attended since her first week in Ingleside. She also had a brand-new patient – a Mrs Lennox, an antenatal case. The address lay beyond the sawmill, a rural area she hadn't visited before. She'd ask Angus for directions; he was often called out that way to the many accidents at the mill. He loved to tell gruesome stories of severed fingers lying in the sawdust.

As she wheeled her bicycle down the village street, the autumn air felt cold and damp, but at least the sky was clear and already she was grateful for a glimmer of sun as it peeped above the rooftops. She felt content as she walked, noting the quiet stirring of the shopkeepers, the straggle of children walking up the hill to school and the steaming breath of two village women who chatted across the street as they swept the stone steps of their cottages. One or two villagers shouted a cheery good morning, which she reciprocated, and by the time she pulled up outside Mr Makepeace's steep-roofed single storey cottage she was humming with energy. As she leaned her bicycle against the newly whitewashed wall – work that had been done by Angus and Leo as a gesture of goodwill to Daniel, who was currently the longest-serving resident of the village, she thought of that first time she'd visited here in the summer after being dropped off by an irascible Bingham.

Briskly, she pulled her leather medical bag from the bicycle basket, glad those early days of settling in felt firmly behind her.

Knocking then entering through the unlocked door, she called to Daniel as she walked through. When there was no reply, she felt a ripple of concern despite knowing her patient spent his days between dozing and waking. She tapped on his bedroom door and called again and still there was no reply, so she pushed it open with some trepidation to find him sitting up in bed wearing a blue knitted woolly hat and matching fingerless gloves. Bright-eyed, he turned to her as a robin redbreast took flight from the sill of the open window, which looked out to the fields and trees.

'Sorry, Mr Makepeace,' she smiled, 'if I'd known you had a visitor I'd have come back later.'

'Don't you be worrying, Nurse Lara. He's a persistent little beggar so he'll be back… especially given the cake crumbs my niece, Esther, brought to feed him up now the colder weather's coming.'

'Yes, there's a decided nip in the air,' she smiled, 'so we probably need to make the most of these fine autumn days.'

'We do indeed,' he grinned, showing his single front tooth, 'because, when the weather gets even colder, Esther won't let me have the window open and that's when she moves me through to the front room so we can have the stove lit. Then that's me for the winter, gazing out to the street. When I had stronger legs and more breath, I'd go and sit by the open window. But last year, with my ticker playing up even more, that was the end of that.'

'Well, like you always say, Mr Makepeace – we can only do what we can do.'

'That's true, lass.' Then, with a wheezy chuckle as she wrapped the blood pressure cuff around his arm, 'Well, it's alright saying a thing... the truth is, I'm as mad as blazes I can't stay in this room.'

She chuckled then. 'I appreciate your honesty, Mr Makepeace.'

As always, she'd have loved to have stayed longer to gaze out of the window to the brown cows that grazed the field and listen to some of Daniel's stories of times gone by, but he was her first visit and not her last, so she had to press on. 'I'll see you again soon, Mr Makepeace. And I hope I haven't scared off your little red-breasted visitor.'

'That's alright, lass. As sure as night follows day, he'll be back for his cake crumbs.'

Setting out now to her new antenatal case – Lydia Lennox – she wheeled her bicycle back up the hill. As she progressed, she called out more good mornings here and there to villagers and the senior vet, Arthur Sullivan, as he bobbed out of his vet's surgery clad in a thick wool overcoat and wellington boots. 'Morning, Nurse Flynn.' He smiled, raising his battered trilby hat. Then she raised a hand to the now familiar milk cart pulled by a skinny black horse as it plodded slowly down the hill. The thin, elderly driver – Herbert Threlfall – was a friend of Daniel's and she often saw his horse tethered outside the cottage when he was visiting. As she passed the Fleece on her left, then the church to her right, she went by the surgery before remounting her bicycle and turning right onto the tarmacadam road that led out of the village and down towards the sawmill. As she passed through the cluster of newer houses, many of them occupied by millworkers, she waved to a young mother, Rose Ryan, whose baby girl she'd delivered back in the summer. They'd almost lost the mother and her baby to a catastrophic haemorrhage, so it was always good to see the red-haired young woman out and about with her baby girl, Cara, who was now thriving. It was tempting to stop and chat for a few minutes but, once she saw the ratcatcher, Septimus Finch, emerge from the side of Rose's cottage with a string of dead rats dangling from his hand, she called a cheery good morning and cycled by instead.

Rose smiled and waved, then she shouted after Lara, 'We've had rats in the backyard but that's the last of them now.'

Heading steeply downhill towards the mill with the screech of the big circular saw and the thump of the engine that drove the machines, she saw a tall metal crane in the factory yard swing round with a huge tree trunk lashed by a chain. The noise grew earsplittingly loud as she freewheeled down towards the mill race where deep gushing water rushed beneath a narrow bridge. She'd got used to the sound of heavy machinery in Liverpool, but it somehow felt more intimidating to be plunged into such industry amid open green countryside. As she reached the bottom of the hill, she pushed against the pedals but then turned at the barely audible shout from a tall, dark-haired fella who raised a hand in greeting from beside the crane. Instantly she recognised Ed Cronshaw, the father of another baby she'd delivered.

'Morning,' she shouted, her voice drowned out by the earsplitting high-pitched whirr of the giant circular saw as it engaged with the tree trunk. Seeing how it cut through the wood so effortlessly, raising sawdust into the air, she felt a shudder go through her knowing how vulnerable the soft flesh of the workmen would be to this savage industrial tool.

Leaving behind the metallic screech of the saw and the thump of the mill engine, she began to push at the pedals again as she cycled towards a large mill pond to her left. Then she needed to work harder to go uphill to her expectant mother. Angus had told her that the address she was looking for – Foxglove Cottage – was a mile or so beyond the sawmill and in a remote place close to the fells. Already she was wondering how any pregnant woman who already had three children was managing out there with no daily contact from other villagers. And, from what Angus had said, the woman's husband had tried but failed to get work around Ingleside, so he worked away, and she only saw him every few weeks.

Her concerns were heightened by the first sighting of the cottage – a single-storey ramshackle building with peeling paint and some broken roof tiles. As she dismounted and wheeled her bicycle to the door, she passed a small, enclosed garden that held the last of the late blooming flowers now withered and dry. But she could see the precision and the tidiness of the planting, and it heartened her as she tapped on the rickety door and heard the noise of at least two small children. The door was opened a crack by a young lad of around ten years who peered from beneath a long fringe of dark hair, his big brown eyes wide but very wary.

'Hello.' Lara smiled, tightening her grip on her leather medical bag as she caught the wail of another child inside the cottage. Then the soothing voice of a woman. But the boy was still standing with the door barely open.

'I'm the nurse from Ingleside Surgery and I've been asked by Dr Bingham to call by to see your mother.'

He twisted his body, called back with the information.

Lara stood calmly at the door, listening to the sharper tone of the woman as she tried to settle the crying child.

The boy narrowed the door even further and said, 'Mum's saying it's not a good time right now. Can you come back another day?'

Lara smiled. 'Well I could, but sometimes it's best to have a chat when things aren't at their best. Tell your mum I'm only here to help.'

The boy opened his mouth to reply, then glanced back. Then she heard a woman's voice say firmly, 'It's alright, Michael, let me speak to her.'

As the door opened wider, Lara offered her best warm but professional smile. Then, seeing the curve of the woman's very pregnant belly, she knew she was almost at term, so getting in to see her properly today was crucial.

'Hello, Mrs Lennox, I'm Nurse Flynn from Ingleside surgery.'

She saw the dark-haired woman glance back to shush her children then she wiped a weary hand around her face. 'I had a letter from that doctor, he said someone would be calling. But I'm up to the eyes with this lot today. So can you come back?'

Mrs Lennox ran a protective hand over her bump and, when she glanced up, Lara saw tears shining in her eyes. 'I never wanted this one so soon after my Ava, but these things happen, don't they?'

Lara reached out a gentle hand to her then and nodded sympathetically. 'Please, Mrs Lennox, let me come in so we can have a proper chat.'

The woman furrowed her brow, glanced back briefly over her shoulder. 'Right you are, but you'll have to take us as you find us. All hell's been let loose in here this morning with the two little ones.'

Relieved to see her step back and open the door, Lara walked through into the dim light of the low-beamed cottage. Michael, the young lad who'd answered the door, was sitting on a low truckle bed at the side of the room with a little girl with blonde curls at one side, and a boy of around four with the same dark hair and big brown eyes as himself at the other. The room was sparsely furnished but it was tidy and scrubbed clean. It felt pleasing to feel the warmth of the cast-iron stove in the corner and she was further heartened to see the metal safety guard that had been fixed to the wall – a good move for any home where small children roamed. Glancing to the cute blonde-haired toddler, she noted her sweet face and rosebud mouth. Clearly by the way Michael snuggled her with a protective arm, the little girl was adored.

'Sit down,' the woman sighed, gesturing to a rickety looking table with the dry, roughened hand of a woman who spent many hours doing the laundry.

'Thank you,' Lara replied, pulling a chair over the worn but scrupulously clean blue linoleum.

As Lara asked her questions about the pregnancy and tried to gently prise some detail of Mrs Lennox's personal circumstances, she sensed the woman's disquiet in her shifting glances to the children. They seemed very well behaved and were all sitting quietly on the truckle bed – the big brown eyes of the two boys taking in every detail as little Ava dozed off in Michael's arms. The scene felt idyllic, especially when she saw Mrs Lennox start to relax. But, when Lara asked the woman about her previous pregnancies, her face clouded over and, as she spoke, her voice broke. 'One bad winter when Michael was four, I lost two younger children – a son and a daughter – to whooping cough.'

Mrs Lennox rubbed a hand around her face, then drew a deep, shuddering breath.

Lara reached across the table, placed a gentle hand on her arm. 'I'm so sorry to hear that.' She knew from experience there were no words that could comfort any woman who had suffered such a loss. So, she sat quietly until Lydia got her breath back and, once her patient was ready, gently continued with her questions. There was nothing else that was a cause for concern apart from Mrs Lennox having come to them very late in her pregnancy, and she was isolated out here with a grocery shop delivering once a week and her only a visitor a kindly neighbour – a farmer's wife, Nora Hurst, who lived down the road. At least, though, it was reassuring to know Mrs Hurst had a telephone and Lydia's eldest lad, Michael, could be despatched to request a call to Ingleside surgery or to the joiner's workshop in Preston where Steven Lennox, the woman's husband, worked. It'd crossed her mind to ask why the family weren't all living in Preston but, when it emerged that Steven was keen to move to Ingleside after he'd completed his apprenticeship, it kind of made sense.

Moving on to the next stage of her assessment, Lara asked, 'Is it alright if I have a feel of your tummy so we can establish which way your baby is lying?'

Mrs Lennox shrugged. 'Of course... but I'm sure this one's head down because I can feel it kicking up here.' She laid a hand on the upper right quadrant of her abdomen.

'You know your stuff, like most experienced mothers,' Lara smiled, 'but I just need to check before you go into labour. Is that alright?'

The woman nodded, then levered herself up from the kitchen chair and waddled to the bedroom. Calling over her shoulder to her eldest, 'I won't be long, Michael. If you want, you can get some more wood for the fire.'

As Lara followed her into the bedroom, she noted a clean space with a large iron-framed bed, some watercolour paintings of flowers on the wall, and a pair of neat blue and white checked curtains at the small window. Once Mrs Lennox was settled on the bed, she palpated her abdomen then used the foetal stethoscope to listen to the rapid thump of the baby's heart. It always gave her a trill of pleasure to hear that sound and sense the new life within. 'That's a good strong heartbeat,' she smiled, 'and you were spot on with your assessment of the position – head down in an anterior position. Your baby's a lively one as well, kicking away in there.'

As Lydia pulled down her cotton dress, she said, 'So it looks like we're all set then,' but her voice held a dullness that felt a little troubling. But, then again, it wasn't unknown for a woman who was dealing with an unexpected pregnancy with three other children to look after to sound weary. Lara made a mental note of it, though, and she'd be on the lookout for any other signs that might indicate a tendency towards melancholia. She'd seen it in other hard-pressed mothers but, with a close eye and extra support after the baby was born, more often than not it was manageable.

'How are you feeling about this pregnancy, Mrs Lennox?' she asked gently.

The woman sat up and began to struggle off the bed. 'Fine, just fine. These things happen, don't they, and we just have to get on with it.'

'Well, there are ways of preventing—'

'I know,' she cut in, 'but Steven won't use anything like that so...'

Lara reached out to her then. 'Look, I've heard many women report the same thing, but it's important for you to have a say in this. So, let's have another chat after the baby's born.'

'Alright,' the woman breathed, and there it was again, that flat, deadpan weariness that set off a bat squeak of concern. But, then, maybe it was pure exhaustion, and the woman was isolated out here apart from the visiting farmer's wife. She'd need to monitor things, but then, as she said her goodbyes and waved to the children, they all responded with a cheeriness that undercut her niggling concerns.

As she freewheeled down towards the screech of the big circular saw at the mill, she could hardly bear the noise. 'For goodness' sake,' she muttered to herself, knowing how she'd managed all manner of loud, industrial noises in Liverpool plus the sound of the docks and the roar of traffic. But she supposed it was the stark contrast with the peace of the countryside that got to her out here. Then, when she heard Ed Cronshaw and Danny Ryan – the husband of Rose, who she'd waved to earlier – yell a cheery hello, she offered a smile and a wave, and it felt good.

Pedalling hard to get up the steep hill at the other side, she left the clatter and screech of the sawmill behind and, once she'd reached the top, pulled over to catch her breath while she thought through her remaining visits. As she stood astride her bicycle, she felt calm amid the gently falling leaves and the spiky shelled chestnuts that lay on the ground. Then, as the sun peeped out and shone through the orange and gold leaves, she felt tears prick her eyes at the beauty of a beech tree across the lane. And the words of a poem she'd learned at school – something about the season of mists and mellow fruitfulness – came back to her then and she felt a warm glow deep inside.

It buoyed her up for the rest of her morning visits and then, as soon as she was back to the surgery for lunch, Mrs Hewitt met her with a beaming smile. 'Dr Bingham was down to the Infirmary this morning and there's good news about young Peter – he isn't quite out of the woods yet, but he's definitely rallying.'

Lara felt her body slump with relief, and she was still smiling as she slid onto her chair at the kitchen table. 'That's such good news,' she murmured, reaching for the hot, sweet tea the housekeeper had just placed in front of her. Mrs Hewitt raised her own cup in a toast. 'Here's to Peter Valentine, let's hope his recovery is swift and he's soon back to the village.'

9

After a few days of brief respite with spells of sunnier, drier weather, it felt appropriate that it had turned cold and wet for James Alston's funeral at Ingleside church. It was a mournful day with big spots of rain and dried autumn leaves blowing around as Lara followed Dr Bingham along a path between the graves. And as they walked together through the heavy oak door of the church where she'd last been to attend the annual Harvest Festival, the contrast felt stark as she recalled the brightness of children singing their Harvest hymns and the sweet, fruity smell of apples and pears. Having been made to attend Sunday services as a child in Liverpool by her Aunt Matilda, she felt comforted by the wood polish smell and the hushed tones of the local folk who'd come to pay their respects and say farewell to a good-natured, kind and hardworking man who had farmed here from being a lad. As she slipped into the back pew next to a silent, stern-faced Bingham, she saw Grace at the front all in black, her hair tied neatly back, her head bowed. And, almost as if her friend knew she'd arrived, she glanced over her shoulder and acknowledged her with a nod. In that split second, Lara noted her ashen face and eyes reddened from crying. Gone was the lightness of being Grace always had; she looked wrung-out. Thankfully, though, right next to her on the front pew was the firm, reassuring presence of Aunt Agnes.

When the white-haired, stick-thin, elderly woman playing the organ launched into a funeral march, a ripple of emotion ran through the congregation and a heart-wrenching sob came from the front. It was Grace, and the sorrowful sound forced tears to Lara's eyes. As she rose with the rest of the congregation in the packed church, she grasped the pew in front, and in moments the pall bearers carrying the coffin were walking slowly down the red-carpeted aisle. As the organ continued to play, Lara felt the music and the grief of the attendees combine as if it were a real, living thing that bound the community together. When she glanced to Bingham, she saw him gripping the pew in front, his eyes shiny with tears.

The rest of the service went by in a blur as she repeated the words, sang the hymns and then, when the first few creaky notes of 'Abide With Me' came from the church organ, her throat felt so tight she could barely join in with the hymn. Grace was sobbing freely now at the front of the church, and Lara felt heavy with the weight of her friend's sorrow. Aware that Bingham was dabbing at his eyes with a pressed white handkerchief Mrs Hewitt had supplied before they'd gone out through the door, she gave his arm a squeeze.

Then, as the elderly vicar, Reverend Hartley, gently brought the service to a close, she began to feel calmer. But, as the four pall bearers made their way steadily back up the church carrying the oak coffin on their shoulders, she sucked in an urgent breath to steady herself. Recognising the dark-haired young coffin-bearer at the head of the coffin as the cousin of Grace's she'd met in the summer, she snatched a breath when she recognised Leo's bowed head as he brought up the rear. Then, as Grace walked slowly by, bent over as if she'd received a heavy blow, Lara needed to fight back tears. As the other attendees filed past, including Alice Taylor – the mother of a very poorly child she'd treated during the summer – she returned their nods and their sorrowful half smiles. As the last few mourners straggled by, she noted a catch in Bingham's breathing as he readied himself to move. When he nudged her gently with his elbow, she held him back for a few moments until the white-haired organist had passed by and then she stepped into the aisle.

As the single church bell continued to toll, they walked out to find the wind had whipped up even more strongly now and there were dried leaves swirling amid heavy spats of rain. She gasped and pointed to the sky when she saw bats flying and swooping overhead.

Dr Bingham leaned in and spoke quietly. 'The bats live in the church tower so, every time the bell is rung for funerals or weddings, out they come for a swoop around.'

Lara gulped back a mildly hysterical noise in her throat as she followed him along the path then down the church steps to the village street. Bingham stopped abruptly and turned to face her. 'I'd have liked to have gone to the grave to see Jim laid to rest, but I make a point of only doing the church services in case there's an emergency call and I need to leave abruptly.'

'I see, that makes sense,' she called through the strengthening breeze, clutching a hand to her district nurse's hat as a stronger gust threatened to send it flying down the village street.

As they turned to walk back up to the surgery, Mrs Hewitt came running with a hand clamped over a black rain hood. 'Nurse Flynn,' she called, as the wind gusted and dead leaves swirled, 'we've had an urgent call from Miss Dunderdale at

Brook House, she's slipped and fallen, and she's had to crawl to the hallway to use the telephone. She was in a bit of state and thought she might have broken some bones. And she was asking for you.'

Lara glanced to Dr Bingham, and he nodded sharply. 'Off you go. I'll see you later.'

Instantly, she was running up to the surgery, her hand holding her brimmed nurse's hat on her head.

Straight in through the front door, she ran down the green-tiled corridor and grabbed her raincoat and waterproof hood from one of the brass hooks. Then she scooped up her medical bag and legged it to the back door. Bingham had just arrived through the front door and, slightly out of breath, he shouted after her, 'I'd run you in the car, but I need to see an urgent case at the cottage hospital in Ridgetown. Angus has the Austin and Marion's already out on her motorcycle. And you'll need to get out on your other visits afterwards, so it's best to use the bicycle.'

'Righto,' she called as she pushed open the door and ran through the dead leaves that lay in a swirled pile in the back yard.

In moments, she had her bicycle pulled from the shed, her medical bag in the basket, and was freewheeling down the cobbled hill towards the hump-backed bridge and out to the country lanes.

She pedalled furiously and it cast her back to her first day at the surgery, when she'd been called to see Miss Dunderdale urgently. The elderly woman had been very hostile to her as a new nurse, and she'd refused all intervention. But things had turned around so much now that she was often the 'chosen one'. It felt good to be accepted, but she was very much aware that nursing and doctoring were always teamwork and, for the best quality of service, all members of that team needed to work together.

Pushing hard against the pedals over the final distance, with leaves swirling and a strong breeze tugging at her rain hood, she felt glad to see Brook House up ahead. She parked briskly and pulled her medical bag from the basket, then went straight to the front door and knocked firmly. When no reply came, she pushed open the door and walked through into the dimly lit stone-flagged hallway.

'Hello, Miss Dunderdale,' she called, keeping her voice steady.

At a moaning sound from the shadows further along, she picked up her pace. Her patient was slumped against the wall next to the telephone. She was clearly in pain and holding her left wrist.

'Miss Dunderdale,' Lara called gently, already on her knees beside her patient.

The grey-haired woman groaned then shot her a sharp glance. 'I'm so glad it's you, Nurse Flynn.'

'Let's have a look at you then... so, you've had a tumble. Where did you hurt yourself?'

'Yes, I was coming out of the kitchen, and I don't know what I was doing but I overbalanced, and I put this arm down to break the fall.'

Miss Dunderdale held up her hand then and sucked in a sharp breath.

Already Lara could see swelling but, thankfully, the wrist didn't seem to be out of shape. 'I'm sorry, Miss Dunderdale, but I'm going to have to examine it so I can check for any displacement. It'll hurt, I'm afraid.'

'Do what you need to do,' her patient said through gritted teeth.

Lara gently took the arm and, as her patient winced and held back a cry, she felt along the bones for any deformity. Nothing seemed to be out of place, so she asked, 'Can you move your fingers for me?'

'Aaargh,' Miss Dunderdale shouted as she waggled her fingers.

Lara pulled the sharpened pencil she used for writing up her notes out of her pocket and gently pressed the point against each of her patient's fingers. 'Can you feel that? Any loss of sensation?'

Miss Dunderdale shook her head. 'But my wrist hurts like the devil all the same.'

'I don't think it's fractured, but a sprain can be just as painful, and take as long to heal. So, first, let me give you some aspirin for the pain, then I'll bandage the wrist, and you can sit with your arm elevated to reduce the swelling. Then hopefully it will feel more comfortable.'

Miss Dunderdale nodded then, with tears shining in her eyes. 'You are my guardian angel, Nurse Flynn. I can't thank you enough.'

'It's all part of the service.' Lara smiled as she helped her patient up off the floor. 'And, as soon as I've got you bandaged up, I'll check your pulse and temperature, so we have the full picture. I trust you're still taking the heart medication you were prescribed in hospital?'

'Yes,' she nodded, 'and, as you know, I'm not always good at following orders... but with the new tablets, I've been a very good girl.'

'Excellent.' Lara smiled.

After she'd left Miss Dunderdale propped comfortably against cushions in her armchair in the kitchen, with a cup of tea and two slices of buttered toast in front of her, she cycled on through squally rain and gusting wind to her remaining visits.

Arriving back to the surgery for lunch with rainwater stinging her eyes, her macintosh and rain hood dripping water over the tiled floor, she felt as if she'd been wrestling with the elements. As she removed her waterproofs and hung them to dry on the brass hooks in the corridor, she heard a screech of pain from the waiting room. Instantly, she ran to see what the matter was.

'Sorry, Nurse Flynn,' a young woman with a squirming red-cheeked child on her lap called, 'this little blighter just bit me.'

It was Ed's wife, Lizzie Cronshaw, with her three-year-old daughter, Sue, writhing on her lap. 'She's got another earache and I've been up all night with her. I'd have been here sooner only I needed to take the baby to Ed's mother, Betty, down the street because I'm darned if I can manage both of them when Sue's like this.'

'Of course, that makes sense,' Lara soothed, kneeling beside the mother and child. Sue held a special place in Lara's heart because she'd been the first emergency case she'd treated in Ingleside. And she'd also delivered Lizzie's baby boy, William, back in the summer.

'The doctor should be calling you in soon,' Lara told her, 'but just shout if you need anything. I'll be in the kitchen.'

'Right you are,' Lizzie called as Sue began to pull her ear and cry miserably.

Angus was already in his seat at the scrubbed kitchen table, and he was piling a selection of sandwiches onto a large white porcelain plate.

'Here she is, another straggler coming home,' Mrs Hewitt called from the Aga.

'That's me,' Lara replied as she placed her medical bag down on the tiled floor and pulled out her chair.

Angus turned to her, still chewing his most recent sandwich. He began to chuckle.

'Whatever is it?' she asked, adding a playfully irritated tone to the question.

'You've got dried leaves in your hair,' he laughed, 'and a smudge of mud on your cheek.'

'Oh, for goodness' sake, no wonder. Unlike you, in the lap of luxury riding around in your little blue car, I'm out on my bicycle exposed to the elements.'

'And it shows,' he guffawed. But then he got up, mid-sandwich, and helped her to pick out the leaves. 'Oh, that's an oak leaf,' he said, still chewing, 'and you've got some broken-up bits of beech in there as well.'

'Thank you for naming them, Dr Fitzwilliam. I'm surprised at your breadth of knowledge given you were born and raised in a city.'

'As were you, Nurse Flynn.' He grinned before sliding back onto his chair and reaching for another sandwich.

'There you go, a nice hot brew of tea.' Mrs Hewitt smiled as she placed the cup down with a satisfying clunk.

As Lara reached for a sandwich, the warmth of the kitchen began to seep through to her bones. And once the autumn shivers had gone, she was able to relax back in her chair and it felt good to know that soon the place opposite would be taken by Marion as she returned from her visits. Then no doubt Dr Bingham would huff his way in from seeing his patients in clinic. And, once Mrs Hewitt had paused her household duties to take a break, she'd settle in her own seat, and the gathering around the table would be complete.

10

Once lunchtime was over, Bingham pushed back his chair and rose from the table. 'So, Nurse Flynn, are you ready to help in the afternoon clinic?' he asked with uncharacteristic good humour.

Instantly, she felt thrown by his exuberance. Often he only showed that side of himself when he was working with his patients. 'Yes, of course,' she replied, narrowing her eyes, wondering if this bonhomie was some kind of trick he was playing.

No, it didn't seem to be, but, still, as she got up to follow the senior doctor, she glanced to Angus and he shrugged, briefly turning down the corners of his mouth. Obviously, he'd also picked up on the senior doctor's jollity. But the whole thing felt very short lived when Bingham turned to Mrs Hewitt with a deep frown and asked, 'Where the blazes is our Nurse Wright? She's even later back than usual?'

Mrs Hewitt looked perplexed. 'She'll be back soon, she had an extra visit added on last minute, if you remember.'

Changing Seasons for the Country Nurse 97

'Yes, of course she did,' he said with gusto, as he strode out of the kitchen with Lara following.

When the telephone began to ring loudly on its small table at the foot of the stairs, he snatched up the receiver, raising a delaying hand. 'Right, so she's definitely in labour by the sound of it. And, yes, I've got the name... it's Lydia Lennox at Foxglove Cottage. I'll send Nurse Flynn right away. Thank you, yes, she will be there as soon as possible.'

'That was Mrs Lennox's neighbour, Nora Hurst. I trust you got the gist of it?' he asked as he replaced the receiver.

'Yes, my patient has gone into labour, so it looks like I won't be assisting you in clinic after all.'

'Quite right.' He smiled, then walked away to his clinic room, quietly whistling. Even the two patients in the waiting room appeared surprised by his cheeriness. There really was no way to fathom the senior doctor.

Already, Lara was heading back to the kitchen to collect her medical bag. 'I'm off to attend Mrs Lennox, she's gone into labour,' she said quickly, then, grabbing her macintosh and rain hood from the corridor, she was straight out through the back door. Even before she set off on her bicycle, she felt heavy spits of rain. And with gusting wind coming at her and slate-grey clouds overhead, it didn't bode well for an easy journey. But, strangely, she felt glad to be out in the open air and not cooped up in the surgery with Bingham. She'd got used to working with him now, but, in clinic, she felt more of a handmaiden. It suited her to be out and about on the district, working independently.

As she pedalled towards the turning for the sawmill and turned right, she was soon freewheeling down towards the mill with falling leaves fluttering all around. Then, as her brain flitted over Mrs Lennox's antenatal detail, there it was again, that bat squeak of concern. Maybe she was niggling because her patient had already lost two small children or was it the ramshackle cottage and poor living conditions that troubled her. But, despite the anxiety she'd sensed in the eldest boy, Michael, the two little ones seemed happy and content. She couldn't put her finger on it, and she'd had similar intimations before with other families, so she knew that often in the fullness of time they didn't lead anywhere. So, she didn't set too much store by it. But one thing she'd learned from her early days of nursing was to never dismiss a gut feeling.

Hearing the thump of the mill engine and the ear-piercing screech of the big saw, she steadied herself to negotiate the bridge over the mill race. Expecting to see Ed Cronshaw or Danny Ryan out in the yard with their cheery hellos and friendly waves, she felt oddly disappointed. But then, as she cycled by the mill pond and gazed over the stone wall, she felt cheered by two ducks bobbing about on the rippling water. It began to spit with rain again then, so it felt harder to pedal up the other side of the steep valley and she needed to dismount to wheel her bicycle over the final stretch. But she was soon on her way and, as she approached Foxglove Cottage, it struck her afresh how exposed and forlorn it was up here, away from the shelter of the valley. Even more so now the light was beginning to fade. Thankfully, she'd recently checked her bicycle lamp battery as inevitably she'd be riding back to the surgery in pitch darkness.

As she leaned her bicycle against the wall of the single-storey cottage, she caught the sob of a child from within and it snagged her heart. Grabbing her medical bag, she walked briskly to the door and knocked. When no one came, she was about to let herself in, but the door swung open to reveal a thin-faced woman with steel-grey hair and a very solemn expression. Lara felt her breath catch at thoughts of a complication in labour, but then the woman smiled and introduced herself as Nora Hurst, the farmer's wife from down the road, and instantly she felt reassured.

'So, you must be the new nurse,' Nora said, not waiting for a reply before rushing in to give the detail of the labour. 'Lydia's waters broke two hours ago, but she waited a while before she sent Michael down to ask me to make the telephone calls, then I came back up here with him. The contractions are strong and regular, so she's making good progress.' Mrs Hurst paused then, knitting her brow. 'I also telephoned Steven, her husband, and he said he'd make it back as soon as possible but he didn't think the foreman of the joinery shop would let him go until he'd completed his full shift.'

'Oh, that's a shame, but it's often the way. And sometimes the men don't mind because they like to be elsewhere when the birthing is going on,' Lara offered as she removed her macintosh and hat, placing them on the back of a kitchen chair.

'Hang them on the hooks behind the door.' Nora pointed to the place where the children's coats and woolly hats were hung.

At the guttural sound of Mrs Lennox in the bedroom, Lara picked up her bag and offered a reassuring smile to the children who were sitting quietly on the truckle bed, Michael with an arm around Freddy at one side and his toddler sister Ava at the other with her blonde, curly head resting against him.

Lara knocked gently on the bedroom door and entered. 'Hello there, Mrs Lennox,' she called, 'sounds like you're well on the way to delivery.'

'Yes,' the woman groaned, then she reached out an arm, her face contorted but not with pain because the contraction had receded.

'Tell me you'll make sure the children are looked after if

something happens to me,' she croaked, her eyes filling with tears, beseeching.

'Yes, of course I will. But you're going to be fine,' she soothed. But the woman clutched at her. 'I'm not sure about this one, I don't know how I'm going to be.'

'There, there,' she murmured gently, feeling her throat tighten at the woman's despair.

'I'm here with you now. I'm going to make sure your baby is delivered safely and that you come through all of it. Is it alright if I call you Lydia?'

The woman gulped, nodded, but her face was still stricken.

'Here, take a drink of water,' Lara soothed as she picked up a spouted cup from the bedside table.

Then, as the next contraction began to build, she held on to the woman, murmured words of encouragement, tethered her as she gasped her way through.

'That's it, you're doing so well,' Lara soothed as she gently wiped the woman's reddened, sweating face. Then, as she accessed that calm place deep within that helped her manage her labouring women, she offered more words of gentle encouragement.

Only then, once she had her patient settled, did she gently palpate Lydia's wrist for a pulse, take her temperature and use the foetal stethoscope to listen to the baby's heartbeat.

'Your baby sounds strong,' she smiled, 'looks like you're about to deliver another little trooper.'

As she settled on a Lloyd loom chair beside the bed, she supported Lydia through every contraction. And, even though she sensed the woman relaxing a little between pains, it felt worrying that her patient still had that haunted look in her eyes. She'd need to assess after the baby was born, but she was increasingly concerned for Lydia. It was reassuring, though, to know that Nora was there with the children, and she was doing a fine job of keeping everything calm. Michael was a very capable older brother, but he was only ten years old, and it was a lot of responsibility for him to bear. When the toddler, Ava, began to grizzle in the next room, she saw her patient visibly twitch with agitation.

'It's alright,' Lara soothed as another contraction began to build. 'Nora has everything under control, and she'll look after your little girl.'

Lydia gulped, nodded, her eyes flitting about the room.

Lara worked hard to contain the woman's knife-edge of tension, but the effort of doing so made her feel increasingly wound up. In her early days of delivering babies, she'd struggled to hide her anxiety, but she was an experienced midwife now, and she took it all in her stride. But everything about this case was telling her she had to be extra vigilant, especially given the cottage was out in the middle of nowhere. When she'd worked in the city, there'd been any number of neighbours and other folk around who'd run to the hospital or call for an ambulance, but out here felt very remote.

At least her patient was progressing nicely and, even as she checked her pulse then reached for the foetal stethoscope to listen to the baby's heart, she heard that unmistakeable catch in Lydia's breathing that indicated a progression to the second stage of labour. 'Your baby will be here very soon,' she said gently. 'Just keep doing what you're doing until the head comes down, and, when the time is right, I'll tell you to push.'

'Aaarghhh,' Lydia shouted out loud, and she was pushing already. Given this was her sixth delivery, she got straight on with it and, in what felt like moments, Lara was delivering a baby boy with a fine head of dark hair, who was taking his first breath and then offering a lusty cry.

The mother lay back with a groan, and closed her eyes. She looked beyond tired, so exhausted she didn't seem to take in whether she'd delivered a girl or a boy. She just lay there, with no energy to welcome her child.

Again, Lara had seen this before, and it wasn't always a worry. Labour was exhausting, especially for an older mother who already had children. So, as she cut the umbilical cord and secured it with suture thread, then cleared the mucus from the baby's nose and mouth, she let Lydia rest. And, as she wiped the baby boy's face and body with a soft towel, he blinked open his dark eyes and wrinkled his brow.

'Hello,' she said gently, smiling as he sneezed.

Then she swaddled the baby in a cot blanket and moved up the side of the bed with him in the crook of her arm. 'Lydia,' she called gently, 'do you want to hold your baby boy?'

Lydia opened her eyes, smiled and took the baby. 'Hello,' she crooned, and instantly her eyes filled with tears, then she began to sob.

Again, this wasn't an uncommon reaction... she'd seen laughs, smiles, sobs, tears. So, she kept a gentle eye on the mother and baby, but had no undue concern.

Once the afterbirth had been delivered, the mother and baby had been washed and freshly laundered bed sheets were in place, the scene was set for the children to meet their new baby brother. So, after speaking to Lydia and getting her agreement, Lara opened the connecting door to find the three children waiting in line with Nora Hurst smiling beside them.

'Well, do you want to come and meet your baby brother or not?' Lara asked.

'Yeah,' Michael called as he led the way with Freddy at one side and Ava at the other.

Lara stood back, watched as each of the children said hello

and kissed the baby on the cheek. Freddy and Ava soon lost interest and were wandering back through to the kitchen to find some toys, but Michael stayed right there beside his mother, stroking the baby's face.

'He's so tiny,' he breathed, 'I don't remember Ava being so small.'

'She was.' Lydia smiled.

Then Michael spoke so gently it almost brought tears to Lara's eyes. 'Can we call him Jamie, like you said, if it was a boy?'

'Yes, of course,' Lydia replied, and, as the mother and son had their heads together gazing at the new arrival, Lara sensed the closeness they had, and it made her push back the niggles she'd felt earlier.

Knowing there wasn't much more she could do now except wait for Steven to arrive, she thanked Nora, who needed to get back urgently to her duties on the farm. Nora had hinted that Michael would be perfectly capable of being left until his father arrived. But the lad was only ten, and without the support families had in the city with close neighbours at either side, she knew she needed to wait. And even as she sat at the rickety kitchen table writing up her notes, the door shot open and a short, stocky man, red-faced and sweating, his pale hair poking from beneath a flat cap, burst in. He was fighting for breath. 'I've run most of the way after getting off the bus in the village,' he huffed with some effort. Then, as the two little ones ran at him, he called across to Lara, 'What is it, what have we got?'

'You have another son, Mr Lennox. A bonny baby boy,' she smiled, closing her notepad, readying herself to leave. 'So, I'll just check your wife and baby for a final time then I'll leave you to it. Lydia's had plenty of practice at this, so she knows exactly what to do. But if there are any concerns whatsoever overnight, run down to Nora at the farm and use her telephone. Ingleside surgery is set up to take calls at any time, day or night. You might get Doctor Bingham with his outdoor clothes over his pyjamas, but you will get a visit from someone.'

'Thank you, nurse. For what you've done,' he croaked, tears shining in his big brown eyes.

'All part of the service,' she replied, pushing her pad and pencil into her bag and clicking it shut. 'I'll just nip in to your wife quickly. Then I'll be back tomorrow for the first postnatal check.'

'Right you are,' Steven beamed, his cheeks shining like red apples as he stood like a rock holding Ava in one arm and Freddy in the other. Michael was standing back a little, glancing shyly at her from beneath his long fringe, but he was beaming a smile, and Lara could sense the strong link he had with his dad. It was a good thing. Often the working fathers of the babies she delivered were distant figures. But, so far, out here she'd found a pleasing closeness within families. That special bond that tied them to each other and to their neighbours as well.

After her final checks on Lydia and baby Jamie were completed, she said her goodbyes to the exultant husband and children. And, as she left the warmth of the kitchen and stepped out into the damp, chill air, she shivered. It was pitch dark, so she appreciated the mellow glow of the oil lamps inside the cottage. And, as she pulled her bicycle away from the wall and switched on the lamp, she felt grateful for its thin light and hoped it had enough power to take her all the way back to the village. That was one thing she missed about Liverpool, the streetlamps, and out here she'd only ridden short distances in the dark. But, as she pushed her medical bag into the basket and secured her rain hood in case there was another downpour, she felt a little nervous about the journey back, but most of all her heart swelled with satisfaction at what she'd done here today.

The baby was strong and healthy and, with his head of dark hair, he was already the spitting image of his two brothers.

Lara pedalled slowly at first until her eyes adjusted to the dark shadows that seemed to loom from the hedges and trees at either side of the lane. And the narrow slit of light cast by the lamp barely illuminated a few feet ahead. Given she didn't feel confident to freewheel in the pitch dark down towards the mill, she dismounted so she could wheel her bicycle. And, even as her sharp ears picked out the gurgle of the mill race further down, she still felt the silence of the fields and the woods around her. At a sudden rustle of roosting birds or maybe wildlife in the hedgerow, she snatched a breath, felt her heart clench. Then a fox shot out across the road right in front of her and she gasped with shock. But the creature was gone so fast, disappearing with a rustle of grass into the dark bank, all that remained was the catch in her breath and the full beat of her heart. It made her feel more alert, stronger somehow, and as she heard the strengthening gush of the mill race and saw the looming shape of the factory buildings, she pushed on.

Her senses were heightened, maybe because of the rapid flowing water. But, at the loud snap of a twig, she startled. And, as she passed down the side of the darkened mill, then out towards the yard, she heard a sharp crackle and saw a flicker of flame. It felt odd. As far as she was aware, there was no night watchman here, why would there be? But then, at a louder crack and a lick of flame that rose higher, she felt her heart jump and her entire body tightened. She knew there had to be a person right there, lurking near the mill. Somebody had set this fire, and clearly it was a threat to the timber in the yard. In the next second, she sucked a sharp breath; she felt sure she'd just seen a fleeting shadow of someone in the flickering light. Then it was gone, and among all the dark shapes around the yard, she knew she could have easily imagined it. Her heart picked up a staccato beat as she wheeled quickly now, her breath catching at every imagined shape.

Once she was over the bridge spanning the rushing mill race, she was running with her bicycle, then she remounted and pedalled hard up the hill. A loud crack behind her. The smell of smoke. And she knew she needed to get back to the surgery as fast as she could.

'Whatever is it?' Mrs Hewitt called as Lara ran in through the back door.

'I've seen a fire at the sawmill!' she shouted. 'I need to ring the fire brigade right now before it spreads.'

Mrs Hewitt was all business. 'I'll dial for you. And we need to call Ridgetown police station as well.'

Once the fire engine had been summoned, Lara blew out a breath as she replaced the receiver with a heavy clunk. 'They're coming right now, and they said a policeman will call here later to ask some questions.'

'Good, that's good. If that factory goes up in smoke, there'd be so many families out of work in Ingleside it'd be an absolute tragedy.' Mrs Hewitt smoothed her apron, lifted her chin. 'Get your coat off and come through to the kitchen, I'll rustle up a bite to eat and have a hot cup of cocoa laced with brandy ready in a flash.'

'Thanks, Mrs H,' Lara breathed, but she already knew that, until she'd heard the fire had been brought under control and all was well, she'd struggle to rest easy.

11

Later, as rain hammered against the windows, a loud knock came to the surgery door and Mrs Hewitt bustled up from her seat at the kitchen table. 'Nurse Flynn,' she called down the corridor as soon as she had the door open, 'it's a police inspector, for you. I'll show him into the sitting room.'

'Right you are,' she called, jumping up from the table.

As she walked down the corridor, Mrs Hewitt was by the sitting room door, holding out her arm to guide Lara into the room where a dark-haired man with an angular jaw stood waiting for her. Lara had expected a policeman in uniform complete with tall hat and silver buttons, but this officer wore a black overcoat and the hat he'd removed out of politeness was a Fedora.

'Nurse Flynn?' he asked, both brows raised, his sharp eyes fixing her with a very direct gaze.

'Yes,' she offered.

'I'm Inspector Stirling, I just need to ask you a few questions about the incident at the sawmill.' He directed her then with his hat to sit in an armchair and it felt slightly odd given he was the visitor here. He looked much younger than she'd expected and, when he spoke, she recognised a Scottish accent.

He pulled a pad and pencil from his pocket and fixed her again with that direct gaze. 'So, I believe you were the one to call the station regarding the fire at the sawmill.'

'Yes, that's correct. I passed by on my way back from attending a birth.'

'Did you see anyone hanging around, hear anything?'

'No, not really, but I might have seen a shadowy figure. It just felt odd, as if someone were watching me.'

He tapped his pencil against his lips, then sighed. 'It's a shame you didn't get a look at whoever it was. The firemen think it was set deliberately to cause harm and, if you hadn't passed by, it could have taken hold and been much worse.'

Even though the information chimed exactly with what she'd been expecting, she still felt shocked. 'In that case, I'm sorry I don't have more to report. But it was pitch dark, I couldn't see a thing.'

He seemed to soften then. 'Of course, I understand. And you did the right thing by raising the alarm.'

'I wish I'd stopped now, tried to make out more detail.'

He twisted his mouth. 'Well, maybe not, because whoever it was had a mind to cause harm. So, who knows what might have happened.'

'Well, I used to work in a city – Liverpool – so I'm fairly streetwise.'

He gave a short laugh. 'Aye, me too. I worked the streets of Edinburgh before I bit the bullet and moved down here to work with the English. So, I know how it feels to be a fish out of water.'

She smiled at their shared experience. 'Well, I'm starting to feel part of it now. But, as you know, it takes a while.'

He nodded. 'It does indeed.' He slipped his notepad and pencil back in his pocket then and pushed up from the chair. 'Well, thank you for speaking to me and if there's anything else you remember, call Preston Police Station and ask for Inspector Adam Stirling. If I'm not there, you can leave a message.'

'Yes, of course.' She was on her feet now and reaching out to shake his proffered hand.

He offered a polite nod, turned and was gone as efficiently as he'd arrived.

As she saw him out through the front door and walked back down the corridor, a smiling Mrs Hewitt appeared instantly. 'He seemed nice, handsome too.'

'Yes, he was nice,' she replied firmly, not taking the housekeeper up on the mention of his good looks. 'And he's new to Preston Police Station, so he's probably trying to prove himself out here in a new post. So, if *he* can't find who set that fire then probably no one can.'

'Well, there's something to be said for having new blood in a team, as you well know, Nurse Flynn,' the housekeeper smiled.

Later, before bed, as she sat at the kitchen table across from Marion and told her about the fire and the young detective who'd visited, her colleague opened her eyes wide, instantly intrigued by the police inspector. 'Scottish, you say. From Edinburgh. Well, that's where I did my nurse training and there were some very handsome men, but I never saw a young police detective ever. So, he must be special, this Inspector Stirling.'

'I'm not sure about being special, but he had a professional and confident manner, and he asked all the right questions. So, I'm thinking he's good at his job.'

Marion leaned across the table, brushing her elbow in the smudge of strawberry jam she'd dropped from her knife earlier. 'So, was he good looking, this new detective?'

'I don't know. I suppose so.'

'What was he like? Describe him.'

'I didn't pay much attention.'

'Oh, go on, Lara. Make something up if you can't remember the exact detail.'

It made Lara smile then, as she recognised Marion's capacity for a story, any story, even if it was made-up nonsense.

'Well, he was wearing a black hat and an overcoat.'

'Not what he was wearing, you numpty. What did he look like?'

'Oh dear,' she sighed, 'you know I'm no good at this kind of thing.'

'Well try, please try. I've had a heck of day with my visits, and I got dripping wet on my motorcycle. Then I had to chase a bunch of sheep who'd escaped from a field up and down a country lane.'

'Alright, alright,' she laughed, 'well, he had dark hair and bright eyes and a nice voice.'

'That's the Scottish accent,' Marion murmured, 'gets me every time... Go on, tell me more. What about his build, is he short, tall, round, thin?'

She began to chuckle; she couldn't help it.

'Lara, please. You need to take this seriously.' Marion grinned deliciously, undercutting what had just come out of her mouth.

Lara cleared her throat. 'He was medium height, ish, I suppose.'

Marion tutted, then asked, 'So taller than me?'

'A bit, maybe?'

'Lara Flynn, you are a brilliant nurse... but you are the worst describer of potentially eligible men that I have ever encountered.'

Then, as Marion took another bite of toast and smeared jam up the side of her mouth, Lara began to laugh.

Marion leaned forward across the table. 'What, what is it now?'

'Yes, what is it, Lara?' Angus called as he shambled through the kitchen door.

'You're back early,' Marion quipped.

He sighed heavily, and slumped down onto his chair next to Lara. 'Not my choice. I've been given what Mrs H calls her final warning. If I'm not back by ten, she said she'll stop brewing my coffee and making my breakfast in the morning, and I will only get one of her delicious sandwiches at lunchtime.'

Marion and Lara laughed together.

'Can't say you didn't have it coming, Angus,' Marion offered, 'but let's face it. Mrs H knows where her power lies. And if her porridge and cooked breakfasts and lunchtime sandwiches weren't the most delicious in the world then there wouldn't be much incentive to change your ways... but she's got you there, good and proper.'

He pressed his lips together, nodded.

Then, as Marion passed him her last piece of toast and jam, he got up to find the supposedly secret bottle of sherry the housekeeper kept in one of the kitchen cupboards. As soon as he had the cupboard door open, he tutted loudly. 'Crikey, there's a dead mouse in here... but at least that means the poison must be working.'

'Yuk,' Marion called, 'pull it out of there.'

'Ugh, I'm not touching it.' He shuddered, as he pulled out the sherry bottle, then poured a glass.

'I'll do it,' Lara said firmly. 'Poor little thing deserves to be treated with respect.'

So, as Angus stood with his glass of sherry and Marion twisted in her chair, she walked to the cupboard, grasped the little dead mouse by its tail then opened the Aga and threw it onto the red coals.

'Yikes, that's a bit extreme,' Marion cried.

'The poor little thing is stone dead so it's only like a cremation,' Lara offered, as she closed the Aga door with a heavy clunk and walked over to the sink to wash her hands.

Marion pursed her lips. 'I suppose... but if Tiddles the cat was just a little bit more tuned into doing what house cats do rather than toasting his toes in front of the Aga all day, then we'd probably keep the mice down without Septimus Finch having to come in and lay his poison.'

'True,' Angus mused as he pulled out his chair and settled with his elbows on the table. 'And that ratcatcher... He's like a character from a Dickens novel. Have you seen him with his strings of mice and dead rats?'

'Yes,' Marion shuddered, 'it's horrible.'

'The other night, he came into the Fleece for a swift pint, and he showed us his catch for the day. Not many of the fellas at the bar could stomach the sight of a bunch of dead rats tied by their necks on a string and they all backed away. So, as soon as good old Septimus had the bar to himself, he turned to us all and said, "Works every time. Best way I know to get served first." It made us laugh, and I went up to him to ask about our mice here at the surgery. He said we're all clear, at least for the time being.'

'Oh, so that's good,' Marion said. But then she turned down the corners of her mouth in disgust. 'He's a bit of an odd character, though, that ratcatcher, don't you think?'

'No odder than our Doctor Bingham,' Angus offered, then

with a mischievous grin, 'in fact, Bingham is probably more eccentric.'

'Mmm, maybe,' Marion mused.

And, when Lara recalled the senior doctor barefoot in his nightshirt the morning she'd come downstairs to rescue Mrs Hewitt from that mouse, she began to giggle.

'What is it?' Angus asked. But she was laughing so much she could barely get her words out.

Then, as she steadied up and told Angus the story, he appeared delighted. 'I'm glad you've given me that information, Lara, because the next time he's giving me a dressing down I'll picture him in his nightshirt with bare feet and it might soften the impact.'

He poured another glass of sherry then and knocked it back. 'Right, that's me done. I'm off to an early night.'

The two nurses shared a wide-eyed glance of disbelief as he exited the kitchen with a cheery goodnight.

Marion scrunched her brow. 'Forgive me if I'm wrong, but that doesn't sound like the Angus we know and love.'

'No, it doesn't,' Lara frowned, 'but maybe he's turned over a new leaf.'

'I hope so,' Marion breathed, her attention seeming to drift for a few seconds.

'Are you alright, Marion?' Lara asked, leaning across the table.

'Oh, yes. Just thinking about new leaves and fresh starts. That's why I came back to Lancashire, for exactly that reason, and I love working here, especially since you arrived...' Marion gulped then, tried to smile but her mouth twisted. 'After you told me your story of what happened in Liverpool, I know there are things I need to say out loud... but I'm not able to do that just yet... so, if that time does come, Lara. Is it alright if I confide in you?'

'Yes, of course it is. Bring it on.'

'Thank you,' Marion replied, offering a wobbly smile. Then she cleared her throat. 'And, in the meantime, we'll just keep jogging along, we two nurses. You on your bicycle. Me on my motorcycle... the one that nearly killed me.' She gasped, then snorted with laughter. 'And I'd probably be back to riding a bicycle if it hadn't been for Angus getting Gloria repaired when I was in hospital.'

Lara blew out a breath. 'I nearly had kittens that day you came home, when he wheeled Gloria out to meet you as a "surprise".'

'Surprise?' Marion gasped. 'Shock. More like.' Then she laughed. 'But it turned out alright in the end. Although, I must admit, that first day I rode her again I dismounted as soon as I got onto the country lanes and wheeled her for a while before I dared get back on. But, good old Gloria, she took it steady, and here we are happily together again.'

'All the same, I wish you'd learn to drive the car.'

'What? Have you seen Angus and Bingham out on the roads and the speed they go at? Swerving and skidding. They're probably far more at risk than I am.'

'True, that's true... You need to come out with me in the little blue Austin some time. I'd like to think I'm an experienced driver but, more importantly, I'm a steady driver. It might give you an idea of how it could be.'

'I just might take you up on that one day,' Marion replied, stifling a yawn, then she murmured, 'Time for bed... so we can be up bright and early and get back out there to tend to our patients.'

Lara rose from the table, linked Marion's arm and pulled her close. And, as they climbed the red-carpeted stairs together, she gazed up to the night sky through the arched window and felt safe here within the thick stone walls of the surgery.

'Goodnight,' she murmured sleepily as Marion left her at the door to her room and continued down the corridor.

'Night, kiddo,' Marion called as she turned to blow a gentle kiss.

12

The next morning, as Lara walked down the cobbled street to Daniel's cottage for her first visit of the day, she was interrupted many times by villagers already out and about. It felt as if the whole world wanted to know about the fire at the mill and there were already numerous theories around who might have done it and why. Some folk even thought the mill owner, Selwyn Barclay, who she'd previously heard described in very sympathetic tones, had set the fire himself to claim the insurance money.

'He wouldn't get much for that ramshackle place,' Sam Collins called from his shop doorway when she'd been stopped in her tracks by Herbert Threlfall parked in the street on his milk cart. And then, with a hearty chuckle, Sam added, 'And what's more, Herbert, that horse of yours probably has more idea of what went on at the mill last night than any of us here in the village!'

'Aye, that's true.' Herbert laughed good-naturedly, his skinny black horse nodding its head and jostling its bit. Then he leaned down with an earnest expression. 'Nurse Flynn, I heard you were witness to the fire, what do you think?'

'Well, as I told the policeman last night... I think I might have seen the shadow of a person, but it was just something I caught in the flicker of flame. It was pitch dark; I couldn't see anything properly.'

Herbert twisted his mouth as if weighing the situation.

Then Miss Frobisher walked up to the group and offered, 'Of course you couldn't see anything in the pitch dark, Nurse Flynn. And all this supposition is no help whatsoever when it comes to working out what happened. Rumours spread like wildfire in this village, so we need to stick to hard facts.' Then, with a firm nod, the retired schoolmistress headed down the street, her metal-tipped walking stick tapping at every step.

Aware of time ticking on, Lara used the moment to step around Herbert's horse and continue her way down towards Daniel's cottage. As soon as she was finished there, she'd be collecting her bicycle from the surgery then back out to her first postnatal check on Lydia Lennox.

Glad at last to reach the bottom of the cobbled street without any further delays, she tapped on Daniel's door and walked in. As she entered, the quiet of the cottage in contrast to the agitated bustle on the street eased her. Then, as soon as she walked through to his room and found him sleeping in his wood-framed bed, she noted for the first time since she'd been visiting that the shuttered window that looked out over the field was closed. She moved quietly, hoping she'd be able to check his pulse and blood pressure without disturbing him. But, as soon as she reached for his wrist, his eyes flickered open, and he smiled.

'Morning, Nurse Flynn,' he breathed so quietly she thought for a moment his fragile heart might be faltering. But then, when he asked her to open the shutter and get his knitted hat and mittens off the dresser, she knew there was enough life and breath there to keep him ticking over.

He didn't mention the incident at the mill, so clearly, he hadn't had any visitors yet this morning. Usually by now, his old friend Herbert Threlfall would have been in, but he was delayed up the street by gossip. She toyed with the idea of keeping quiet about the fire, but then Daniel would wonder why she hadn't told him. The rapport they had felt too precious to risk so, as she completed her observations, then straightened his bedding and made sure he'd taken his morning digitalis, she told him the story.

He scrunched his brow, pushed his blue knitted hat further back on his forehead, leaving a single tuft of white hair sticking out. And, as he gazed out through the open shutters, he said, 'It makes me very sad to hear about that fire... years ago in this village we never had anything like that. Then again, what happened to you with that Vic Taylor... I still haven't got over the fact that he'd threaten a lovely nurse, a ministering angel like you...' He sighed, shook his head. 'It feels as if we're living in a new age where anything goes. I don't know what to make of this modern world with its motor cars and electric lights and all the things that should make life easier... It feels as if good old-fashioned values are going down the swanny.'

Lara squeezed his hand. 'I hear what you're saying, Mr Makepeace, and you're right. But how can any of us hold back progress?'

He pressed his lips together. 'We can't, nobody can. It's just oldies like me who wish it were so.'

His eyes filled with tears. 'Some days, I'm glad my Martha's already gone. Her father worked for the Barclays at the mill his whole life without a spot of bother. She'd be appalled by what's going on now.'

Lara patted his hand. 'It's hard to make sense of things sometimes. And I'd like to stay longer and talk it through, but I'm hard-pressed with visits this morning. But Herbert's on his way down, he shouldn't be long.'

Daniel cleared his throat, then he had a twinkle in his eye. 'Aye, lass, and he'll be bobbing in thinking he's the first with the news about the fire. And he might be a bit put out when I tell him I already know. But that's alright, me and him have known each other our whole lives, so we'll soon be talking about other things.'

'That's good,' she breathed, picking up her medical bag and saying her goodbyes. But then, when she noted his very pale face against the white pillow, she hoped the news of the fire hadn't hit him too hard. But he always wanted to know every detail of what was going on in the village, so she'd done the right thing by telling him.

Just as she reached the front door, it clicked open, and Herbert bustled in with a cheery good morning. He barely broke his stride with his eagerness to get in and tell his friend the news.

As she exited the cottage, she saw Herbert's horse tethered to an iron ring and the creature snorted gently and flicked its ears back and forth. 'Hello,' she said with a smile. 'I'm assuming you already know the story of the fire?' And the horse snorted and nodded its head.

Still smiling, Lara kept her head down and walked briskly back up the street to the surgery. Responding to a good morning here and there from the village women sweeping their steps, bustling to the Post Office or across to the butcher's shop with their baskets. As she passed by the vet's surgery, the door opened abruptly, and Leo shot out, his dark hair dishevelled, his eyes bleary. 'Morning, Lara,' he called over his shoulder, 'I'm just off to get the van. An obstructed labour. A cow at the Alstons' farm.'

'Give my best wishes to Grace,' she called after him.

'Will do,' he shouted as he ran up the hill.

She hadn't seen Grace since the funeral, but she'd be calling by soon to make sure she was alright.

Increasing her pace as she walked by the butcher's shop, she stopped briefly to exchange a few words with Lizzie Cronshaw as she stepped out of her terraced cottage with baby William on her hip and Sue by her side. All seemed to be well despite Ed having got back to regular attendance at the Fleece and the Old Oak. However, since the birth of his baby son and now with his drinking buddy, Vic Taylor, off the scene, it seemed Ed's behaviour was much improved. It felt satisfying to know she'd played a part in stabilising the family, but this was just the start of her story here with all the families in the village. And with each new baby she delivered, she hoped she'd become a stronger part of the community. As she crossed the street, she glanced to the sky and felt glad of those patches of pale blue that peeped through the grey clouds. Hopefully she'd get out to Lydia Lennox before it rained again.

As she pedalled away up the hill towards the turning for the sawmill, she felt relieved to be leaving the agitation of the village behind. But, once she was freewheeling down towards the screech of the big saw, she spotted the blackened remains of the fire and the sooty mark on the mill wall and felt a stir of unease in her stomach. There were men in the yard working the big saw and, as the crane swung round, the driver began waving at her. It was Danny Ryan, and his warm smile lifted her spirits.

The mill race was full this morning and it was loud. And, as she cycled over the bridge, she sensed the power of it. As she reached the other side, she saw the police officer who'd visited the surgery last night, Inspector Stirling, climbing out of a car. He raised a hand and shouted a good morning, and she called a greeting, but it was swallowed up by the rush of the mill race and the heavy thump of machinery. What struck her, though, as she pedalled away from the noise of the heavy machinery, was the calm she felt as she approached the still waters of the large, flat mill pond. And, as she gazed over the stone wall, a wild deer stepped shyly out from a thicket of trees at the far side, then dipped its head to take a drink of water. She gasped with pleasure and would have liked to have pulled over, but there was no need, the deer lifted its head with water still dripping from its muzzle and, in a second, it had gone back into the shadow of the trees. So quickly she almost wondered if it had been a mirage. But, no, it had been real, and it made her smile. As she pushed out into open country, she felt the pale autumn sun on her face, and it lifted her. It was good to note the play of light on the leaves with their burgeoning red, brown and gold. And, at the chatter of lapwings in a field, she felt a sense of escape.

Arriving at the Lennoxes' cottage, she tried to hold on to that calm but, as she propped her bicycle against the wall and pulled her nurse's bag from the basket, she heard the high-pitched wail of a child, and the moment moved on. Tapping on the door, she was greeted by Steven Lennox's warm smile as he held Ava against his shoulder, soothing her, and as she stepped through to the flicker of fire in the stove, it was good to see Michael and Freddy settled on the truckle bed, playing with their toys.

Knowing she needed to get on with the rest of her visits, she politely declined the cup of tea Steven offered and went straight through to the bedroom to see Lydia. And what struck her instantly as she closed the door behind her was the contrast in atmosphere. Lydia was lying back, pale against her pillows with dark smudges beneath her eyes. And, even though Jamie was sleeping peacefully in his crib, she kept glancing to him, her brow furrowed as if she were deep in thought.

'How are you doing?' Lara asked gently.

For a second, Lydia stared blankly, then she offered a brief smile and cleared her throat. 'Still very tired. But I'm alright.'

They were the right words, but something about the way they were spoken gave Lara pause.

'Is it OK if I have a feel of your tummy?' she asked gently, rubbing her hands to warm them up. 'Sorry, my hands might be a bit cold.'

'That's alright,' the woman said, her voice deadpan.

As Lara did her routine examination, Lydia lay very still and stared up to the ceiling. Then, as she gently examined the sleeping baby and called across to the newly delivered mother how bonny her baby son was and how well he was doing, that's when her patient began to show some interest.

'You look exhausted,' Lara said, when all her checks were done.

Lydia sighed, offered a wry smile. 'I'm worn out, that's why. But thank goodness Steven has been able to get a few days off work.'

'Yes, that is good... but it'll only take you up to the end of your first week of lying in.'

'Yes, I know... but Michael's very capable and then Nora will be bobbing in and out.'

'Is there anyone else, any family who could come? Just so you'd have someone here.'

She pressed her lips together, shook her head. 'It's a long story but my family didn't approve of my choice of husband, so they cut me off completely.'

'I'm sorry to hear that,' Lara breathed. 'Would it help if I tried to contact them?'

Lydia coughed out a short laugh. 'You'd be hard-pressed to do that, they don't have a telephone and they're across the border in Yorkshire.'

'Ah right, bit of an obstacle… Anyway, I'll be coming in for my routine visits and maybe we could get someone to help with the housework?'

'Michael will take it on, with Nora's help.'

'I was just wondering, though… And I know Michael's probably been kept back from school because of the new baby… But have you any idea when he might return?'

She shrugged. 'No. And I wouldn't manage without him here. We're just hoping that Steven will get work in Ingleside and then things will change for the better.'

'Alright, sounds like a plan,' Lara said, but she knew she'd have to keep a gentle eye on the situation with this family.

'I'll see you again tomorrow,' she called before walking back through to the warm kitchen.

Steven was at the stove, and he turned with a smile. 'Everything alright?'

'Yes, all fine,' she said.

The toddler, Ava, missed her footing then and fell nose first to the linoleum floor. Instantly she was screeching but Michael was straight there, picking her up, soothing her.

'Let's have a look at you, young lady,' Lara said, crouching beside the two children. 'Well, you might have a bruise on your forehead, but your nose is still straight, so that's good.'

'She's always falling,' little Freddy said, crawling by with his toy truck.

'Well, she'll steady up when she gets a bit older.'

Freddy nodded and continued with his truck.

Steven called, 'Thank you, nurse... Are you sure you don't want a cup of tea?'

'I wish I could, but I need to get on with my other visits. See you all tomorrow.'

Riding back down past the mill and seeing the blackened ash from the fire being shovelled away, she steeled herself. After all, it was probably just some random happening and once the charred remains were gone and other news took precedence, the whole thing would blow over. But, then, on her other visits, as she continued to field questions about the fire and was forced to listen to more theories of who was responsible, she felt so weary of the issue she knew she had to push it right away, today.

Arriving back to the surgery, she bobbed in through the door and it felt heartening to hear chatter from the kitchen punctuated by Bingham's gruff laugh and Angus's snort of merriment. She could tell by the voices around the table that Marion wasn't back yet but, as she entered the kitchen and saw Mrs Hewitt turn from the Aga with a warm smile, she felt instantly soothed. This was her safe haven, her shelter from the storm, and right now, she felt as if she wanted to stay forever.

13

It had rained solidly since yesterday afternoon, and Lara was grateful for her wellington boots as she sloshed through rainwater gushing down the street to see Daniel. He was quiet today, as if he were in tune with the dark clouds and the weather, but at least it was still warm enough for him to have the shutters open for a brief time so he could watch the Shorthorn cattle that belonged to Leo wander back and forth in the field. He told her that his niece, Esther, who visited daily to provide care had been very firm with him about the shutters. Last year, they'd stayed open too long, according to her, and that's why he'd ended up with a bad chest and been very poorly. 'I'll have to do as I'm told,' he said, his voice flat. Then he gazed wistfully out through the open shutter and sighed heavily. Just then, as if it had been summoned, a white cow with crooked horns shoved its head boldly through. It caught Lara by surprise, and her heart jolted in her chest. But Daniel began to chuckle. 'There she is, my beauty, coming to say hello to an old farmer.'

If he'd been stronger, she'd have encouraged him to get out of bed to give the creature a scratch behind its ears. But now the weather had turned cold, he seemed even frailer, and he was stick thin with an almost otherworldly translucent pallor to his skin. Mostly, though, he kept up his cheery demeanour and she loved to see him propped against his pillows wearing his bright blue knitted hat and mittens. She'd been hoping to catch Esther for a chat, needing to check if she was aware that Daniel's heart condition was slowly deteriorating. Even thinking about it made tears prick her eyes – she'd always treated her patients equally, but secretly he was one of her favourites, of course he was.

Due to the heavy showers, the street was deserted as she trudged back up the hill, apart from one or two women sweeping the rainwater from the stone steps of their cottages. One of the women, sleeves rolled above her elbows, shouted cheerily, 'Morning, Nurse Flynn. Good weather for ducks.'

'Yes, indeed.' She laughed as she left the worst of the flooding behind and made her way up the cobbled street. Just as she was walking by the stone steps of the Fleece, a slight figure wearing a waterproof coat ran down and, when the person pushed back a rain hood to reveal a head of red-blonde hair, she recognised Ada.

'I've been hoping to catch you, Nurse Flynn. Come up, will you, just for a minute.'

Once they were through the pub door, Ada swore gently as she struggled out of her still wet macintosh, dripping water over the stone-flagged floor. 'What weather we're having. It's not usually like this until November. How are you managing, Nurse Flynn?'

'I'm fine. I was born and raised in Liverpool and it's very wet at this time of year.'

'So, you're used to it then?'

'Yes, I am,' Lara replied, noting the dark smudges beneath

Ada's eyes, the line between her brows. 'What is it, Ada, are you alright?'

The barmaid began to shake her head. 'Not really... That's why I stopped you. I've only got my dad, and he's always busy and I can't talk to him about much anyway because he's only ever half listening. And so, given I've heard that you're a level-headed person and the issue I want to broach relates to you anyway... I saw you walking up and thought, sod it, I might as well speak directly to Nurse Flynn.'

'Well, I'm intrigued now... so, what have you got to say?'

Ada snatched a breath. 'So, this relates to something I heard when I was working behind the bar the night of the Harvest Ball.'

'Right... well, fire away.'

For a fleeting moment, Ada appeared unsettled, then she moved in close. 'We had a different mix of customers that night and it was quieter than usual, so I overheard two of the fellas from the sawmill talking about Vic Taylor. They were chunnering on about how unfair it was he'd been cast out and they were saying he was living rough out near the fells somewhere, just biding his time to come back to Ingleside and finish off what he'd started... And it's been niggling at me ever since and I didn't want to scare the living daylights out of you, given he attacked you. But I just wanted you to know.'

Shocked, Lara felt a watery feeling of anxiety spread up from her stomach and she swallowed hard to quell it. 'Thank you for telling me, Ada. I've been having those creepy feelings at the back of my neck when you think someone's watching you. And, if nothing else, it's good to have confirmation I'm probably not imagining things.'

'Like I say,' Ada said with a sigh, 'I held off a bit because I didn't want to scare you and, given the amount of gossip that goes around this village, there's every possibility that it's all hot air anyway.'

Lara reached out to her then. 'Thank you for telling me. Even if it is just gossip.'

Ada shrugged. 'Well, I had to say something, because if there's anyone in this village that is honest and straightforward, it's you, Nurse Flynn.'

Lara took the compliment, it boosted her. 'Thank you for that. And I appreciate the information because we're a bit out of the loop at the surgery.'

'True... except for young Dr Fitzwilliam, I suppose. But, then, he's only interested in chatting to Leo and Ed, so not much else gets through to him.'

'Sounds like a fair assessment,' Lara offered, preparing to make her way back out to the street.

'Oh, and before you go, there is one more thing from that night of the ball – a posh fella came in the pub, soaked to the skin. He seemed charming and he was very handsome, but there was something about him that felt a bit off. Anyway, bold as brass, he was standing at the bar in his expensive coat asking the customers about *you*. And, of course, they were telling him everything they knew, including what happened with Vic Taylor.'

Lara sighed. 'Well, that sounds about right for a man like him, because there's no mystery there. That was Patrick, my ex from Liverpool. And you're spot on with there being something off about him. I just wish I'd acted on my instinct and never agreed to go out with him in the first place.'

Ada groaned. 'Don't beat yourself up. I'm currently involved with something similar – it's easy to get caught up with the wrong sort, particularly if they're handsome.'

'Hmph,' Lara offered, and she almost told Ada about the

confrontation at Ingleside Hall but, glancing to the clock above the bar, she realised she needed to get back to the surgery to assist Dr Bingham with the morning clinic. 'Thanks for that, Ada. I'm grateful for the information you've given me. If you see or hear anything else about Vic Taylor or Patrick, please let me know.'

'Of course,' the barmaid said firmly. 'It's one of the perks of the job, being able to listen in to conversations at the bar. They stand there after their tongues have been loosened by a few pints and everything comes out. And behind the bar we're just like part of the furniture, so they have no idea we're soaking up the detail. I could write a book with all the stories I've heard over the years.'

'I bet you could, and I'd probably like to read it… But, thanks again, Ada, hopefully I'll see you again soon.'

As Lara nosed out of the pub, the rain was hammering down again, and it made her feel overly annoyed. She knew instantly it mostly related to her aggravation at Patrick's intrusion into her new life, but hopefully she wouldn't have to see him ever again. As she ran across the street to the surgery, she cursed quietly under her breath, knowing if it hadn't been for her keeping the necklace then none of this would ever have happened. 'But here we are,' she muttered to herself. And that's when she felt a spark, like quicksilver, run right through her and she stopped for a few seconds with the rainwater sluicing over her and vowed she would not let Patrick ruin things for her here. And, if that Vic Taylor reared his head again, she'd fight back at him as well.

In through the front door of the surgery, she walked briskly up the corridor, passing by the huddle of patients waiting to be seen in morning clinic. One or two raised a hand and Lizzie, back again with Sue, called out a good morning, which she returned with a smile. Shrugging off her macintosh, Lara hung it to dry with her rain hood, then after a nip into the kitchen to wipe the rain from her face, she was back out to assist Bingham with the clinic.

At lunchtime, she was grateful to find the little blue Austin was free in the afternoon and she could use it for her visits. The driving wouldn't be easy in this rain, but at least she wouldn't be exposed to the elements. So, after two thick-cut egg sandwiches, a piece of spicy fruit cake and two cups of hot, sweet tea she was in the car and heading out to see Grace Alston for the first time since the funeral. Bingham had implied she wasn't doing all that well, but then he had such an abrupt manner sometimes, and he'd been a close friend of her dad's, so maybe she would find a different scenario. As she drove slowly over the hump-backed bridge, she felt shocked at the height of the fast-flowing river and some of Angus's stories of getting bogged down in ditches and caught in floods came at her. She drew a slow breath, gripped the steering wheel more firmly and felt the little blue car putter bravely out towards the country lanes. But, even with the wipers working as hard as they could, it wasn't vigorous enough to fully clear the rainwater from the windscreen.

Thankfully, the rain was easing off as she bumped her way up the potholed track that led to Grace's farm. It was strange to see the fields empty of sheep and cows. No doubt they were sheltering, but the landscape felt even bleaker without them. The yard was deserted, the barn door closed and the fierce farm dog hunched inside its kennel emitted no more than a low growl. As she parked up then waded across the waterlogged yard, once again she felt the stark contrast to her visits in the summer, when she'd felt the life of the farm all around her. There was no response to her firm knock on the farmhouse door, it made her feel mildly agitated but she sensed Grace wasn't far, probably in the barn or the shippon.

But at least it'd stopped raining now and, as she made to walk back across the yard, a ray of sun peeped out briefly from behind a dark cloud and it cheered her.

'Ah, it's good to see, isn't it? After all the rain,' Grace called as she emerged from the shippon. And then she was striding across the yard in her boots and brown corduroy pants, her hair sticking out in tufts as she shaded her eyes at the sudden ray of light.

'You've brought the sun with you, Lara. And it's a good sign.'

'I hope so, and I hope it's good for you too.'

Grace began to nod slowly. 'It's been very grim. It still is. But, just the other day when I came out to the yard, I was sure I heard my dad's voice, and I had an even stronger sense of him... Does that make sense?'

'Every bit of sense.' Lara smiled. 'Like I've said before, he'll always be with you. Especially when you're out and about on the farm.'

Grace sighed, dropped her head and, when she looked up, she offered a wry smile. 'Oh no. Don't tell me he'll always be going on at me about what to do when and how?'

'Yes. He will, I'm afraid.' Lara chuckled.

'Well, in that case, I need a big mug of sweet tea and a piece of Aunt Agnes's Victoria sponge right now. What do you think?'

'I think it's the only medicine for the situation,' Lara replied as Grace took her arm, and pulled her close. As they walked back towards the farmhouse, Lara still sensed the residual sadness in her friend, but she knew now that Grace had begun to pick up and it was the work on the farm that would bring her through.

Later, as she drove back down the potholed track en route to her next visit, the sunlight cast a shimmer through raindrops on the turning leaves of a tall oak, and it made her feel hopeful.

The information about Vic and Patrick she'd received from Ada was still with her like a tight ball deep inside, but her next visit was to Lucy Taylor at Fell Farm for the monthly check on her still-healing scar, and it felt positive.

As she parked up next to the ramshackle barn in the shadow of the fells, she took a few moments to gaze down towards Ingleside. Visibility was poor, but she could pick out the cluster of houses and the church spire, tiny in the distance. And, as she walked the familiar path by the now empty pig pens, she felt as if Marion were guiding her in the same way she had on that very first day she'd visited here on the back of the motorcycle. When she tapped on the farmhouse door, it was opened almost immediately by Lucy's brother, Robin. He was grinning and standing back for her to enter. After tending Lucy in a truckle bed upstairs while the deep wound on her leg had been healing, it always felt like a lovely surprise to see her downstairs in the kitchen with the rest of the family.

'Hello, Lara,' Alice and Lucy called together, the girl dodging past excitedly to greet her. 'We've sold the house. We're moving to Ingleside.'

Alice was kneading the bread dough in its earthenware bowl, a dusting of flour on her cheek. She was grinning, exultant.

'So, when did this happen? Who's buying it?'

Giving the dough an extra vigorous knead, Alice gasped a little as she replied, 'Some fella looking for a place close to the fells so he can build a launch strip. He wants to fly gliders from here, apparently.'

'Oh, that's unusual,' Lara offered, not sure if she liked the idea of a piece of machinery hovering overhead, frightening the livestock or crashing into the fells.

'He's giving us a good price and he's going to sign a paper to say they can only fly one contraption at a time. And it has to be done with respect to the local farmers and their livestock.'

It eased her a little to have that information, but she felt surprised at how protective she already felt of the fells and the farms and the people who lived out here.

'So, you'll be moving to that cottage next to the Old Oak?'

'Yes... It's where the landlord before Ted used to live, so it's been empty for quite a while. We'll be there on a trial basis initially, but, if it works out for us and for him, he says we can make it permanent.'

'Sounds like a good deal. And did you tell me you're thinking of opening a bakery?'

Alice laughed as a burst of flour puffed up from her earthenware bowl and dusted her hair. 'Yes, given I've always got my hands in a bread bowl, I think I might as well.'

Robin brought a towel then, to dust his mother's face.

And when Alice spoke again, she dropped her voice. 'It'll be good for these two as well. They can walk up to school and they've both missed so much with Lucy's injury and Robin being kept back to help on the farm.' Alice seemed to shudder then, clearly she was thinking back to how threatening Vic had been before he'd moved out.

'You and the children deserve a fresh start,' Lara said firmly. 'And what a good idea to open a bakery. Mrs Hewitt is always complaining about the bread she gets delivered from Ridgetown... she says it's like wire netting.'

'Well, that's good to hear.' Alice laughed as she gathered the dough and lifted it onto a wooden board where she kneaded it vigorously.

By the time Lara was ready to inspect Lucy's leg, the girl had already unravelled the bandage and removed the dressing pad. The scar extended down the full length of her shin, and it was still an angry red, gouged-out mark but it was very well healed now. 'It's good, Lucy. You're doing all the right things to protect it with the bandage and are you still dressing it yourself?'

The girl opened her blue eyes wide and smiled. 'Yes, of course I am. And, when I'm old enough, I want to train as a nurse, like you.'

'You will make an excellent nurse,' Lara offered unreservedly.

Alice glanced up with a smile as she wiped her flour-dusted hands on a tea towel. 'She will, won't she?' she said, walking over to put an arm around her daughter's shoulders. 'That's what comes of the experiences – good and bad – that we have, even as children.'

Robin piped up then. 'Does that mean I'm going to be mucking out pigs when I grow up?'

'No, you munchkin, of course not. You'll be mucking out sheep, cows and pigs.'

They were all laughing together when Alice's Uncle Josh pushed open the door – a tall, grey-haired muscular fella with a snake tattoo on his forearm, who Lara had met briefly in the summer. He nodded to Lara. 'Alright there, Nurse Flynn.' And when Robin told him what had just been said about him mucking out the pigs, Josh smiled wryly. 'Well, don't tell your mother, but I'm training you up to be a prize fighter.'

Alice was shaking her head. 'Oi, Uncle Josh, none of that talk. I don't want my beautiful boy ending up with a crooked nose like yours.'

Josh offered a deep belly laugh as he grabbed for Robin and put him in a playful headlock.

'You two, stop that.' Alice laughed. 'And for goodness' sake, don't knock into my bread bowl.'

Lara was laughing with them, and she would have loved to

have had time to stay longer in this house that was now the opposite of what it had been under Vic's suffocating, iron rule.

After she'd rebandaged the girl's leg and she was preparing to leave, she told Alice, 'The good news is I can discharge Lucy now, but if there are any problems with the scar, I can easily bob in to see her once you're in the village.'

'Well, that's another good reason to move,' Alice said firmly. 'This farm has been in my family for generations and I'll miss that view of the valley and the fells, but I feel as if I can't breathe here now, I have to get away.'

Lara nodded and, as she said her goodbyes, she reached out to give Alice's arm a reassuring squeeze. Then she was out to the yard and, oddly, just as she took the track that led by the now empty pig pens, she felt the hairs at the back of her neck prickle as if someone were watching her. She shook her head, telling herself it was just a throwback to when Vic had been here. But it unsettled her, and as she walked to the car she still glanced around – all the outbuildings were closed, and the pens were empty. But the barn door was half open and all she could see in there was black, empty space. She felt a dull thud in her chest at the thought of going anywhere near there. And, even as she slipped into her car and slammed the door, she couldn't shake that feeling of being watched. She reversed quickly and only began to ease once she'd bumped and manoeuvred her way back down the full length of the potholed farm track.

14

Days and weeks ticked by as the weather grew much colder, with vicious winds and heavy rain that stripped the autumn leaves from trees and hedges. And as Lara cycled or drove the little blue Austin to her visits, the leaves fluttered or squished beneath her tyres. Often, unless it was sheeting with rain, she preferred to be out on her bicycle so she could breathe the damp air and revel in the red, gold and brown of the leaves. She often stopped at chestnut corner to pick up fallen conkers, which she stashed in her basket, then left by the bright red post box halfway down the village street for the local children to find when they came out of school.

By the beginning of November, a huge bonfire had been built on a patch of ground next to the village hall for Guy Fawkes night. For weeks, children and grownups had been dragging branches, piling up old fence posts and any waste wood they could lay their hands on. There'd been a rumour that someone had taken the vicar's blue-painted wooden wheelbarrow, thinking he'd left it out for the fire. No one ever owned up, but there was plenty of gossip over who might have done it, and some shards of blue wood were found mixed into the ever-expanding bonfire pile. Of course, nothing was proved, but it was a nice gesture that, on mischief night – the fourth of November, a new wheelbarrow freshly painted blue and barely dry was left outside the vicarage door. Rumour had it, Reverend Hartley had tripped over it and almost broken a hip but that had never been substantiated. And Lara had seen him in the churchyard happily wheeling his new barrow as he collected fallen leaves.

It felt like a perfect night for a bonfire – cold, bright, with that dank smell of wood and breath steaming in the air. Then the excitement of that first crackle of fire and whiff of woodsmoke as newly lit petrol rags spread their flames greedily to timber that had been piled and re-piled to provide the maximum draught for what was hoped would be the best bonfire Ingleside had ever seen. To be part of this excitement was a first for Lara. She'd seen bonfires in the city, but they'd been small, scrappy, hastily put together by the kids who roamed the streets. Nothing like the scale of this. And, as the first big orange flame licked skywards, she grabbed Marion's arm.

'It's the biggest one ever this year!' Angus whooped, raising the glass of ale he'd brought from the Fleece.

'Don't be ridiculous,' Bingham chimed. 'Last year's was just the same. And in my youth, we built them even higher.'

Mrs Hewitt, out of the house for once, offered a mischievous glance in Lara and Marion's direction and mouthed, 'He says that every year.'

Lara stifled a giggle. Then, at a loud crack of wood as sparks shot high into the air, she yelped and grabbed Marion's arm.

Some children were whooping and dancing in what felt like

an ancient ritual that went back to even before Bingham had been born.

Marion told her then, with an excited gleam in her eye, 'The kids always go crazy like this, I used to do it at the bonfire in Ridgetown.'

Lara thought back to herself as a child, and she knew she wouldn't have been one of the dancing children. She'd have been like those who stood close to the adults, their eyes wide and reflecting the flames. At each loud spit from the fire, the shock went right through her and she grabbed Marion's arm even tighter. 'You're like a fine-bred horse, Lara. Just try to relax.'

She nodded, gulped, but then with the next crack of wood she did it again. And it all felt heightened by the fire she'd seen at the mill that night she'd cycled back from delivering Lydia Lennox's baby. At least there hadn't been any further incidents and Inspector Stirling had telephoned the surgery to inform her that the case had been closed for now. As the fire burned hotter, fiercer, with flames licking up to the night sky, the crackle and spit strengthened. And she glanced about to see children and grownups dancing, shrieking and getting way too close to the fire, some of the men sloshing their glasses of beer, and she prayed everyone would stay safe tonight.

Marion nudged her then, offered a sip of whisky from her hip flask. Dr Bingham was on call tonight, so she took it readily, not to fight the cold, her thick district nurse's coat over the tweed pants and woolly sweater Mrs Hewitt had issued kept her warm. The whisky was to settle her jangled nerves. Then, as thick, chewy wodges of parkin, toffee apples and home-made treacle toffee were handed around, she loved the sweetness of the snacks and that sense of sharing with this community. And when she saw Alice Taylor and family at the far side of the fire, she waved and told Marion, 'I'll just go over to say hello to the

Taylors.' Marion offered an unintelligible response due to the big piece of treacle toffee she was chewing, but she nodded her head and motioned her away with a sticky hand.

'Nurse Lara!' Lucy and Robin shouted together as they ran to greet her. They took her hands, one at either side, excitedly jumping up and down as they shouted about the bonfire and hoped there'd be good fireworks this year.

Alice and Uncle Josh were smiling in her direction. 'Good to see you,' Alice called, 'have you heard we moved into Old Oak cottage yesterday?'

'No,' she gasped, her response exaggerated by shock at another loud crack of wood from the fire. 'But I knew it would be soon. Is everything alright there?'

'Yes,' Alice said with a grin. 'It's still chaos with bags and boxes everywhere, but there are three bedrooms, and they have some good, solid furniture that's been left behind. So, Lucy has her own room.' She glanced to her daughter then with a smile. 'Robin shares the biggest room with Uncle Josh, and he's thrilled about that given the man is his all-time hero. And I've got a small room with a single bed and it's perfect. I have a dresser so my stuff's all in there and to have a room of my own...' She offered a wobbly smile, tears shining in her eyes.

Lara grabbed her arm and gave it a squeeze. 'This is a fresh start for you, Alice. And I'm so glad you're happy with everything, even on the first day.'

'I am happy, yes,' she croaked.

It felt strange and a shiver ran down her spine, but as Lara said her 'goodbyes for now' and walked back to Marion and Mrs Hewitt, she was almost certain she saw the shadow of a lurking figure silhouetted against a wall in the light of the flickering bonfire. It flashed in her brain, a tall man, unruly hair, and she felt sure it was Vic Taylor. A second later, when the same spot flashed bright again, there was no one there. She told herself it had to have been her imagination because why would Vic come to the bonfire when he had, in effect, been banished by most of the villagers. But, then again, he was just the type to bear a grudge over far less than his family selling up and moving.

As soon as she got back to her Ingleside surgery group, the first rocket went up with a loud swoosh and an earsplitting bang. She squealed excitedly, she couldn't help it, and it made Marion cackle with laughter, then shout, 'It's a good job you're making the most of it because we never have all that many fireworks.' Instantly, there was the wild swoosh of another, and it went high this time, bursting into blue and red flame. Angus cheered and sloshed his pint, then he turned with a grin and linked Lara's arm. 'This takes me back to the bonfires on my grandfather's estate in Scotland – huge affairs with friends and relatives and all the local gamekeepers and deer stalkers.'

'It must have been amazing,' she called back to him through another burst of firework, a fountain spewing silver sparkles.

'It was, but you know how it is when you're a child – everything is marvellous. But, then, you grow up.'

'Well, that's life, isn't it?' she said, giving his arm a squeeze.

He shrugged, raised his tankard, called out a cheer with, 'Here's to life,' then he swigged the remains of his beer.

Once the fireworks were done, Angus released her arm and Lara felt herself relaxing as she gazed to the slowly dying bonfire. Marion stood quietly beside her staring into the flames until Angus called, 'Who's for a pint at the Dorchester?'

'We are,' Marion cried, grabbing Lara's arm and raising it with her own.

'We both need to get back to the surgery,' Mrs Hewitt said, with a nod in Bingham's direction. 'But you three get yourselves out there and enjoy it.'

Linking Marion's arm, Lara followed behind Angus, who strode ahead with the empty tankard swinging in his hand. He turned to grin over his shoulder as they climbed the stone steps to the Fleece and then, as he pushed open the door, he called over his shoulder, 'What're you both having? I'll get them in.'

'That'll be a first, Dr Fitzwilliam,' a man's voice called from the bar, and she saw Leo turn with a grin.

'Yeah, yeah, that's a bit much coming from you, Mr Scrooge.'

Leo cackled with laughter, his eyes bright and alive. She still didn't quite know what to make of the young vet, but the timbre of his voice felt warm, and it made her smile.

'A port and lemon for me, please,' she said, when Angus shouted for their orders. But then, when Marion asked for a pint of bitter, she remembered she'd drunk beer in the summer when she'd attended the local show with Grace. 'No, make that a pint of bitter for me too,' she called, and Angus grinned.

As Ada acknowledged her with a smile, she recalled that last time they'd spoken, about Vic and Patrick. It made her stomach twist a little with anxiety, but she felt sure Ada would have got in touch if there'd been any more information. Nevertheless, when she briefly caught the barmaid's eye, she mouthed, 'Any more news?' and Ada shook her head.

'Phew,' she said out loud.

Instantly, Marion picked it up. 'What you phewing for, are you alright?'

'Yes, I'm fine,' she replied forcefully.

Then seeing Marion frown, she added, 'Well it's just so good, isn't it? To be out here with you and Angus.' Then quickly, to shift attention, she took a snack from the brown paper bag Marion thrust towards her.

She bit into it without thinking. It was hard, greasy and

tasted horrible. Instantly, she pulled out her pocket handkerchief and spat it out.

Marion was chuckling. 'You're not a fan of pork scratchings then?'

'Yuk, no. Most definitely not.'

She wiped her mouth, then with the foul taste still in her mouth she gulped down a few mouthfuls of beer. 'Ahh, that's better,' she offered, setting her glass down.

'Wow.' Leo grinned. 'I never thought I'd see you drinking ale like that.'

'Just shows you've got a lot to learn,' she replied with a grin, grabbing her glass for another go.

The evening progressed and she felt happy, relaxed and, as the bar quietened, Ada's dad Sid was able to manage the serving alone, so Ada came to sit at the piano tucked against the wall right next to a blazing fire stacked with wood.

'Who wants a sing-song?' she shouted, and all the customers roared in response.

As she opened with 'Roll Out The Barrel', the whole pub stood up to sing with their pints in their hands.

That's when Lara noted Angus singing along raucously next to Leo without even glancing to Ada. It sunk in then that the devotion to the barmaid the young doctor had confessed abruptly in the summer must have run its course. She didn't think he'd set his sights on anyone else, and she still felt keen to see him with Sally Greenwood, the nurse from the cottage hospital who'd helped at the surgery over the summer when Marion had been recovering from her accident.

Marion nudged her arm gently and murmured, 'What you thinking about, dreamer?'

'Oh, nothing,' she replied, smiling when she realised her Aunt Matilda had often called her 'dreamer' when she'd been silently mulling things over. Maybe she'd have grown up differently if she hadn't been the only child of a mother who'd eloped to New York with an American ship's captain after her father had died from pneumonia one freezing Liverpool winter. It had been a quiet household with just her aunt, and she often wondered if that had shaped the person she'd become. But then she'd visited enough raucous, lively families on the district to know that there was often a quiet one. She wasn't shy, she'd never been shy in the way Izzy Valentine was. She'd just been quiet.

The noise of the pub crashed back at her then as the rabble of locals shouted out for the final tune and the barmaid led them into a rendition of 'Goodnight Sweetheart'. Then, as Ada closed the piano lid and walked back to the bar, Angus called, 'Come on, you lot, let's go down to the Old Oak.'

Leo was at the bar talking to some fella and, when Angus shouted to him, he raised a hand and called back, 'I'll see you down there.'

Then Lara linked Marion's arm, and they followed Angus down the stone steps to the cobbled street. After the warmth of the pub, the cold air felt fresh and invigorating. And, as Marion told the story of Angus slipping on ice last winter and sliding down the street on his backside, Lara laughed all the way down to the Old Oak. As she walked through the pub door, she felt surprised at the open space with a broad wooden bar. And there was plenty of room on the benches and wooden chairs around the tables. It was full of smoke though, much more so than the Fleece. Probably all down to the two elderly men at the bar puffing on their pipes. Instantly, she recognised Daniel's friend Herbert Threlfall as one of them, but the short, dumpy other fella with a cap pulled low over his brow was new to her. Sitting at a table to the side, away from the cold draught from the door, she settled beside Angus, as Marion went to the bar.

'See her go?' Angus grinned a little blurrily. 'She's full of it, isn't she? Keen to get on. And just look around, there's only one other woman in here tonight and that's you.' He pointed his finger at Lara then and grinned.

'Oi, I'm not a woman. I'm a nurse. So, I don't count, and neither does Marion.'

He emitted a belly laugh then and he was still shaking his head when Marion came back with the beers. In the quieter atmosphere of this pub, Lara began to feel a little sleepy and, as Marion and Angus chatted on, she almost nodded off. That's when the door burst open, and Leo strode in, slightly out of breath. 'Sorry about that,' he called as he walked to the bar. 'That farmer has a poorly bull and he wanted to give me all the detail. I'll get out there tomorrow, get it sorted.'

The energy Leo brought felt loud, too loud, and Lara instantly roused up at the strident edge to his voice. Once he had his pint in his hand, he plonked himself down beside her, then turned with a mischievous glint in his eye. 'So, Nurse Flynn, what do you think of our Bonfire Night in Ingleside?'

'I like it very much,' she replied. And when he began to grin unreservedly, she saw the boy in him, and it made her warm to him.

'Do they have a bonfire every year?'

He took a sip of beer and nodded as he swallowed. 'Yes, and every year the fire seems to get just that bit bigger. And for those of us born and raised in Ingleside, it's a reliable event that marks the turning of the seasons and it brings the whole community together. I say whole, but of course it's not attended by everyone.' He offered a mischievous grin before he spoke again. 'But I don't regret the absence of good old Miss Frobisher – my retired headmistress.'

Lara could understand why he was saying that, especially since her first impression of the woman had been that she was outspoken, overbearing. But, in the summer, when Vic Taylor had spread his vicious rumour that she was an incompetent nurse, Miss Frobisher had stood up for her when many of the villagers had sided with Vic.

Leo swiftly moved on to other topics and he was recalling former bonfires now, when he and some of the lads from his gang had set off bangers before dark and Herbert's horse back then, a feisty white gelding, had broken its tether and set off at a gallop up the street with the milk churns rattling. 'It took us ages to find that horse, but thankfully no damage was done to any person or property. But I never joined in with anything like that ever again, not after the good hiding my dad gave me. After all, he was right to point out that the horse might have sustained a terrible injury. And after what he went through as an army vet during the war, he finds it hard to put down any badly injured animal.'

Lara nodded, felt her throat tighten as she recalled what Mrs Hewitt had told her about Arthur Sullivan and Dr Bingham being involved with the shooting of army horses.

Marion waded in then. 'Well, I think you deserved a good hiding... But, then again, me and my two brothers used to get up to all sorts in Ridgetown... and not just on mischief night. We once tied string to door knockers all the way down the street so we could knock on a door then hide. And we strung bed sheets in trees to look like ghosts. Some of the more short-sighted locals had a real fright.'

Angus was chuckling now; he was really enjoying the stories. 'I wished I'd lived out here back then, sounds like you had a great time. I was stuck in boarding school with a load of other boys and some very strict and nasty schoolmasters. Not much fun there.'

'That's why you're making up for it now, Fitz,' Leo called across to him, raising his pint, sloshing it a little. 'Here's to Ingleside life!'

They stayed on in the Old Oak until last orders, and by that time Herbert and his friend had gone from the bar and there was only one old gent sound asleep in the corner. Ted the landlord came out from behind the bar muttering good-naturedly. 'He does this every night. And sometimes I need to walk him back up to his cottage.'

'I'll take him tonight,' Leo offered, up on his feet, ready to help, and it pleased Lara to know he had such a kindly side to him.

'What do you want?' the old fella groaned as Leo and Ted hauled him up from the bench.

'It's me, Albert. Leo Sullivan the vet.'

'I don't need a vet. What do I want a vet for?'

Ted laughed then ran a hand through his chestnut hair. 'Can you manage him, Leo?'

'Yes, I think so,' Leo wheezed as he took the weight of him and led him towards the door. Then he called back over his shoulder, 'But if you find him out in the street in the morning, sleeping on the cobbles, you'll know it didn't go well.'

Lara and her group began to chuckle and, when he glanced to her with a broad smile, she felt her heart warm to the young vet.

'We're coming out behind you anyway,' Marion said. 'So, if you need any help just holler.'

'Will do,' he grunted, but Albert seemed to be struggling to break free.

'Get off me,' he shouted, 'I can find my own way home.'

Leo glanced back and turned his mouth down at the corners, but the old fella was huffing and puffing and staggering off in front.

As Lara's group got up from their table to follow, Ted beckoned to her. 'Alice tells me you were a godsend when young Lucy was sick.'

'Well, I was doing my job... but I'm so glad things seem to be working out for her and the family now.'

Ted nodded, then his eyes shone warmly. 'I still sometimes hear a few mutterings at the bar about the new nurse, a city girl, all that rubbish. But I always set them straight. I won't have such talk in my establishment, not when I was once a newcomer too.'

'Ahh, were you?'

'Yes, I moved here from Preston... I know, not anywhere near as far as Liverpool, but still, in this tight-knit community, I was seen as an outsider. In fact, I've only just been properly accepted since I took over the pub these last few years.'

'Hah,' she said with a laugh, 'I've got quite a way to go then.'

He smiled. 'Don't lose heart. These folk, once you get to know them, they're the best in the world.'

'Yes, I've already seen enough of that to stay put for at least a year.'

'Good, that's good,' he breathed as he walked her to the door.

The others were at the top of the street now, clustered around a low doorway helping Albert access his cottage. And, as she called her goodbyes to Ted, then heard him lock the door behind her, she focused her attention on her friends. Then, at the edge of her vision, she felt sure she glimpsed a shadowy figure slip back into a doorway across the street. It could have been a trick of the moonlight, but it made a shiver run through her. It crossed her mind to go over there, face her demons, but when Marion called and beckoned to her, she walked up to join her friends. She glanced back though, just as she reached the top of the street. There was nothing to see.

'You alright?' Marion breathed.

'Yes... just thought I saw somebody down there, across the street. But it's just shadows, I think.'

'Yeah, I don't like the dark either. And I can't see anything down there,' Marion said, narrowing her eyes to gaze down the street.

Leo glanced in her direction then, an unasked question in his eyes.

'I'm alright, we're just going to get back to the surgery. Goodnight.'

'Goodnight,' he called after her as Angus stayed chatting.

Lara pulled Marion close, and they walked the remaining distance. The smell of the bonfire still hung in the air, reminding her of the good night out they'd had, and the shining light in the surgery window made her feel safe. Then, as Angus came running up behind, ridiculously out of breath with a cigarette clamped in the corner of his mouth, Leo shouted another good night as they went in through the door.

'Mmm, what's that?' Angus said, lured, as they all were, to the kitchen and the smell of freshly baked ginger cake. Three slices had been cut and left out by the housekeeper.

'Good old Mrs H,' Marion grinned as she picked up a piece of the sticky cake and munched a big bite, leaving crumbs stuck to the corner of her mouth. Angus took his piece and chomped through it with the remains of his smoke between his fingers.

'Lara, have some. It's such a delicious recipe she has for this cake; it's one she keeps secret,' Marion called between bites. And, as Lara picked up her own piece and took a delicate nibble,

Marion began to chuckle. 'Get stuck in there, girl. Go on, a big bite, take a big bite. As if it's a slice of life.'

15

The smell of the bonfire still lingered in the air the next morning and a light mist had settled over the village. As Lara cycled towards the bridge to her visits, the world felt oddly hushed. Even the gushing brook, full of water at this time of year, seemed muted. So, when a voice called from behind, she felt a little startled. It was Alice, waving a good morning from outside her new home. Lara pulled over and twisted in her bicycle seat. 'Sorry about that, I was miles away.'

'That's alright.' Alice smiled, walking to catch up to her. 'I'm still getting used to being here in the village. It's a novelty to see people out and about and be able to talk to them.'

'It must feel strange, having always lived in a remote place.'

'Yes, it's a whole new world, and it does feel odd. But, right now, I'm enjoying the company, and it's so easy for Lucy and Robin to walk up to school.'

'How are the children doing? I suppose they're on catch up after being kept off for so long.'

'Oh, they're fine. Lucy's enjoying the reading and writing,

and the whole of the school can't get enough of seeing her scar. You know what children are like.'

'And how's Robin managing?'

'Oh, he's loving the football in the schoolyard and he's turning out to be a bit of a bright spark. I mean he's barely had any schooling with how restricted things were up at the farm. But he's lapping it up now. I taught them both to read and write, so they were alright there, but there's something to be said for formal education, unless you get a bad teacher.'

'I suppose you had Miss Frobisher, what was that like?'

Alice glanced over her shoulder, then leaned in. 'She was a battle-axe, very strict. But she only used the cane if the issue was severe.'

'Fair enough, I suppose.' Lara smiled, recalling the discipline at her boarding school and the sting of the slipper she'd got across her hand for being caught at a midnight feast in the dorm. 'I suppose it's good to have strict teachers, but if they're brutal, that's a whole different matter.'

Alice was nodding. 'I don't know if you've met Mr Armistead, the new headmaster? He's young to be in charge, but he's kind and softly spoken and he lives right next to the school in that end cottage. Moved across the border from Yorkshire.'

'Ah yes, I met him briefly in church at the Harvest Festival and I've seen him out and about in the village, but I haven't had any real conversation with him. Sounds like he's doing a good job, though, at least with your two.'

'He is... And I know you need to get on with your visits, but I just want to say thank you again for what you did for Lucy when she needed to be rushed to the Infirmary... And I'd also like to apologise for Vic's behaviour.'

Lara was already shaking her head. 'None of that was your fault, there's no need to say sorry for anything.'

Alice smiled. 'I know, but I owe you a great deal, Lara. And I'd like to think we are friends.'

'Of course we're friends... And I'm so happy you've moved to the village because now I can see more of you. You've done the best thing ever by selling the farm and making this fresh start.'

'Yes, it feels right... and I'll let you go now, but thanks again and I'll see you soon.'

As Lara cycled towards the bridge, she noted the disused building at the other side of the road where she thought she'd seen a shadowy figure last night. A shiver flashed through her, and it made her push hard against the pedals until she was riding free on the country lanes. And, as the gentle mist cooled her face, she felt soothed, unencumbered, out here with the big sky above. Her first patient was Robert Thompson, a gamekeeper who lived in a tenant cottage on the Ingleside Hall estate. Marion had done the initial visits, and she'd reported that Mr Thompson required the redressing of an injury caused by catching his foot in a trap set by poachers. The wound was nasty, and it was being treated aggressively to stop the infection from spreading.

Lara was looking forward to cycling through the tall gates and along the tree-lined drive. 'Just like a lady of the manor,' Marion had joked when she'd handed over the detail of the visit. Lara toyed with the idea for a moment but a flashback to Lady Harrington's almost smile at the Harvest Ball made her shudder. And, of course, she would never desert her patients... plus the only other thing that seemed to matter right now was the pale sun that peeped out from behind cloud to illuminate the last of the turning leaves as they clung to the branches.

Then, as she cycled closer to the hall, she looked forward to seeing the warm glow of the stone walls and the carved oak front door. But, just as the stately home came into view, she was distracted by a woman on horseback. And as the black horse pranced and snorted, she knew instantly the rider was Philippa Harrington. Lara tried to ignore her but, as she dismounted to wheel her bicycle over the gravel drive, she heard Miss Harrington calling a good morning.

Lara had no choice but to turn around and return the greeting with a raise of her hand and she felt surprised when Philippa offered the semblance of a smile. Lara pushed on then, towards the gamekeeper's cottage, but Miss Harrington called to her again. 'Just a moment, please, nurse.'

'Yes?' Lara replied, turning.

As Philippa trotted over, her flighty horse shied and danced sideways. Then, as the horse and rider halted, the horse stamped and snorted, and Philippa leaned down from the saddle. 'Sorry, nurse,' she said, barely holding the horse in check, 'what is your name again?'

'Nurse Lara Flynn.'

'Lara. That's quaint.'

Something about Philippa's tone made Lara even more impatient to get to her patient. And she was about to push on, when Miss Harrington leaned closer, narrowing her eyes. 'I saw you at the ball, didn't I...? And I do believe you had a couple of dances with Leo Sullivan.'

Lara felt instantly affronted. What did it matter if she'd danced with Leo?

Philippa offered a tight smile. 'So, given I've bumped into you, I thought I'd have a quiet word... just to let you know that I've known Leo for many years, and he isn't looking for anyone right now.'

What Miss Harrington had just said had sounded off skew, but Lara had grasped the gist of it. 'Well, neither am I,' she replied, fighting to keep her voice level. Then she quickly followed up with, 'I'm here to attend Robert Thompson, one of the gamekeepers. So, I need to get on.'

In a very odd moment, Lara found Miss Harrington still holding her gaze in a piercing kind of way, as if she were desperately trying to read her thoughts. Lara broke eye contact then and said, 'I need to see my patient.'

The young woman straightened in her saddle, and with a nod of her head she spurred the skittish horse towards the open green parkland that surrounded the hall. Lara didn't glance back, but she heard the thump of the horse's hooves on the turf as Miss Harrington galloped away.

How ridiculous. Who did the woman think she was? Then instantly she thought of how pleasant Leo had been in the pub last night, the potential he had. *Was it possible he was involved with Philippa Harrington. Him and her, as a couple?* It didn't feel right and not just because of the yawning gap in their status.

Lara shook her head. None of this was her business and she'd keep it to herself because it was very possible that what Miss Harrington had just said, hinting at some level of intimacy with Leo, might be something that even Angus, Leo's closest friend, didn't know. In fact, it was highly likely because the young doctor could never keep anything to himself, so, if he'd known, he'd have spilled the beans for sure. So, she wouldn't speak of this, not out of any consideration for Philippa Harrington, but for Leo. Hopefully if he *was* involved with the woman, he'd see sense and ditch her. An image of Philippa falling from her horse into an actual ditch played through her head and she tried not to let it, but it made her smile. Perhaps, though, she shouldn't judge Miss Harrington too harshly, after all she didn't know her. Maybe she was high-handed because she was insecure. No, Lara didn't really think that was the case. But she was prepared to keep an open mind – of sorts.

By the time she was knocking on the gamekeeper's cottage door, her thoughts were fully focused on her patient. Robert Thompson opened the door with a ready smile, his brown hair tousled and sticking out to one side. And, as he limped back to his chair, the detail of his wound and the plan she'd formed for his dressing clicked through her head. Already he was propping his foot on a worn leather stool so she could have easy access to unravel the bandage. 'How is it doing?' she asked. 'Is it throbbing with pain or comfortable?'

'Comfortable,' he smiled, 'but if I catch it on something it hurts like bloody hell.'

'Well, that might be a good sign. It's a deep wound so having pain shows that there's probably no nerve damage.'

He grinned then and tapped his forehead. 'Except up here. I mean, how the heck could I have missed that poacher's trap? I've got sharp eyes. I'm trained to find them.'

'All it takes is a moment of inattention, for anyone trained to do a job.' She glanced up then with a smile and said, 'Even us nurses can slip up... I mean, it's rare, and I probably shouldn't have even said that on my first visit. But stop beating yourself up, we're all human.'

'Aargh,' he shouted, as she quickly pulled the final bit of the dressing away.

'That's the worst done. It should be plain sailing from here.'

He winced, then grimaced as she gazed at the mangled mess of his foot. 'That's a sight for sore eyes... and I'm thinking it's not going to be quick to heal up.'

She reached out to pat his hand. 'I'm afraid you're in this for the long haul, Mr Thompson.'

He sighed. 'It's just that Lord Harrington might cut back my wages, given I'm not able to do much.'

Lara felt her heart twist and she glanced up instantly. 'If he does that, tell me. I'll have a word with him. Accidents happen and, by the sound of it, you've been a good, loyal worker for many years.'

'That doesn't matter to them who run the show, does it? All they want is to get the job done. But I started here straight from school – trapping moles at first, drying the skins and sending them down to London to make moleskin gloves. It brought in the first real money I'd ever earned and when Mr Ambrose, the senior keeper back then, saw how good I was with the traps he offered to train me up as a gamekeeper. I've worked fifteen years since then and hardly taken a full week off each year. It's just so busy from one season to the next and then, of course, we've got a constant battle to keep the poachers at bay.'

'Right, so, here's what we'll do, because you deserve to be treated well after your years of service. If you run into trouble, I'll speak to Dr Bingham about it and I'm sure he'll have a word with Lord Harrington.'

When Robert spoke again, his voice sounded throaty. 'I've never had anyone look out for me before... so I'm very grateful for that.' He tried to say more but his voice choked up.

Lara kept going with cleaning the wound and replacing the dressing. 'This will feel stingy,' she said, wiping with carbolic solution. Then, as she doused the wound with plenty of iodine, he sucked in a sharp breath and gritted his teeth.

Once the bandaging was done and she was packing her bag to leave, she told him again, 'Don't forget. If Lord Harrington starts to give you grief, you let me know. When I worked in Liverpool, I had an accident on my bicycle, and I was off for weeks. All that time, my employer, the hospital, looked after me and paid my wages. Matron wouldn't have had it any other way.'

'Maybe I should train as a nurse and work with your matron

in Liverpool,' Robert offered with a chuckle as he struggled to get up from his chair.

'Well, you might make a better nurse than a patient.' She laughed. 'Sit back down, will you? And keep that foot elevated on the stool provided for the purpose... I'm more than capable of showing myself out. The dressings will have to be done daily for a while yet, so it'll be me or Nurse Wright tomorrow.'

'Right you are.' He smiled, then raised his hand in farewell.

As she walked away wheeling her bicycle, she gazed out to the park. The huge trees had mostly shed their leaves, they lay on the ground with their colours fading to shades of brown. She didn't know much about stately homes and parks, but these trees must have been planted centuries ago. It awed her to think of the hall and its estate in continuous use for all that time. And her imagination ran wild as her eyes scanned the parkland and the precise way the chestnut, beech and oak had been positioned. Everything here on the estate had been built to endure and, if the end of the world came, she felt sure Ingleside Hall would remain. That was the thing about having money, she supposed, it didn't just bring entitlement, it also brought security.

As if in need of a stark contrast, her mind flicked back to an account of one of the hunger marches she'd read in a Liverpool newspaper. An image of the ragged, determined working men had stayed with her. Those workers had shown incredible spirit, but she wondered if what they'd done had made any difference to their pay or working conditions. All it would take was for the very rich to pay their employees fairly and not profit from cheap labour. Some areas of Liverpool were so poverty-stricken it had felt as if little had changed since Queen Victoria's time. It was better out here in the countryside, but she'd seen poverty in the Lennox household.

Wheeling back across the gravel, she glanced to the big house, its door closed, windows tight shut against the autumn weather. When she'd attended the ball, she'd loved being inside the grand building, seeing the sparkle of the crystal chandeliers, the deep, ancient glow of the antique furniture. But, now, as the colder days crept towards winter and the hall would soon be shut up and empty for months, she had a creeping feeling that times were changing and maybe the Harringtons of this world might not be as secure as they'd always been.

Listening for the dull thud of hooves on grass, she felt relieved that Miss Harrington was nowhere to be seen. The young lady of the manor had seemed troubled and there was still something haughty about her. And what she'd said about Leo had been ridiculous. Maybe Philippa needed to spend less time peering down from the back of a horse, it might give her a whole new perspective on life. Lara twisted her mouth then, knowing it was very possible she'd be the same if she'd been born into a privileged family. And she might even have learned to ride a horse. She smiled to herself then as she recalled a donkey ride across Southport sands on a Sunday school trip to the seaside that had been more than enough for her.

Once she reached the drive, she mounted her bicycle and freewheeled down the gentle incline to the lane. The sky was still clear but there was a breeze now and a stronger nip in the air. Glad of her woollen vest and thick coat, she pushed on to her next visit to check on Miss Dunderdale at Brook House. From there, she'd see a new patient on the outskirts of the village and then make her way back to the surgery for a bite to eat.

Her mind was ticking over her next patient as she rode towards the village. But, when she heard a familiar voice calling her name from behind, she pulled up immediately and twisted in her seat. It was Grace on her bicycle, and she appeared distressed.

Instantly, Lara jumped off her bicycle.

Grace came to a halt with a screech of brakes and a spray of grit. Rapidly dismounting, she let her bike fall to the side of the road. She doubled over then, struggling to catch her breath.

Quickly, Lara moved to support her. 'Grace, whatever is it?'

Grace sobbed; she couldn't speak.

Lara put an arm around her, spoke softly, tried to soothe her. Then, as her friend's chest heaved with another sob, she held on to her.

When at last Grace could straighten up, her eyes were red-rimmed, glazed with tears.

'What is it, Grace? Please, you must tell me.'

Grace cleared her throat, then she croaked, 'My father, grandfather and great grandfather have been tenant farmers at Manor House Farm for the best part of a century. And, this morning, I got a letter...' Her voice choked up; she sucked in a breath.

'This morning, I got a letter from the Harringtons' solicitor telling me that, now my father is deceased, as a female relative I am not entitled to inherit the tenancy, so the estate will be selling the farm.'

'What?' Lara shouted, instantly outraged. 'You've run the farm all those years that your dad wasn't fit to work. They can't do this.'

Grace coughed out a bitter laugh as she pulled a letter from her trouser pocket. 'Well, there's a letter here from a fancy solicitor in London saying that, yes, they can do just that.'

Lara grabbed the letter, scanned it. Then she reached out to her friend. 'Never. We're not having this. As soon as I get back to the surgery, I'll speak to Dr Bingham. We'll get our own solicitor if needs be.'

Grace was shaking her head. 'I wish I had your confidence, Lara, but I've been going out of my mind since the postman delivered the letter this morning. What if they *can* do it?' Her voice broke when she spoke again. 'What if I've lost my dad... and now I'll be turfed off the farm as well?'

Lara's heart twisted with pain for her friend, she had to find something for Grace to cling onto. 'Come to the surgery at lunchtime or go there now if you want, Mrs Hewitt has already said you can call for a cup of tea anytime. We'll do everything in our power to help you, Grace. I promise we will.'

Grace doubled over to catch her breath. 'I'm so glad I ran into you, Lara. I didn't know where to go or who to turn to when I set off on my bicycle. I just knew I had to find somebody. So, I'll get back to the farm now, finish my chores, then I'll be down to the surgery.'

'Right, yes. That's the plan and we'll take it from there,' Lara said, lifting her chin, making her voice confident. And, as Grace slowly wheeled her bicycle away, she called after her, 'We'll help you fight this, Grace. We're in it together.'

Her friend turned, offered a smile, but her eyes were filled with so much sorrow it tore at Lara's heart. She felt outraged and, if she hadn't had more visits, she'd have gone back up to Ingleside Hall right now and hammered on the door until someone let her in.

16

As Lara got on with her remaining visits, she was fully functional, capable, doing her job. But she was still grappling with Grace's issue. To see her cheerful, happy-go-lucky friend hit hard by her bereavement and now the threat of eviction felt cruel. And, when she arrived back at the surgery and saw her friend's bicycle parked against the wall, she knew she had to help in any way she could. As soon as she was in through the back door, she picked up the noise of a lively discussion. And, as she entered the kitchen, all those gathered around the table looked to her. Grace was sitting between Marion and Mrs Hewitt, her face flushed, her eyes shining. 'Well, what do you think?' Lara called and Bingham slammed his fist down, making the plates jump. 'It's outrageous. I knew James Alston my whole life and there was never any suggestion of Grace relinquishing the tenancy if something happened to him. What the blazes is Lord Harrington up to?'

'Well, I don't think there's much of a mystery there,' Marion called, glancing around the table. 'He's thinking of his purse. He needs the money, and he'll get it any way he can.'

Bingham tried to speak but emitted an agitated noise.

Mrs Hewitt reached out to grab his arm, then rose from her seat. 'I'll get one of your calming down tablets. You'll not be any use to Grace or anyone else if you go off at the deep end.'

Bingham grabbed his tea, took a slurp and began to cough. 'Damn and blast,' he gasped as he leaned back against his chair. Mrs Hewitt tipped a white tablet out of the bottle and handed it to him.

Lara felt heartened by Bingham's strong response and, as she sat down in her place, she reached across to give Grace's hand a quick squeeze.

'Help yourself to more sandwiches before Dr Fitzwilliam scoffs the lot,' Mrs Hewitt called as she put those she'd plated up in front of Lara. Then, as she placed a large sugar-dusted Victoria sponge in the centre of the table, she said, 'I always think cake is an absolute essential for any stressful situation.'

'Hear, hear,' Angus called, already reaching for a slice. And, as the conversation moved back to Grace's tenancy, the young doctor quietly devoured his piece, leaving a delicate dusting of icing sugar on his top lip. But he'd clearly been taking in what was being said because, as soon as he'd finished eating, he scrunched his brow and said, 'I've got a friend from boarding school who's a damned good solicitor. He lives over the border in Yorkshire, but we could get him onto this if required. And, if I asked him nicely, he'd charge a nominal fee only.'

'Sounds like a good plan,' Marion grinned, 'you've got more going on inside that dishevelled head of yours than anyone might imagine.'

Angus laughed. 'You ain't seen nothing yet, Nurse Marion. I'm a wolf in sheep's clothing.'

'Oh, I think I've seen all there is to see,' she teased.

As Angus laughed and Mrs Hewitt cut more cake, Lara sensed Grace relaxing. And, when Dr Bingham glanced down the table to round up the detail of what had been discussed, his eyes blazed in Grace's direction. 'We're with you on this,' he said firmly, 'and, as soon as Lord Harrington is back from London, I'll be hammering on his door to ask what the ruddy hell he thinks he's doing.'

Marion coughed on her cake, but Bingham's fierce expression didn't falter.

Grace heaved a sigh, then offered a smile as she rested back in her chair for a few moments before rising from the table. She still looked pale and exhausted, but the light had returned to her eyes. 'I can't thank you enough, all of you. I felt crushed this morning when I received that letter and now you people have given me hope.'

Then, as Grace rose from her seat and walked to the door, Lara linked her arm to escort her out. 'Are you really alright?' she asked gently as they walked down the green-tiled corridor.

'Well, I'm still in shock... but, thanks to you and your team, I can now see some light. I know I'll have a tough fight on my hands, but, with you lot behind me, it just feels easier.'

'That's the spirit,' Lara grinned, sensing for the first time since James had died that the old Grace was on her way back. And, when Grace offered a smile as she said goodbye, Lara noted a flash of brightness in her eyes, and it felt heartening. 'So, I'll see you soon then, Grace,' she offered. 'And I hope all the thrashing out around the table was OK. It's just sometimes when the whole team get together it can be a bit daunting.'

'Oh no, not to me,' Grace smiled. 'When my dad was fit and well, we often went hammer and tongs over some issue related to the farm. Aunt Agnes used to think we were arguing... but we were making decisions, getting things done. And, right now, I'm glad of the thrashing out. Hopefully I'll see you again soon for more of the same.'

Pulling her bicycle from the wall, Grace blew a kiss before setting off down the cobbled street towards the bridge at some speed. Lara gritted her teeth, hoping her friend would judge the angle just right, but Grace had lived here her whole life and she'd probably cycled into Ingleside for school, so she deftly negotiated the hump-backed bridge.

'Phew,' Lara breathed, turning then to make her way back into the surgery. But, just as she did so, a shiny red sports saloon pulled up beside her and the driver wound the window down. She waited, thinking it was a sightseer looking for directions, but, when a head bobbed out, she wished she'd gone straight back inside. It was Patrick, and he was gazing at her and smiling as if she ought to be delighted to see him again.

'What are you doing here?' she hissed.

'Just passing through. Thought I'd come to let you have a look at the car that emerald necklace helped to buy for me.'

'You mean you sold it, just like that. I thought it was a family heirloom.'

'It was,' he smirked, 'but there's nothing wrong with turning old stuff into ready cash. And, besides, a man about town needs a decent set of wheels. Fancy hopping in and going for a spin?'

'No. Of course not,' she said sharply. 'In what world do you think, after what happened at the Harvest Ball, I would want to speak to you ever again. Never mind go for a drive in your car.'

He shrugged, pulled his mouth down at the corners. 'Your loss. Maybe I should call by the pub across the road and see if the lovely Ada will take me up on the offer.'

'You can try, but I can guarantee she'll have nothing to do with you either.'

'Oh, so you two girls have been swapping stories, have you?'

'That's none of your business and you need to leave right now,' she called over her shoulder as she turned to stride back into the surgery.

Just at that moment, Sam Collins pulled up in his van and jumped out of the driver's seat. 'Is this fella causing trouble, Nurse Flynn?'

'Not anymore,' she said.

'Well, I don't like the look of him. I didn't take to the man that night he cadged a lift to Ingleside Hall. So, I'll wait here until he's gone, if that's alright with you.'

'Yes,' she said, 'that's absolutely fine.'

At that, Patrick grunted, stuck the car in reverse and zoomed off in a spray of grit. It was a relief to see him go, but she was left with a niggling thought telling her this was no trip out to socialise. He'd come here, all this way, for a reason. She swallowed hard as she made her way back into the surgery, and not wanting to get the team riled up in her defence, she decided not to report the incident. But, as soon as Marion saw her face, she said, 'What's up with you? You look like you've seen a ghost.'

There was no point in making up a story, Marion knew her far too well to be fobbed off. So, as soon as she'd slipped back into her chair, she said, 'It was Patrick. When I was saying goodbye to Grace, he pulled up outside in a new car, one he'd bought with the proceeds of that necklace.'

'What the blazes does *he* want?' Bingham spat as Marion shouted, 'If I see him anywhere near here again, I'll hit him harder next time.' And Angus swore and muttered under his breath.

Lara didn't have an answer to Bingham's question, but she knew without a shadow of doubt that there had to be a reason. She just didn't know what it was yet.

17

After lunch, Dr Bingham headed out in the Rover to visit his poorly patients at the Infirmary and Angus had an urgent case to attend at the cottage hospital. As the young doctor waved a jovial goodbye, Lara and Marion were scrutinising their lists of afternoon visits when they heard him rev the little blue Austin and reverse at speed down the side of the surgery. Mrs Hewitt offered a wry smile, and was about to make some comment probably related to the young doctor's driving when the telephone rang. The housekeeper walked briskly to the hallway to answer. In seconds, she was calling through to the kitchen, 'It's an emergency. Be ready to go out.'

Lara and Marion grabbed their coats and waited for instruction. In moments, Mrs Hewitt was shouting, 'There's been a motor accident just past Ingleside Hall, two male casualties, sounds like one fatality, another badly injured. The ambulance has been called but the injured man needs emergency assistance right now. A farm labourer, Jack Bradley, heard the smash when he was out in the fields, and called it in. He's going back now to see what he can do. You both need to go right now, as fast as you can.'

'Roger that,' Marion said. Then to Lara, 'Let's take the motorcycle. You alright on the back?'

'Yes,' she called as she ran full pelt, following her colleague to the back door.

Gripping a bag of extra dressings and bandages Mrs Hewitt had thrust at her, Lara leapt on the back of the Norton as Marion kick-started it into life, and shouted back, 'Hold tight,' then skidded out onto the road. Lara gritted her teeth as they shot down the hill, adjusting her position to match her colleague's as they swerved over the bridge. Once they were out on the country lanes, she tightened her grip around Marion, the bag of dressings wedged firmly between them. It felt like too slow progress at first, as they made their way uphill with the motorcycle engine screaming like a banshee. But, once they were out on the flat, she felt Marion's body tighten as she leaned forward across the handlebars. Then they were hurtling along the narrow lanes with autumn leaves flying up and around. She gritted her teeth, willing the motorbike to go faster, praying the injured casualty would survive.

Once she spotted the gates to Ingleside Hall, she knew they were almost there. But time seemed to stretch on painfully slow until Marion swore, then shouted back, 'I can see the accident up ahead... It's horrendous.'

Lara felt an increase of tension building in her chest as she ran through emergency procedures in her head. And, as soon as Marion skidded to a halt, she leapt off the motorcycle and sprinted with her bag of dressings, yelling, 'You check the car, I'll go to the casualty on the road.'

Jack Bradley jumped up from his tending of the injured man – his face ashen, almost as pale as his white-blond hair. He was visibly shaking; he could barely get his words out. Lara called out to him, 'It's alright, Jack, we can take over from here. You stand by so you can flag down any vehicles.'

He nodded, and silently complied.

The front end of the car had been destroyed by a stone gatepost, so it was only a moment before Marion shouted to confirm the driver's death. Lara was on her knees beside the twisted body of a male casualty – he was unconscious but breathing. His head was bloodied, but the injury looked minor compared to the slick of bright red blood oozing briskly through his trouser leg. Quickly, she noted deformity of his shoulder and the distorted angle of one arm. Fractured arm, fractured shoulder. His right leg didn't look out of alignment, but it was where she needed to focus her attention before the young man bled out here at the side of the road. She pulled scissors from her pocket, cut open his trouser leg. A deep wound above his knee was gushing blood.

Marion was by her now, a catch in her breath when she spoke. 'The man in the car must have died on impact. His chest's been caved in by the steering wheel. Didn't stand a chance.'

Lara heard the words, nodded, her attention fully focused on the casualty in front of her. Then she was speaking rapidly, 'We have an unconscious patient with a head injury, left fractured humerus and shoulder. But, right now, this upper leg wound is our major concern. I've put pressure on, padded it up with gauze, but the dressing is soaked already. We need to apply more pressure, bandage firmly.'

'What about a tourniquet?' Marion shot at her as she pulled new dressings from the bag.

'We might have to resort to that, but I'm worried because it could cut the blood supply off completely... but, then, if the ambulance doesn't get here soon...'

Marion cleared her throat. 'They never get here soon. Not their fault, that's just how it is.'

Still holding a bloodied hand to the leg wound, Lara held fast while Marion applied two more dressing pads and a crepe bandage. Then she held the dressings firmly as Marion bandaged. Lara blew out a breath then and shifted her attention to the head wound. 'It looks clean enough, no foreign bodies, so let's bandage.' As Marion grabbed another dressing pad and bandage, Lara pressed her fingers to the man's neck to palpate the carotid artery. 'His pulse is rapid and thready.'

Glancing down the lane, straining her ears, she needed to hear that ambulance bell.

'We can only do what we can do,' Marion said firmly as she bandaged.

Lara nodded, knowing it was the reality of their situation. But a painful ache throbbed in her throat at how young the handsome, dark-haired casualty was. And, if he survived, he'd need to learn of his friend's death.

A shiver flashed through her but, when she heard the putter of a vehicle heading in their direction, she instantly jumped up, praying it was the ambulance. However, it didn't sound like an ambulance, and a moment later, when a low-slung, blue MG sports saloon came around the corner, she knew there was no assistance there. Instantly, Jack was flagging the vehicle down. The car swerved, then stopped abruptly and a young woman in a fur coat was clambering out, shouting.

'What the heck?' Marion cried.

But Lara had already recognised the driver, it was Philippa Harrington, and it felt wildly inappropriate that she'd stopped to cause a scene. But, when the young woman emitted a gut-wrenching sob, sank to her knees on the rough road, shouting, 'I know these men. They are my friends,' Lara felt a painful lump in her throat.

Miss Harrington was struggling to get up, and as Lara tried to assist her, the young woman seemed to panic, and pushed hard against her. Lara spoke firmly then. 'I know it's hard, Philippa. But you must calm down.'

The young woman shot an unseeing glance in Lara's direction. Panicked, she was trying to struggle free. As Lara grappled with her, she begged her not to go near, because she wouldn't be able to unsee what was there. Philippa dropped her head then, as if all the air had been knocked out of her. 'The driver?' she croaked. 'What about the driver?'

Lara was shaking her head. 'He didn't stand a chance.'

Philippa doubled over, as if she'd taken a punch to the gut. 'Quentin, it's Quentin. He visited me at the hall this morning. He is my dearest friend.'

'I'm so sorry,' Lara breathed.

Philippa was fighting for air, wracked with deep sobs. Then, needing to get back to the casualty, Lara called over to Jack. 'Please can you look after Miss Harrington. The men in the car are her friends. She's had a terrible shock.'

Jack took Philippa's arm, then spoke gently to her.

Lara was heading back to assist Marion with the casualty, but then she realised she'd have to move Philippa's car off the road so the ambulance could get close. She ran to the car, jumped in, turned the key then reversed into a field gate.

When she returned, she sensed Marion's agitation even before she knelt down beside her. 'He's worsening, there's too much blood,' Marion said, her voice taut. 'We need to use the tourniquet right now.'

They fought with blood-slicked hands to apply enough pressure to slow the bleeding. But the man's face was chalk-white now.

'What's happening?' Philippa wailed in their direction.

'He's still breathing, we're doing our best to save him,' Lara called back to her. 'What's his name? Do you know him well?'

Between sobs, Philippa shouted, 'He is Alastair Bowley. He's not a friend like Quentin, but I've known him for a while.'

Lara used his name then as she whispered, 'Stay with us, Alastair. Keep fighting.'

He made a tiny noise at the back of his throat as if in reply, but, given the pallor of his skin, it could have been his final breath.

She needed to get through to him, so desperately she used anything that might help him cling to life. 'The ambulance is coming, Alastair. Right now. They're almost here.'

Strangely, right then, she did hear the ambulance bell, and she called to Alastair, 'They're here. The ambulance is here.'

Moments later, the ambulance men were running with their stretcher, the driver listening as Lara rapidly ran through the details while Marion assisted with the loading of the casualty onto the stretcher then into the back of the ambulance. 'We've put a tourniquet on the leg, so it needs to be checked. And there's another casualty in the driver's seat, but he was already deceased when we arrived.'

The ambulance man sucked in a breath. 'Right you are. I'll have a quick look, and if we can't easily pull him out of there, we'll have to leave him for the tow truck.'

It felt awful to do that, but there was no choice. The priority was to get Mr Bowley to hospital.

As Lara helped to settle the casualty on the stretcher, the ambulance driver quickly checked the deceased. He walked back briskly, shaking his head. 'He didn't stand a chance, poor sod. Must have died instantly.' He grabbed the bottom of the stretcher then and in moments their casualty was loaded, and they were heading down the lane with the bell clanging.

It felt so quiet once they'd gone. They all stood silent, as if frozen in some horrific tableau, Marion kneeling at the side of the road covered in blood, Philippa still clinging to Jack.

'We did all we could,' Lara breathed, reaching out to put an arm around Marion's shoulders.

Marion heaved a ragged sigh, and nodded.

Then Philippa began to sob, a deep, guttural, broken sound.

Despite everything she'd wrangled with regarding the Harringtons, Lara went straight to the young woman, tried to hold her back as she struggled free from Jack and staggered towards the wrecked car.

'No, don't look!' Lara shouted, catching up with her, grabbing her arm.

But Philippa turned with unseeing eyes and Lara held back.

'Just let her go,' Marion said gently.

When Philippa emitted an unearthly wail, Lara walked over to support her, held on to her. The horror of the dead man in the car made her stomach plunge as if she were in freefall. But Marion was also there now, giving support. And when Jack glanced beseechingly in Lara's direction, she went to him. 'What an awful thing for you to witness, Jack. And I'm so sorry to have to ask you this... but the police will need to know the details of what you heard and saw.'

He ruffled his white-blond hair, blew out a breath. 'I was walking across the fields on my way to check the sheep and I heard a loud screech then a huge bang. I ran straight towards it... and saw the man in the car first, knew he was dead. So, I went to the fella on the ground. He was still breathing, and he was awake, so I legged it fast to a nearby farm where I knew they had a telephone. There was nobody in, but the door was unlocked, so I called the ambulance.'

Jack paused then and, when he spoke, his voice broke. 'When I got back here, I could see the fella on the road was still breathing but there was so much blood... and he kept drifting in and out and asking over and over about his friend, Quentin. I kept saying don't worry, he'll be alright, because I needed him to stay calm. Then he passed out before you came... And that was it really.'

'You did a good job,' she told him, 'you did everything you could.'

Jack pressed his lips together, nodded. But, when he spoke again, his voice sounded taut with nerves. 'I'm not sure about that, you start going through it in your head. Wondering if there was anything else you could have done.'

Lara reached out to place a gentle hand on his arm. 'Trust me, there was nothing more you could possibly have done.'

He dropped his head and, by the time he glanced up, his breathing had steadied. He wiped a hand around his face. 'I need to get off, my boss'll be wondering where the heck I've got to.'

Lara pulled her pad and pencil out of her pocket. 'Before you go, give me your name and address so the police can contact you if need be.'

He nodded, quickly told her his details. Then, with a half-smile and a raise of his hand, he was away across the fields.

Marion had an arm around Philippa's shoulders now and the young woman looked broken, as if she'd taken a heavy punch to the gut. Her head bowed, her make-up smeared across her face, Lara couldn't help but feel for her.

But Lara needed to organise next steps, she had to get things moving. So, she walked over, spoke gently to the young woman.

'If you'll give permission for me to drive your car, I'll run you back up to the hall. And then I can use your telephone to report back to Ingleside surgery.'

Phillipa opened her mouth to reply, but no words would come, so she nodded.

'That makes sense,' Marion sighed, with a glance to her motorcycle. 'So, you get off and I'll be tidying up the kit here and waiting for the police.' Her friend mustered a smile then, but her eyes were wide and full of sorrow. Lara felt sure she'd been triggered back to her own accident in the summer, and she reached out a hand to her then. 'Are you alright?'

Marion cleared her throat, nodded. 'Yes. Now you get off. Let's get sorted.'

Moments later, Lara was in the driver's seat of the blue sports car with a shocked Philippa silent and heavy-eyed from crying in the seat beside her. She couldn't help but feel concern for this broken woman who was unrecognisable from the haughty horseback rider she'd previously encountered.

Once she'd parked up and guided Philippa in through the door of the hall, she called for assistance, and at the sound of running feet was met head-on by a very concerned housekeeper, who immediately led a sobbing Philippa away. After calling the surgery, Lara walked back through the entrance hall and saw the crystal chandeliers she'd marvelled at the night of the Harvest Ball. Without their rainbow light, they were just glass now, as if what had been displayed had been a trick of the eye, a mirage.

Closing the heavy door with a firm clunk behind her, she began to walk briskly back down the drive and out to the lane. Still fired up with adrenaline, her mind flitted over details of the accident. The shock of it was still with her and it made her breath catch, but she just kept on walking. The difference between attending an emergency out here and in Liverpool was stark. In the city, the ambulances were quick to arrive, and hospitals were close by. All of what she'd just done out on a lonely, country lane felt raw, cut to the bone. And in the next breath other snapshots of her own accident in Liverpool and finding Marion after her motorcycle crash came at her. All of it cohering into a mess of flashbacks. Glad of this time alone before she got back to the accident scene, she halted for a few moments beneath a barely leafed oak tree. Its scarred trunk rose strongly from the ground, the branches ragged with the bulk of their leaves gone. But this tree was strong and, in the spring, new life would come. She pressed a hand to the rough bark, felt the texture. The dried, fallen leaves were sparse now, blown about and a dull brown, but, as she rustled through with her foot, she saw a tiny wood mouse startle and run. The suddenness of it made her breath catch, sent a gentle stab through her heart. But it helped to lighten her and spurred her on.

Arriving back to the smashed-up car, she felt relieved to see two uniformed police officers inspecting the scene, their small black car parked up in the gateway she'd used earlier for Philippa's vehicle. Marion was waiting by her motorcycle, and she raised a hand to Lara then motioned to the men. 'They need to have a word with you, to corroborate the story.'

'Right,' she said, walking over, ready to answer their questions.

'That all seems to be in order,' the taller policeman said as he finished scribbling his notes with the stub of a pencil. 'So, now we've spoken to you both, you're free to go. We'll wait here for the tow truck so we can get the deceased moved...' He was shaking his head then. 'Sadly, this kind of thing is now routine. We had another one like this yesterday on the outskirts of Ridgetown. It's crazy, the way these young folk drive their cars.'

Lara nodded, 'Maybe they should make the driving test more difficult to pass.'

'Well, the fella we attended yesterday hadn't even bothered with a test. It's madness, absolute madness.'

She drew a slow breath, walked over to Marion, who was ready and waiting astride the motorcycle. As she clambered aboard, Marion called over her shoulder. 'I don't know about you, but I feel like I've done a full day's work already even though we've got the rest of our patients to see. Hopefully, we can get some tea and toast before we head back out.'

'I think Mrs Hewitt will be already onto that.' Lara sighed, grateful for Marion's sturdiness as she put her arms around her waist and relaxed. And, as they rode back to the surgery with leaves dancing in the narrow lanes, she felt the reassuring thrum of the motorcycle and breathed the damp, earthy air and it calmed her.

18

Later that day, as the Ingleside team gathered for their evening meal, for once Marion was quiet at the table and Lara felt grateful for the matching of their moods. They'd both pushed on to catch up with their visits but, with the demands of the emergency call, it had taken every drop of energy, seemingly from them both. They'd answered questions from Dr Bingham and had some level of debriefing, but Mrs Hewitt had insisted her 'girls' were allowed to relax after what they'd dealt with this morning. Once Bingham had retreated to his room for his glass of whisky and Angus had told them he was going for a walk around the village – which was of course code for him going to the Dorchester for a few pints of ale, Mrs Hewitt pulled the sherry bottle from the cupboard and brought three glasses to the table. 'I'm not going to be asking you about what happened this morning, I can see you're both exhausted. But you two are my beautiful angels and I'm so proud of you both.'

'Steady on, Mrs H,' Marion offered but Lara could tell her colleague was pleased by the accolade.

'So, here's to you both,' the housekeeper called, raising her glass and clinking it first against Marion's, then leaning across the table to Lara. 'Cheers.'

Even after a single glass, Lara began to feel sleepy, so she made her excuses and almost crawled up the red-carpeted stairs on her hands and knees. With barely enough energy to wash and clean her teeth, she slipped into the nightdress she always placed on the cast-iron radiator and felt glad of its warmth. Sure she'd fall fast asleep as soon as her head touched the pillow, she was quickly exasperated by the explosion of thoughts as her brain replayed scenes from the accident. She lay on her back, turned on her side, but she was uncomfortable now and needing to get up and sit at the side of the bed. Glad of the glass of water she always had on her bedside table, she took some sips then tried to settle again. But still sleep evaded her.

Drifting in and out all night long with flashbacks of the accident, she fell asleep in the early hours only to startle awake with Philippa's scream playing through her head. When at last she did doze off again, it felt as if she were woken instantly by the loud trill of her alarm clock. She gasped, reached to switch it off, then groaned when she heard the patter of rain against her window. 'Not again,' she said out loud, knowing today of all days she needed clear sky and the feel of the late autumn sun.

'Morning,' she called to Mrs Hewitt, arriving first to the breakfast table.

'Good morning,' the housekeeper called breezily from the Aga, but then she narrowed her eyes and peered closer. 'My goodness, Nurse Flynn. You're a bit peaky this morning.'

'Yes, I think that's a fair assessment,' she sighed, 'I couldn't sleep last night and I'm exhausted. But that's not going to stop me getting out to see my patients.'

Mrs Hewitt leaned in, her voice softer. 'What if I speak to Dr Bingham and see if we can shift you to the clinic. I'm sure

Marion wouldn't mind; she's always itching to get out on her motorcycle.'

'Oh no, please don't do that. It'll probably make me feel even worse. At least when I'm out on my bicycle, I'm getting exercise, and it might revive me.'

Mrs Hewitt pressed her lips together for a second, then she said, 'You and Marion had a heck of a time yesterday morning. So, if you start nodding off at the table and slump face first into your porridge, you have no choice, I'm shifting you to lighter duties.'

Lara giggled then. 'There is every possibility I might just do that.'

But, by the time she'd eaten her breakfast and downed two cups of strong Lancashire tea, she was feeling much more functional. And when Marion ran in late, closely followed by Angus, to grab their usual sup of tea and quick slice of toast and jam, she began to feel even better.

'Just a moment, Dr Fitzwilliam,' Mrs Hewitt called as Angus made to dash out of the kitchen.

He turned wide-eyed as if he'd just been found out for some misdemeanour.

'No need to worry,' the housekeeper cackled, pulling a clean handkerchief from her apron pocket. 'It's just that you've got a big smudge of strawberry jam at the side of your mouth.'

He grinned then as she dabbed it away. 'Thank you, Mrs H.'

Lara and Marion exchanged a relieved glance. They had a strange, unspoken pact to support the young doctor. Which didn't make much sense because usually he deserved the tellings off he got from Mrs Hewitt. Not always those he got from Bingham, though, and having sometimes found herself on the wrong side of the senior doctor she knew what that felt like. Whereas Marion could do no wrong in Bingham's eyes. It had niggled her at first, but from the beginning she'd felt close to Marion, and she'd sensed her vulnerability. So, despite her colleague's lively demeanour, she knew Marion would struggle if Dr Bingham ranted at her in the way he sometimes did with her.

As she pushed back her chair, she thought again of their young, male casualty from yesterday. She knew the housekeeper would have reported any information straight away, but she still asked, just in case.

'No news yet. So that means he's alive,' Mrs Hewitt called from the Aga.

'Good, that's good,' Lara breathed, as the housekeeper began to slowly shake her head as she stirred her pan. 'What a tragedy, though, for the young man who died. He had his whole life ahead of him. They should do something to stop these youngsters speeding in their cars. Once they've passed their driving test, they're off, driving like the devil.'

'Yes, you're absolutely right,' she replied, 'but it's tempting to push on at some speed once you get the hang of driving. And, of course, we all should be more careful, but I've seen horrific accidents in Liverpool involving horses and carts. So, I suppose in a way it's not what you drive, but how you drive it that matters.'

Mrs Hewitt tipped her head to the side. 'I think you might be spot on with that, Nurse Flynn. But, even so, we should remind our doctors not to drive so fast. And Marion has only just recovered from her motorcycle accident, so maybe she should slow down as well.'

'Yes, she's nippy alright. But the few times I've ridden pillion with her, she's been a steady, competent rider. So, it's hard to figure out what happened to her that day she had the accident. Maybe she was distracted by something, she still can't remember anything about it.'

'I hope it never comes back to her, some things are best left.' Mrs Hewitt sighed, then pursed her lips. 'Anyway, me and you discussing traffic safety issues won't help me finish making this soup... or the batch of scones I promised Dr Bingham. Ooh, but there is one good thing... your friend Alice Taylor, she's already started baking her bread and it's excellent. I've got an order in for a regular delivery. I just don't have time to bake the bread as well as everything else and that stuff we get from Billington's in Ridgetown, it's like wire wool compared to Alice's.'

Lara giggled at the housekeeper's colourful analogy, and felt pleased that Alice was already up and running with her bakery. Then, glancing to the kitchen clock, she knew she needed to get going. 'See you later, Mrs H,' she called as she grabbed her medical bag from beside her chair then ran to the pegs in the hallway to gather her macintosh and rain hood.

It was a relief to be out in the open and, although the sky was darkening with heavy, grey clouds, the rain had eased off for the time being. First on her list was a check on Miss Dunderdale's badly sprained wrist, then she'd be back to the village to see Daniel Makepeace and, finally, out on the road to Ridgetown to visit Peter Valentine. It had all been overshadowed by the car crash yesterday, but the young lad had got back from hospital in the afternoon, so he was down for a check today.

As she freewheeled down the hill with her brain still ticking over her cases, she didn't see the bulky frame of Alice's Uncle Josh until he shouted out a greeting and flagged her down. She pulled up fast, skidded a little, thinking there might be a medical issue with Alice or one of the children. 'Is everything alright?' she asked urgently, further triggered by his anxious expression.

'Oh, yes. Sorry,' he said quickly, then he leaned in rather awkwardly due to his bulky, muscular frame. And when he spoke, his voice was hushed. 'I've not told anyone about this yet, not even Alice. But I need you to know that Vic Taylor has been seen in the village. And I've heard he's living out in the wilds somewhere near the fells. I don't know what he's up to, but I'm damned sure it's nothing good.'

Instantly, she felt a painful lump in her throat. He'd caught her in an unguarded moment, so she was shocked, but, given the half sightings of the man she'd had, she wasn't surprised by the news.

'I'm glad you've told me. I've just had that feeling at the back of my neck and that night of the bonfire I was sure I saw him in the shadows, but I told myself I was probably imagining it.'

He was shaking his head. 'No, you were spot on. And rumour has it that he was the one who set the fire at the mill.'

She felt a flush creeping into her cheeks. 'But why would he do that?'

'To cause trouble, to get back at the fellas he thinks turned against him. Think about it this way, if the mill burns down, then half the village including his old buddy – now enemy – Ed Cronshaw will be out of work. Ingleside would be devastated – no work, no pay, just poverty.'

'I see what you're getting at,' she said, but still she couldn't comprehend the lengths Vic might go to, given his children now lived in the village. Then, alert to a high-pitched gleeful shout from the alley by the Old Oak, she saw Lucy and Robin run past in their coats and knitted hats, clutching their school bags. They called out merrily, 'Morning, Nurse Lara.'

'Morning, you two,' she shouted after them, but they were already halfway up the hill.

Uncle Josh was gazing after them with more than a hint of pride. 'Look at them go. They're thriving here in the village.'

'Well, you don't look like you're doing too badly yourself,' she said, smiling.

He wiped a hand around his face, then grinned. 'I've never felt so settled in my whole life. I'd warn anyone away from a life of prize fighting and tell them to help run a village bakery instead. Alice has got me kneading the bread and I like the work, and I'm very settled here.'

'I'm so glad to hear that and I'm grateful for the information about those rumours... but, right now, I need to get on with my visits. Please let me know if you hear anything else.'

'Will do,' he called after her as she cycled away, her breath coming quick with an extra stab of anxiety as she pedalled hard to try and rid herself of worrying thoughts.

Later, after she'd checked in on Miss Dunderdale and given her a set of light exercises for her healing wrist, she headed back to the village to see Daniel and he was very concerned and visibly upset at the news of the young man who'd died in the car crash. Since the weather had got much colder, he'd been moved by Esther to the front room so the stove could be lit, and he could keep warm. But it felt dark and closed-in for him away from his beloved window and she sensed him fretting. Even though he could see out to the street, it was nothing like being able to gaze over the fields and have the cattle come to the window. So, as she checked his pulse and measured his blood pressure, she let him talk on and vent some of his frustration.

His pulse was very thready today and his breath seemed shallow, but she spoke gently, trying to reassure him. 'You're doing as well as you possibly can, Mr Makepeace. And I know you miss the back room, but it's nice and warm in here at this time of year.'

He heaved a slow breath. 'I know what you're up to, Nurse Flynn, trying to jolly me along.' He emitted a low chuckle then that left him breathless, then he wheezed. 'And all I can say is... your tactics do seem to be working.'

He smiled deliciously then, showing his single front tooth.

'Do you want your woolly hat and gloves on?' she asked.

'Not really, I'm warm enough... but Esther will be in soon and she'll be telling me off if I'm not properly wrapped up.'

'They look good on you,' she offered cheerily, as she helped him pull the blue knitted hat over his white hair. Then she held out the matching mittens one at a time for him to slip on.

'Thank you, Nurse Flynn... and, I know I've been a bit down today, but don't be worrying about me. I've got Herbert in for a daily chat, and I know I complain about Esther being a bossy boots, but she's good company and I couldn't manage without her.'

'You're doing as well as you possibly can be,' she offered as she picked up her medical bag and prepared to leave.

He fixed her with his bright eyes then. 'But I just can't wait for the spring. Once the warmer weather comes, I'll be in my room again and back with Martha.'

'But your Martha is with you here, in this room as well.'

He smiled then. 'Aye she is, but she never liked cooking on that blasted stove... as she used to call it. She was a free spirit, at her happiest when she was out in the open air tending the cows and the sheep and the shire horse we kept back then. Or off up the village for a natter with the women.' His voice tailed off then as he offered the shadow of as smile and said, 'I wish I could hear the sound of her voice... just one more time.' Then, as he sank back against his pillows he blinked slowly once, twice, then drifted off to sleep.

The coals in the grate gently hummed and spat as Lara slipped out through the door and clicked it firmly shut behind her.

And as she walked up the hill, wheeling her bicycle, the smoke from many chimneys swirled and settled in the cold air, making her breath catch. It made her yearn even more for the clear spring skies, but there was a good way to go yet. She did enjoy feeling the changing of the seasons. Out here it felt unsheltered, the stone walls and tiny cottages offered minimal protection, so she was fully exposed to the elements. She'd read *Wuthering Heights* at boarding school and fallen in love with the image of Catherine and Heathcliff roaming the moors. She loved that combination of romance and tragedy.

'You look miles away. Where are you?' a voice called abruptly.

She startled. It was Leo at the door of the vets, and he was beaming a smile.

'What do you mean? Sorry, yes. I was just thinking about my visits,' she blurted, thrown off by the brightness of his gaze.

Instantly, she felt flustered, so she raised her hand and moved on quickly up the street.

'I heard about the motor accident,' he called after her. 'It must have been horrendous having to deal with such carnage. Hope you're alright?'

She stopped, turned to face him as she held on to her bicycle. 'Yes, I'm fine. It's all part of the work.' It was a stock phrase she used to deflect similar questions.

'Mmm,' Leo said knowingly and, by the sceptical look in his eye, she knew he could see right through her bluster.

'You take care, Lara, and you can always talk to me. I know my line of work is livestock, and it's not the same, it can't be, as working with humans. But it can still be harrowing.'

He seemed to be tying himself into knots and his face flushed a little. Seeing this softer side of him made her smile.

Then she said, 'I'm just off to the Valentines' farm, so I need to get on, but I'll be seeing you around.'

He offered a single nod. 'Yes, you will... Oh, and give my regards to young Peter, he's such a good help when I visit the farm. A lovely, bright young lad.'

'Will do,' she called.

Then it seemed as if he made to raise a hand in farewell but changed his mind and blew her a kiss instead. And the dazzling smile he offered felt like a shaft of sunshine on a cloudy day.

19

A chilly gust of rain sent her scurrying towards the door at the Valentines' farm and even the yard dog was keeping to his kennel as Lara waded through a slushy mix of manure and mud in the yard. All she knew of Fly was a thin whine and the tip of his nose peeping out just for a few seconds. Glad of her rain hood and macintosh, she kept her head down as she reached the farmhouse door and knocked firmly. There was no reply for a few moments but then the door creaked open, and Izzy was there offering her shy smile.

'Hello,' Lara said gently, 'I'm here to see Peter. Can I come in?'

The girl nodded, twisted her body away, then said, 'Follow me. Mam's in his room right now.'

Lara glanced to her mucky boots. 'Oh dear, shall I take them off?'

'Nah,' Izzy said, 'just give them a good wipe on the mat like Dada does.'

Lara felt pleased to have easier communication with the girl and, as she followed her through the kitchen then down the hall to the sitting room where Peter was being nursed, she noted the determined set of Izzy's shoulders.

The door was closed but, as Lara reached to knock, Izzy pushed it open and announced their presence. Sally Valentine stepped away from Peter's bed and turned with tears in her eyes and a broad smile. 'It's so good to see you, Nurse Flynn. Come in,' she urged, beckoning with her hand.

'Thank you,' Lara replied, catching her first glance of Peter and needing to use all of her external calm not to show on her face the shock she felt inside. The young lad had lost so much weight during his hospitalisation that his face and arms were stick thin, his cheekbones sharp, and his eyes appeared over-large and sunken. He smiled though and then propped himself up on one elbow to say hello.

'It's so good to see you, Peter.' Lara smiled genuinely. 'I hope they looked after you in the Infirmary.'

'They did,' he said, with a lopsided grin. 'And, when I was getting better, they wheeled me out into the grounds so I could see the street with all the cars, and I saw an ambulance coming in with its bell ringing and everything. Is that what it's like at the hospital in Liverpool?'

'Yes,' she said, recalling Peter's fascination with the city of her birth.

'I've told him we'll take a trip to Liverpool, once he's stronger. It's early days yet to be making any plans... but we'll get there,' Sally said, gulping back tears.

'I'll be up and about soon enough,' Peter called, then he glanced to Lara. 'She's worrying about me because I've lost so much weight, but I'll soon put it back on.'

Sally pulled a white handkerchief from her apron pocket

and dabbed at her eyes. In the next moment, Izzy was by her side, linking her arm. 'Peter's going to be alright, Mam. I know he is. And Fly thinks so too.'

'Yes, of course he is,' Sally hiccupped. 'It's just been so hard having him away from home. Then only being able to visit once or twice because of the farm and stuff.'

'Don't fret, Mam, I'll be right as rain soon enough and I'll be up to mischief again and, once you're telling me off, I'll know I'm fully better. My doctor at the Infirmary told me not many survive the lockjaw and those that do come back stronger than ever.'

'Well, young man,' Lara said, 'you've still got a fair way to go, but you're making an excellent start. I just need to check your temperature, pulse and blood pressure, then I'll have a look at that leg wound, if that's alright.'

'Fire away,' the lad said, trying a cheeky grin but already he seemed to be tiring.

'Come on, Izzy, let's go and put the kettle on,' Sally said. 'Do you want a cuppa, Nurse Flynn?'

'Yes, please.' She smiled, knowing it would be good to sit down with Sally to give moral support and listen to any concerns she might have.

By the time she'd finished her checks, Peter was nearly asleep, but she told him his leg wound had healed up well, considering they'd opened it up and debrided it. His observations were satisfactory, but he'd need to pay attention to his diet – plenty of fluids, fruit if they could get it, and good, plain food rich in carbohydrates.

He nodded sleepily, then reached a thin arm out to her. 'I can't remember that day I got very sick, but Mam told me you and Nurse Marion came on a motorbike, and you fought to bring down my fever. You looked after me... and Izzy said you saved my life.'

'Well, that was down to the hospital as well. And, whatever we did, I'm so glad you're back home now.'

He was already asleep, but she spent a few moments watching his eyes flicker beneath blue-veined eyelids. 'You're going to be fine, Peter,' she breathed, not fully sure that was the case, not yet. But, with the spirit the lad had, well, it made it so much easier to predict a good outcome.

In the kitchen, Izzy was busy setting up a tray with cups and saucers and a plate of biscuits, which she brought to the table. Sally was at the stove pouring boiling water into a teapot and then she turned and gestured for Lara to take a seat.

'Can I sit next to you please, Nurse Flynn?' Izzy asked as she slipped round to her side of the table and took a biscuit from the plate.

'Yes, of course you can.'

Izzy sat then, her back straight, her hands folded neatly in her lap.

'My word, Isobel,' her mother called as she approached, 'you're very neat and tidy today sitting next to Nurse Flynn.'

Izzy sighed then. 'Well, I've been thinking I might not want to be a farmer like Dada after all. I think I want to be a nurse or a doctor.'

'Well, well.' Sally smiled as she slipped into her seat opposite, glancing at Lara. 'What do you think, Nurse Flynn?'

'Good choice, Izzy, and I think you'd excel in either of those roles. But you'll have to work hard at school to pass your exams.'

Izzy nodded. 'I can do that, and our new teacher, Mr Armistead, he thinks my marks are excellent.'

'Well, it sounds like you might be all set then. But it's probably a bit early to decide.'

The little girl nodded again, then she sighed. 'The only thing is, can nurses and doctors have dogs...? Because I'd want to take Fly with me.'

'Well, I'm not sure you could have a dog while you were training, you certainly couldn't take one into a hospital. But you could get one when you were qualified, maybe have someone look after it while you're at work.'

Izzy waggled her head. 'I don't think Fly would mind, he spends a lot of time in his kennel, so it should be alright.'

Lara tilted her head to the side. 'Well, that seems fairly settled then. But, it'll be a good few years before you'll be making that decision. However, it pays to work hard at your lessons anyway, whatever kind of job you'd like to do.'

Sally was shaking her head. 'The things this lass comes out with, honestly.'

'Nothing wrong with thinking ahead,' Lara said. 'Hopefully there'll be a whole new world of opportunity waiting for young women by the time Izzy gets there.'

'Yes,' Izzy grinned, 'and I'll grab it with both hands. That's the kind of thing Mr Armistead would say.'

Lara had only seen the new headmaster in passing, but, if what Izzy said was a true reflection of his attitude to teaching girls, she was all in favour of the man.

It was so good to sit around the table with Sally and Izzy that Lara almost forgot she needed to go back to the surgery for lunch. And this afternoon, she'd be working alongside Dr Bingham in clinic to book in a new antenatal patient from the village, before setting out for another postnatal visit to Lydia Lennox. In the time since her baby boy had been born, Lara had been increasingly concerned by the isolated situation of the newly delivered mother. Nora Hurst called daily with milk and eggs and of course the eldest boy, Michael, was very capable. But it didn't feel right that he was kept back from school to take care of his siblings. And there was still something unsettling about Lydia that she couldn't quite put her finger on.

The damp and cold clung to Lara as she cycled to the turning that led down to the sawmill. And as she freewheeled towards the high-pitched screech of the big saw, she saw men in the yard, hunched in their thick wool coats with caps pulled low over their faces. Then, inevitably, as she cycled by the factory, her eyes were drawn to the black smear of soot on the wall next to where she'd seen that fire. It sent a shiver through her, especially after the suspicions Josh had shared with her the other day. Most frustratingly of all, it made her feel as if she'd never be free of Vic Taylor and the grudge he held against her. Just as she got ready to negotiate the bridge over the mill race, she heard a voice shouting her name and a tall man waving energetically caught her attention. It was Ed Cronshaw, his breath steaming as he hollered a greeting. She waved back, amused to see many of the other workers who she didn't know also waving. Once she'd passed by the side of the mill, she cycled towards the dark, glassy expanse of the mill pond. Then, as the lane grew steep, she pushed hard at the pedals to get as far as she could before being forced to dismount and wheel her bicycle. As she walked, she gazed over the crumbling drystone walls to see a few scraggy sheep with meagre grazing. The fields were stubbly compared to those lower down and right now they felt eerily quiet. It made her feel tense. Until a magpie chattered as it settled on a bare branch of a tree. One for sorrow popped into her head but, even as she thought it, she was grateful for the two for joy second magpie that landed for a squawk and a squabble.

Arriving at the Lennoxes' cottage she noted a thin spiral of smoke from the chimney and hoped the family had enough fuel to keep warm, especially with a new baby in the house. As she propped her bicycle against the wall, she noted a neatly stacked woodpile beneath a lean to at the side and knew this had probably been brought up from the mill. The way these folk looked after each other reminded her of some of the streets in Liverpool, but out here the ties were even stronger because they stretched between villages and small towns and out to isolated farms and cottages.

As she tapped on the cottage door and stood with steaming breath waiting to be admitted, she heard the low murmur of a voice inside and knew it was the eldest boy, Michael. In moments, he opened the door and he was smiling, with little Freddy at one side and Ava clinging to him at the other. Lara secretly adored all of these children, and she would never have said it out loud because it always felt wrong to have a favourite, but every time she saw Ava with her big eyes and rosy-cheeked face surrounded by blonde curls, her heart almost melted.

'Hello, Nurse Flynn,' Michael and Freddy trilled in unison.

'Hello.' She smiled, glancing around for Lydia, who had been sat at the kitchen table nursing the new baby the last time she'd visited.

'Ma's in bed today,' Michael told her matter-of-factly.

'Oh, is she alright?'

'Yes, she said she's very tired. She's like that some days.'

'Alright, I'll just go in and check on her.'

He nodded, took the hands of the two little ones and led them over to the truckle bed at the far side of the room. 'Come on, let's build a tower,' he called gently as he tipped out wooden blocks from a cloth bag.

The rattle of the blocks on the linoleum floor sounded loud in the confined space so she could perhaps understand why Lydia was spending quieter time in the bedroom. As she tapped on the door and waited, she listened for a voice telling her to enter, but all was silent. She tapped again more firmly, then called out, 'Mrs Lennox. It's me, Nurse Flynn. Is it alright if I come in?'

She heard a groan then and a voice called a slurry assent.

It was dark in the room with the curtains drawn and it took a moment for Lara's eyes to adjust. When she saw Mrs Lennox lying flat with no attempt to get out of the bed, she felt instant concern. But the mother and new baby were still in the lying-in period, so this wasn't untoward. She glanced to the crib where the baby slept peacefully and, even before she pulled out her weighing scale, she could tell by his chubby cheeks that little Jamie was thriving. So, shifting her attention back to Lydia, who was now swinging her legs out of bed. She asked gently, 'How have you been?'

Mrs Lennox cleared her throat, seemed to force a smile. 'Oh, you know what it's like. I'm not getting much sleep, but I think I'm doing alright.'

The rising intonation at the end of her remark set off a bat squeak of unease. And given the dark smudges of exhaustion beneath the woman's eyes, she made a mental note to increase the frequency of her visits here, just until she felt more settled about her patient's condition.

'I'm aware you've got a lot on and you're a bit out of the way here.'

'Oh, I prefer it that way,' Lydia replied, a bit too quickly. 'And Nora's very good, she comes in most days. And I've got Michael, I don't know what I'd do without Michael.'

Today didn't feel like the right time to gently remind Lydia that her eldest son might benefit from being back at school, even if it was on a part-time basis. So, she gently asked her patient to lie back down on the bed so she could have a feel of her tummy. It was over ten days now since the delivery and the fundus of the uterus could no longer be palpated. 'Everything's back in place. So that's all fine.'

Lydia offered a perfunctory smile and quickly pulled her nightdress down. Lara felt another grumble of concern. Even for a mother who already had the demands of three other children, Lydia's mood seemed very flat.

'Are you alright?' she asked gently, reaching out to her.

The woman shook herself. 'Yes, of course. It's just tiring, that's all. But Michael's very good.'

There it was again, that emphasis on Michael.

There was nothing she could pin down beyond the woman looking exhausted, but she felt confident in her need to increase her visits. Straightening up from the bed, she went back to the crib. 'So, let's have a look at this little one. I'll try not to disturb him, but we do need to weigh him today.'

Not getting any response, she glanced back to the bed where Mrs Lennox lay staring at the ceiling. Then, quickly, her patient roused, turned her head. 'Yes, of course, Nurse Flynn. Do what you need to do.'

Once she was back in the light and the warmth of the kitchen, the niggles she had seemed to lessen. Especially when a knock came to the door and Nora bobbed in with a basket over her arm. 'Oh hello, Nurse Flynn,' she called cheerily, despite the deep frown that Lara had now become used to. 'I'm just doing my daily round – first here with the milk and eggs – and I've brought a cake today. Then I'm off further up the road to Mrs Walker – her arthritis is terrible at this time of year, so I go in twice a week to help with the chores she can't manage and have a chat.'

'Ah yes, I've heard my colleague talk about Mrs Walker, but I haven't visited her myself as yet.'

'Well, I've told her all about you and she very much approves.'

'Oh, that's good.' Lara smiled, walking to the sink to wash her hands before she left the cottage for her next visit.

'I'll pour you some hot in there, Nurse Lara,' Michael called as she ran cold water.

'Thank you,' she said as he used the potholder and carefully grasped the kettle off the stove. The two little ones stood back, Freddy holding on to his little sister's hand as they'd been trained to do.

'Good lad,' Nora offered, ruffling Michael's hair after he'd put the kettle back on the hob.

As Lara scrubbed her hands, she glanced to the shelves above the sink. At the very top, she noted a tin marked with a skull and crossbones. RAT POISON. It felt stark to see it in the kitchen but, from her experience, it wasn't untoward to see strychnine or other poisons stored like this, especially in such a small cottage with no outbuildings. It was well out of reach though, even for Michael. Sensing her disquiet, Nora offered, 'We've been overrun with mice and rats this year. How's it been in the village?'

'The same,' she said, 'I suppose they're just trying to keep warm like the rest of us.'

'True,' Nora smiled, 'but when they're gnawing holes in my hen cabins to get to the eggs, I'm not feeling favourably disposed towards the blighters.'

'Oh dear. Yes, of course, you need to keep them at bay,' she said, drying her hands, preparing to leave.

As she picked up her medical bag, Ava gazed to her, before shyly burying her face against Michael. And it felt like the sun coming out when the little girl peeped back with her cherubic face and blonde curls and smiled.

'Bye, Ava, I'll see you soon,' Lara called gently.

Then, as she shrugged into her macintosh and pulled the door shut behind her, she felt the cold air meet her. She'd be back to check on Lydia and she'd report her niggling concerns to Dr Bingham. But, as she cycled away, she felt content with her assessment and the warmth of the little girl's smile stayed with her all the way to her next visit.

20

It was heartening to know Dr Bingham instantly understood Lara's concerns about Lydia Lennox, and he readily agreed to accompany her on the next visit. So, following a busy afternoon clinic two days later, she was waiting outside the front door as Bingham rapidly reversed his black Rover down the side of the surgery. She had every hope this journey would be slower and calmer than the tense emergency dash to James Alston they'd shared back in the summer. They'd both come a long way since then in their professional relationship, and it heartened her to realise that, even though they sometimes had differences of opinion, they were able to thrash things out. Equally stubborn, they sometimes ended up with an impasse and needed to look for common ground, but she appreciated the cut and thrust of the relationship. There'd been no difference of opinion regarding Lydia Lennox, however, and given Dr Bingham was an excellent practitioner of physical ailments, he also shared her interest in maladies of the mind. She appreciated his breadth of expertise, especially out here in this remote rural environment where difficult decisions had to be made on the spot.

Given her previous stressful experience of Bingham's fast driving, she gripped the leather seat with both hands and steeled herself as he revved the engine then skidded onto the gravelly road that led up to the turning to the sawmill. They were running late, so the autumn light was beginning to fade as they sped down towards the mill and, given the speed they were going, the slope felt precipitous. And she so wished the doctor would keep his eyes firmly fixed on the road instead of glancing to her as he chatted about previous cases of perinatal mood disorder he'd treated.

She nodded and tried to reply, but they were motoring at quite a pace, and the lights of the sawmill were rapidly approaching. She gritted her teeth, clutched her seat. Then, as he slowed his pace in preparation for negotiating the bridge, he jammed on the brakes and she lurched forward. He dropped his voice then, switched his topic of conversation. 'That fire you saw at the mill... it was a strange business. But maybe it was a bonfire that hadn't been put out properly?' He glanced to her then as he jarringly changed gear to go over the bridge.

'Yes, it might have been. But I've heard any number of theories since it happened.' And she had, but the one she'd latched onto was that some human had been out to make trouble. There was certainly no weight whatsoever to the version claiming the mill owner, Selwyn Barclay, had attempted to set a fire so he could claim the insurance money. That didn't make any sense because currently the sawmill was booming, and they'd recently expanded with a workshop to make chairs.

Accelerating away from the factory building, they were soon whisking by the mill pond, then emerging from the cover of trees at the top of the hill. She felt relieved, but the thought of the journey back in the dark made her breath catch. Arriving at the cottage, she hoped Nora had passed on the message to let the family know she'd be visiting with Dr Bingham. But, as soon as Michael opened the door, she could tell instantly that notice of the senior doctor's visit had been received. And, for the first time since the baby had been born, the whole family were gathered in the living area. The room was warm and well-lit, the kettle was singing on the hob. Lydia was sitting on a kitchen chair cradling baby Jamie on her knee and little Freddy's eyes were wide as he sat next to her, staring at a large chocolate cake on a white plate in the middle of the table. 'Nora made a cake,' the little boy grinned, 'and she said I could have a big piece.' Then, as Michael picked up Ava and carried her over to sit on his knee at the table, the family group was complete.

It was good to see, but it frustrated Lara because she knew that what she'd observed previously had predominated since her first antenatal visit. Instinctively, she knew Dr Bingham would understand the context and there would be no problem with the visit being labelled as a waste of his time. But, as she smiled and accepted a slice of cake, she hoped there'd be enough evidence of her concerns for him to give useful input. There was some chit chat back and forth and, once the slices of cake had been consumed and Freddy and Ava both sat with chocolate smeared mouths, Michael took the little ones in hand and led them to their wooden toys.

And that's when Lara noted the brightness of Bingham's gaze and the careful questions he began to ask Lydia in a kindly but expert way. She knew then he hadn't dismissed her concerns. It felt like a warm conversation, but all the while he was assessing Lydia's state of mind. He was good at what he did and, as he brought the chat to a close, he reached out to Lydia with both arms. 'Let's have a hold of the little fella,' he smiled. That's when she saw Lydia's eyes flash with pain, or it could have been anxiety. But it was gone so quick it was hard to pin down. And Lydia was smiling as she got up from her seat and handed baby Jamie to the doctor. 'You're a strong little fella,' Bingham crooned as he expertly tucked the baby into the crook of his arm. And, as she watched, she saw him run a gentle hand over the infant's dark hair. He glanced up then with a warm smile. 'These tiny ones are so special at this stage, aren't they?'

The warmth, the tenderness of him was all on display and it made her wonder why he'd never married and had children. Mrs Hewitt probably knew the answer to that question, and she'd ask her when they had one of their chats in the sitting room. The housekeeper was often tight-lipped about her own history, but she never held back from answering questions about Dr Bingham.

'Well, we'd best get on,' Bingham said, standing up from his seat to pass the baby back to the mother.

Lydia nodded, and offered a smile that didn't quite reach her eyes. 'Well, it was lovely to meet you, Dr Bingham.'

'Likewise.' He smiled.

It was pitch dark as they drove away from the cottage, guided solely by the weak light of the headlamps. There was no choice but for Bingham to drive slowly and, as they progressed along the narrow lanes, Lara listened carefully to his summing up of the visit. 'I know where you're coming from with your concerns. It felt as if there was an emptiness at times and the mother is pale and exhausted. But probably no more than any other woman who's just given birth to her fourth child. And, taking into consideration her history of having lost two young children to whooping cough, the picture feels complicated. But, I have to say, right now, I don't think there's enough out of the ordinary to cause concern. However, keep visiting regularly and, of course, I'll come out to see Mrs Lennox again if need be.'

'Yes, thank you,' she said, feeling a little disappointed but needing to swallow it down out of respect for the senior doctor's judgement. Then, as the headlights picked out a bright red fox leaping out in front of the car, a dead rabbit clamped in its jaw, her heart jumped, and she screeched out loud.

'Steady on, Nurse Flynn... just an example of nature red in tooth and claw,' Bingham chuckled, as they plunged through the darkness on their way down to the mill.

Lara sat quietly as they passed by the mill pond, but, as they approached the dark, looming shape of the mill, she was sure she'd seen another flicker of light that might be a fire. She leaned forward in her seat. 'Did you see that?'

'No, what...?' Then Bingham shouted, 'What the bloody hell!' and slammed on his brakes as they approached the mill yard.

It was a fire, just like the one before. But this one was much bigger. 'I'll get out, see if I can get some buckets of water?' Lara offered instinctively.

'No, you will not,' he shouted, 'I'd rather see it all burn down than risk leaving you here alone to tackle that blaze. We need to get back to the surgery to raise the alarm and then we'll drive back together.'

He pushed ahead, accelerating over the bridge and flying up the hill, swinging around corners, going as fast as he possibly could. As the car skidded to a halt outside the surgery, Lara leapt out and ran inside. Mrs Hewitt was there instantly. 'Call the fire brigade and the police,' Lara shouted down the corridor. 'There's another fire at the mill.'

When she ran back out to Bingham, he already had Ed Cronshaw in the back seat of the car. 'He's coming with us. Let's get down there, see what we can do before the fire brigade arrive.'

'Right you are,' she called as she slipped into the passenger seat.

'We'll pick up Danny Ryan as well,' Ed called. 'His cottage is on the way, so we won't lose time.'

This fire was substantially bigger than the first one and it'd taken a good hold of the wood in the yard. Tall flames were licking the front of the mill building. Ed and Danny jumped out and Ed soon had a hosepipe trained on the flames and then Lara and Bingham helped Danny to haul buckets of water up from the mill race. Lara was coughing on smoke, saturated and shivering, but she kept going. When she heard the fire engine bell and the shape of the vehicle loomed in the darkness, she almost doubled over with relief. But she kept filling and carrying buckets, and they soon had the fire under control with the support of the firemen and their hoses.

Once they were down to the smouldering remains of wood in the yard, Ed walked over with Danny in tow. They were still coughing on smoke, soaked to the bone, and Ed said, 'This must be linked to that last fire. What the bloody hell is going on? Does somebody want the whole village out of work?'

Lara grabbed Ed's arm. 'We need to wait for the police, see what they say. But I agree, this must have been deliberately set and probably by the same person.'

Ed nodded, then wiped a hand around his face. She didn't want to aggravate him further by repeating Josh's speculation over Vic Taylor, but she was sure there were grounds for thinking he was involved.

Bingham walked to his car and returned with a hip flask. 'Here, have a sup of this then pass it round,' he ordered, thrusting it into Ed's hand.

He took a good swig then croaked, 'Just what the doctor ordered.'

Bingham coughed out a laugh. 'Exactly.'

Lara shook her head when it came to her turn with the flask but, on the next round, she took a swig just to warm her bones. Then, at the sound of an approaching vehicle, she saw a police car looming. It was Inspector Stirling and, as he walked towards her, he called, 'So it's you again, Nurse Flynn.'

'Yes, it is.'

'I can vouch for her,' Bingham offered. 'She was in the car with me, and we saw the fire when we were driving back from visiting a patient.'

The detective turned his mouth down at the corners. 'I didn't for one moment think Nurse Flynn would be involved.' Then he turned to Lara, 'But it's good you have a solid alibi... so there's no need to take you in for questioning.'

'No need,' she said, watching the detective then as he stood surveying the scene. Now the fire had been extinguished, the lights inside the mill had been put on, so it was easy to see the pile of smouldering, blackened wood and grey ash in the yard.

'It looks very similar to last time, but much bigger,' Lara offered.

'Mmm...' the detective mused. 'But what I'm wondering is why do half a job. If you want to burn the mill down... why not smash a window, light a fire inside.'

'Clearly it's someone sending a signal,' Lara replied.

'Yes, I think you might be right,' Inspector Stirling called over his shoulder as he walked towards the building.

Suddenly feeling very cold, with shivers running through her body, she felt relieved when Bingham motioned for her to get in the car and he clambered into the driver's seat. 'Ed and Danny are going to stay on to assist Inspector Stirling and apparently Mr Barclay has been called, and he'll be coming down. So, we might as well get back to the surgery.'

As she settled in the passenger seat, she felt cold to the bone, and she was shivering violently.

'I'll soon have you back in the warm at the surgery,' Bingham said gently as he turned the ignition then began to pump the accelerator.

Her teeth were chattering violently now, but her mind was still whirring with the incident. 'It's odd though, isn't it?' she stuttered. 'That each time I've been returning from the Lennoxes' in the dark... this has happened.'

'Yes,' he said, glancing to her. 'But it could also just be a coincidence.'

Her logical mind told her he was right, but her instincts pulled her in the opposite direction. She felt in her gut that this was no coincidence. And, even if the link wasn't her, there had to be a connection between the two fires.

Once they were back to the surgery, it felt like heaven to be in the warmth and the light. And, as soon as her macintosh and nurse's hat were drying in front of the Aga, Mrs Hewitt shepherded her through to the sitting room and into an armchair pulled close to the open fire. As Lara sat with a blanket around her shoulders, nursing a steaming cup of cocoa, she felt like a waif and stray who'd found shelter. The warmth of the coal fire was luxurious, and she revelled in the lick of the flames. And, when Marion bobbed into the room and pulled up a chair, they sat huddled together as Lara told the story of what had happened.

Marion listened carefully, her brow knotted. 'How strange, what the heck is going on?' Then she twisted her mouth into a wry smile. 'So, I know it's been a stressful evening for you... but, I'm just wondering if that detective is coming here to ask more questions?'

'Not that I know of,' Lara replied, 'and even if he did come, he'd only be asking about the case. Plus, for all we know, he might have a wife and children.'

Marion turned down the corners of her mouth. 'Oh well... I was just wondering, that's all.' Then she began to chuckle. 'It's just that, when I was on a visit home to Ridgetown, my friend who lives next door but one to my mum's was talking about the handsome, young detective and word is he's either single or recently divorced. Anyway, whatever... he seems to be causing quite a stir.'

'Poor man.' Lara sighed. 'He already sticks out like a sore thumb, but to also be subject to idle speculation.'

'Quite right he sticks out, he's absolutely gorgeous.'

Lara frowned, she couldn't see it. 'Well, I'd say he's moderately good looking.'

Marion spat out a laugh.

'Mmm, well. You met Patrick at the Harvest Ball, so you know where my antagonism to handsome men is coming from. I just can't get worked up about relationships anymore and I'm not sure I ever will again.'

'You sound like an ice queen.'

Lara shrugged. 'It just makes sense right now. I'm focusing on my career... other things aren't a priority.'

Marion tipped her head to the side. 'Well, I suppose that makes sense, given we work in a profession that is only just coming around to the fact that married women can still carry on working. It's nineteen thirty-six, we've come through a world war, yet in terms of our work we're not far removed from the days of Florence Nightingale.'

'I agree, and we do need to move into the modern world... But, right now, for me, I celebrate the values of Miss Nightingale.'

Marion began to shake her head, then she lifted her cup of

cocoa in a toast. 'Here's to good old Florence... we'd still be in the dark ages of nursing if it hadn't been for her, but sometimes those rules and regulations are just a bit too strict... So maybe it's time to recognise that nurses are hot-blooded women who need a bit of loving. We're all doing it anyway, apart from Nurse Lara of course, so let's cast aside our regulation navy-blue knickers, loosen our stays and step out into the modern world.'

They were both giggling now and Lara almost choked on her tea. And, when a knock came to the front door, they exchanged a wide-eyed glance like two naughty children and Marion hissed in a theatrical voice, 'Maybe it's the ghost of Miss Nightingale come to discipline us.'

Lara clapped a hand over her mouth to stop herself from laughing out loud and, when she heard Mrs Hewitt opening the door then calling, 'Nurse Flynn, Doctor Bingham. It's Inspector Stirling come to ask a few questions,' Marion's face flushed bright pink.

'Can I stay with you, when you're being questioned?' Marion whispered.

'Most definitely not.' Lara swatted at her. 'The Inspector's here on professional duties.'

The sitting room door was thrust open then by Mrs Hewitt. 'Inspector Stirling's here to ask questions, Nurse Flynn. I've no idea where Dr Bingham is, he's probably soaking in a hot bath, so are you alright to speak to him first?'

'Yes, of course,' she said, standing up with Marion, wide-eyed, beside her.

'Nurse Wright,' Mrs Hewitt said firmly, motioning with her head for Marion to leave.

Then, as the detective entered and removed his black Homburg hat, Lara couldn't be entirely sure, but she thought she saw a saw a spark of something in his eye when he glanced to Marion and acknowledged her with the hint of a nod.

And, as Marion sucked in a quick breath and exited the room, he gestured with his hat for Lara to sit back down. 'So, Nurse Flynn, sorry to trouble you again and I won't keep you long. But just a few more questions...'

By the time she'd answered everything, Bingham was at the door in his full-length plaid dressing gown and red carpet slippers, his usually tousled hair damp from the bath and sticking flat to his head. It reminded her of when she'd seen him in his nightshirt and, despite the potential seriousness of this occasion, she felt the pit of her stomach tickle with amusement.

Exiting quickly, she headed for the kitchen.

Marion was sitting at the table, and she was grinning.

'Right,' Lara said, pressing a finger to her lips, then dropping her voice to barely above a whisper, 'I'm not prepared to answer any of your questions about Inspector Stirling until he's out through the door. So shhh.'

Marion nodded, then whispered back, 'That's OK. But you have to promise we'll talk later, when he's gone.'

'Yes,' she nodded, 'but I need to put a time limit on it... I don't want you going on and on right up to bedtime.'

'Oh, you know me, why would—'

'Exactly, I do know you. That's why I want you to agree.'

'Alright, alright, Nurse Frumpypants.'

'What?' she gasped, then they were both laughing.

'Whatever's tickled you two?' Mrs Hewitt called as she came into the kitchen.

'Oh, nothing,' they said, giggling.

The housekeeper narrowed her eyes. 'It wouldn't take a detective to work out that it is definitely not nothing and therefore assume it's something to do with the handsome policeman in the front room.'

'Shhh,' Marion hissed, pressing a finger to her lips. 'Lara says we're not allowed to talk about it until he's gone.'

'Quite right too... But you both know how our senior doctor likes to chat. So that young man will be in there for a good while. So, in the meantime, who's up for a glass of sherry?'

'Me,' they both cried together as Mrs H went to the cupboard to collect the bottle and glasses.

Even as she poured the first glass, the door pushed open and Angus bounded in. 'What's up? There's been talk in the Dorchester about another fire at the mill? Leo's heard it nearly burned down.'

Mrs Hewitt held up her hand. 'Well, yes, there has been a fire, but the mill has nowhere near burned down so that's an exaggeration for a start... And I don't know whether your friends at the pub told you this or not, but our Nurse Flynn and Dr Bingham were the ones who discovered the fire, and they helped to put it out.'

'Well, well.' Angus grinned. 'We are amid heroes, right here in our very own surgery.'

'Anyone would have done the same,' Lara said, but nevertheless she felt pleased by the young doctor's recognition.

In the next moment, Mrs Hewitt knotted her brow, then directed a piercing gaze in Angus's direction. 'I thought you were off out to a meeting at the village hall tonight, something about the football team, or was it rugby?'

He gulped in a breath. 'Oh, well, the meeting was cancelled.'

'So, you went to the pub instead.'

'Correct,' he grinned, 'and I know I said I'd cut it down during the week, but...'

'But what? And don't lie.'

'I just fancied a pint?' he said, as if he were asking a question.

'Oh, for goodness' sake, I'm just going to have to leave this with you. But, if you're struggling to get up and out to your visits in the morning because you're hungover or too exhausted, then I'm coming down on you like a tonne of bricks... Understood?'

'Understood, Mrs H,' he breathed, as he slumped down in his seat next to Lara.

He took the glass of sherry handed to him, raised it in Lara's direction and downed it in one. 'So, what's the score then with this fire at the mill?'

And as Lara filled him in on the detail, he scrunched his brow, and at the end of it he said, 'The fellas in the pub are thinking the most likely candidate for setting the fire is Vic Taylor. But why the heck would he do that? What does he hope to achieve? Alice and the children are living in the village now and she's just opened a bakery. If the mill burns down, most of the village are out of work and it won't go well for anyone.'

Mrs Hewitt sucked in a breath. 'Exactly... but he's a man and after being forced to leave by his wife and ostracised by most of the village, his pride has been badly dinted. So, he's unpredictable, vengeful even... But I don't think there's anything to gain from going over theories. We need to leave this issue to the police, there's enough to do here without us becoming amateur detectives.'

Angus downed another glass of sherry before heading to bed, and the women stayed longer to chat, forgetting until they heard voices in the corridor and goodbyes at the front door that Dr Bingham and Inspector Stirling had been in the sitting room all that time.

As Bingham called down the corridor for Mrs Hewitt and she exited the kitchen, Marion seemed sleepy, almost ready for bed. But, then her eyes sprung wide open as she leaned across the table and dropped her voice theatrically. 'So, Inspector Stirling's gone now. Tell me everything you know about him.'

Lara hardly knew anything, but a promise was a promise, so she repeated what she'd already said then told Marion how the inspector had seemed when he'd interviewed her. When there was nothing more she could possibly say, Marion leaned back in her chair, stifling a yawn. 'Thanks for that, Lara, you're getting better at dishing the gossip. But, that's me done for another day. Time for bed.'

Lara rose from her chair and waited for Marion, and they walked together out through the door, then up the red-carpeted stairs. After they'd called their goodnights, and Lara had clicked her door shut behind her, she felt grateful for the silence of her room. And, as soon as she had her clean uniform ready and her medical bag sorted for the morning, she washed then donned her white cotton nightdress and slipped gratefully between clean sheets. Just before she tipped into sleep, she heard the crackle of fire at the edge of her consciousness, but she was too exhausted for it to stop her from drifting into a deep, dreamless sleep.

21

It was the first time Lara had seen a member of the Harrington family out on the street in Ingleside. But, as she exited Daniel's cottage and began to walk up to the surgery, she saw a lithe young woman in a red and gold checked wool coat with matching hat step out of the vet's surgery and she recognised Miss Harrington. Leo was still at the door with a hand raised in farewell and he offered a nod in her direction as he stood watching Philippa go. Lara followed the young woman as she picked her way up the cobbled street in high-heeled shoes. And that's when she was able to observe the turned heads and raised eyebrows of the villagers the young lady of the manor left in her wake. When Lizzie Cronshaw met Lara head on with baby William cradled in one arm and little Sue tagging along behind, she gestured with her head up towards the visitor and muttered, 'What the heck is her ladyship doing on our street?'

Lara shrugged, then smiled. 'I've no idea. But maybe it's a good thing she's seen out and about in the village.'

Lizzie barked a short laugh and shook her head as she

walked on, calling over her shoulder, 'I'm not sure there'd be many in the village who'd agree with that, Nurse Flynn.'

Of course, Lizzie was right, and she supposed the softening of her own opinion towards Philippa was linked to how vulnerable she'd been at the scene of the accident. But, the moment she saw Philippa heading into the surgery, she picked up her pace, curious to find out what the young lady of the manor was up to.

As soon as she was in through the front door, she found Dr Bingham and Miss Harrington in the corridor, deep in conversation. 'Ah, here's one of the nurses now,' the senior doctor called as he gestured for Lara to approach. 'Nurse Flynn. Miss Harrington wants to see you and Nurse Wright.'

'Oh,' she said, surprised, then intrigued to find out exactly why.

Philippa offered a smooth, practised smile that gave nothing away. 'Ah, Nurse Flynn. I was in such a state of shock the day of the accident, I can't even remember if I thanked you properly.'

'Yes, I'm sure you did. And, as you know, it's all part of the work we do, so...'

'Well, I need you and Nurse Marion to know that the family of Alastair Bowley are incredibly grateful for what you did that day. And they asked me to thank you both personally.'

'Well, thank you,' she said, then laughed, 'and now *I'm* thanking *you*... But, please, do you have an update on Mr Bowley's condition?'

'Yes, of course. He's making an excellent recovery; he still has some memory loss due to the head injury, but his leg wound is healed and the fractured arm is doing very nicely. In fact, he's about to be discharged for convalescence to a wonderful facility in the Lake District.'

'Oh, that's good to know.'

'Yes, it is, isn't it?' She smiled. 'And I'd like to thank Nurse Wright too, in person. When is she expected back?'

'It's difficult to say. She's often running late when she attends the more remote farms on her motorcycle. But, if you're not able to wait to catch her, I can pass on what you need to say.'

Philippa hesitated then, her breath held, then she glanced at the dainty gold watch on her slim wrist. 'Well, my chauffeur will be here to collect me in twenty minutes or so, but he has instruction to park up and wait. So, it should be fine.'

It felt very strange to be leading the way to the kitchen with Miss Harrington in tow and Lara wished she'd been able to warn Mrs Hewitt, but there hadn't been a chance. So, when the housekeeper turned from the Aga with a tray of scones, her eyes widened and she cried, 'Blooming heck,' almost dropping the tray as Philippa breezed through as if she were used to visiting here.

'Ah, Mrs Hewitt. The scones smell delicious.' Philippa smiled, standing by the table as if waiting for something. And, as Bingham asked if he could take her coat and then pulled out a chair for her, Lara had to stifle a giggle. And she was so glad Marion wasn't there because she knew it would have been so much harder to hold back her laughter at Dr Bingham's chivalry.

By the time Miss Harrington was settled in Angus's chair, sitting precisely at the table with her hands folded in her lap, Mrs Hewitt had made a recovery, and she now had full control of the situation. 'Why don't you go and hang Miss Harrington's coat in the hall, Dr Bingham...? Oh, and Nurse Flynn, please could you take this plate of sandwiches to the table and provide an extra place setting.' Then the housekeeper switched her full attention back to their visitor. 'So, Miss Harrington. Would you like tea and a sandwich or a freshly baked scone?'

'Tea and a buttered scone would be delightful.' Philippa smiled, then, just for a second, she dropped her head and seemed at a loss for more words.

As Lara sat quietly eating her sandwiches, a strange, stilted conversation took place between Dr Bingham, Mrs Hewitt and their visitor. She wasn't really following most of it, but, when Grace's name cropped up, she tuned into what was being said.

'Yes, he was a very good tenant, Mr Alston. I knew him all my life and I visited Manor House Farm many times with my father.'

Did you now? Lara thought, instantly annoyed at the young woman's glib reference to a family who had just been served with an eviction notice. How could Miss Harrington not see how insensitive it was to sit here glowing over her childhood memories of visiting a family who were about to lose the farm they'd tenanted for generations. She opened her mouth to challenge Miss Harrington, but Dr Bingham caught her eye and shook his head just once. And there was something about the glance he gave that told her he had this in hand.

He gazed kindly then towards Miss Harrington, raised his eyebrows and, with a semblance of innocence, asked, 'So, you must know the Alston family very well?'

'Yes, indeed I do. We were hoping to attend James's funeral but sadly we were detained in London.'

'That's a shame,' he breathed, 'the whole village turned out for it because James was a good, honest man and he was very well liked. As is his daughter, Grace. And she's been running the farm for all the years her father was too sick to even get out to the yard.'

'Yes, so I've heard.' Philippa nodded, reaching for another sip of tea then taking a delicate bite of her scone.

Lara saw Bingham's eyes narrow, then he spoke firmly, 'So it seemed quite a shock that Grace received a letter of eviction just the other week.'

'What?' Philippa gasped, lowering the buttered scone halfway to her mouth.

'Oh, apologies, Miss Harrington. I assumed you'd know about the issue and therefore would be able to offer an explanation.'

Two red spots instantly appeared on Philippa's cheeks, and she swallowed hard before she spoke. 'I'm afraid I am unable to comment on the matter. But clearly my father has made the decision for a reason.'

Bingham twisted his mouth. 'Well, I'm wondering if it's because the new tenant of Manor House Farm will be a woman?'

Philippa pursed her lips before she spoke. 'Well, I can't say. But, if that is the case, then there might be...'

'Oh, so you would be prepared to have a word with him on Grace's behalf. That would make sense, given she's an independent young woman, just like yourself.'

Philippa reached for her tea, took a sip. When her voice came, it was measured, deliberate. 'I can see what you're trying to do here, Dr Bingham. But I am not party to any of the decisions my father makes regarding the estate.'

He tipped his head to one side. 'Well, maybe you should be. After all, it'll be you who will inherit the tenancies when something happens to your father. So, surely it makes sense for you to be involved with the dealings now. After all, you are woman living in this modern world of ours.'

Philippa narrowed her eyes. The whole table fell silent, waiting for her to reply.

She cleared her throat, looked uncomfortable, but when she spoke her voice was clear. 'Maybe you're right, Dr Bingham. And I *will* take up Grace Alston's case if you wish. The whole thing will of course have to be approved by my father.'

'Yes, of course. And I trust Lord Harrington is all about doing the right thing by his loyal tenants,' he said, narrowing his eyes before reaching for the teapot. 'More tea, Miss Harrington?'

As she opened her mouth to reply, Angus burst in through the door. 'Sorry I'm late, bloody lane full of bloody sheep. Aren't the blighters all meant to be tucked up inside—'

He clamped a hand over his mouth when he spotted Miss Harrington. But, in the next second, he was grinning and calling out to their visitor, 'Pip! What the heck are you doing here? I didn't realise you were back from London.'

'Yes, I've been back for a few days...' And as they began to chat like old friends, Lara shared an amused glance with Mrs Hewitt, as she knitted her brow and mouthed 'Pip?' Then the housekeeper rose from her seat, motioning for the young doctor to sit down. Bingham was quiet now, but Lara noted the determined thrust of his chin and the twinkle in his eye, which indicated that he knew he'd made a strong case for Grace to stay at the farm.

Just as Lara began to relax a little, with Angus and 'Pip' still chatting across the table about shared acquaintances from the boarding schools they'd attended, she heard running feet in the corridor. Thinking it might be an emergency, she was about to jump up from her seat when Marion burst through the door. 'What the heck is that big posh car out front?'

'Oh, that'll be mine. Is the chauffeur still in there?' Miss Harrington turned in her seat to offer a sweet smile.

'Yes,' Marion replied, still wide-eyed, her unruly hair

sticking out at all angles as she pulled her brimmed nurse's hat from her head.

'In fact, Nurse Wright. You and your colleague, Nurse Flynn, are the reason for my visit. I've come to commend you personally for your sterling work on the day of the accident. I know there was nothing you could do for poor Quentin, but your efforts undoubtedly saved Alastair.'

Flustered, Marion mumbled a thank you as she slipped into the chair opposite, still aghast. 'Well, yes, I suppose. I'm just glad we could help.'

'That may well be,' Miss Harrington said firmly, 'but I've come here today to say thank you and offer an invitation for you and Nurse Flynn to visit me at the hall for afternoon tea.'

Marion swallowed hard, glanced to Lara. 'Yes, that would lovely.'

Lara was forcing a smile, feeling a little flustered by what seemed an extravagant gesture.

Dr Bingham and Mrs Hewitt were nodding their approval, then Mrs Hewitt glanced to Lara and Marion and said, 'Providing it's at the weekend, we can make sure you both get the time off.'

Philippa offered a single, precise nod. 'Well, sounds like it's settled then. I'll ask our housekeeper, Mrs Stewart, to call with some dates... It won't be for a little while because I'm going to join my parents in London, but we always come back up to Ingleside for Christmas, so we can firm up our plans later if that's alright?'

She rose from the table then and offered her goodbyes. 'No, please, Dr Bingham, I can see my own way out and I'm very capable of getting my coat from the hall,' Philippa told him when he rose from his seat to attend her. Then, with a glint in her eye, 'After all, as you pointed out earlier, I'm a modern, independent woman of the world.'

Bingham chuckled, bowed his head.

'Wow,' Marion mouthed to Lara across the table.

Then, Miss Harrington was gone. And, once they'd heard the click of the front door, Bingham leaned forward conspiratorially and gently thumped the table with the flat of his hand. 'I think we've done it... It sounds like there might be a good chance Grace will keep her tenancy.'

Angus cheered. 'She's a good sort really, isn't she, Philippa?' he stated, glancing from one to another when he didn't get a reply.

'Well, of course you'd think that way, posh boy.' Marion grinned. 'And what's all this chit chat with Miss Harrington about your shared connections.'

'Oh, it's nothing really. I only know Pip through the sister of a friend I was at boarding school with.'

'So, why is that not a connection?' Marion asked, scrunching her brow.

'Well, I suppose it is.' He grinned.

'We won't hold it against you, Angus,' Mrs Hewitt smiled, 'because, when you're here with us at the surgery, you're one of our team.'

They were running late after their unusually extended lunch, so, as Lara freewheeled down the hill to her afternoon visits, she was grateful for the clear November sky and that nip in the air that signalled she wouldn't be slowed up by rain this afternoon. Her cheeks were already stinging with cold, but she savoured the crisp autumn days. Already ticking through her list of visits in her head, she felt startled when a voice called her name from the side of the road.

It was Alice Taylor striding towards her with a basket of

bread balanced on her hip. 'Sorry, I didn't mean to give you a shock,' she laughed, 'but I've been so busy with setting up the bakery, I haven't seen you for ages. How are you doing?'

'Fine, yes, I'm fine. How are you? How are the children?'

'So good. It's all good. I should have moved years ago instead of sticking it out at the farm with the place dropping to bits around us.'

'Well, you seem to be doing well with your business. Mrs Hewitt never stops singing the praises of your bread.'

'That's good. And I'm just heading up to her now with free samples of the barm cakes I've been making.'

Instantly puzzled, Lara asked, 'What's a barm cake?'

'Oh, well. Like this,' she pulled a bread roll from the basket.

'Ah, you mean a teacake.'

'Barm cake is what we call them round here, Nurse Flynn.' She laughed. 'These are my first batch, so I'd like Mrs Hewitt's opinion. She's a straight-talking woman so, if they're not up to scratch, she'll soon tell me.'

'Yes, I can guarantee she will.' Lara laughed, readying herself to push off as she asked after Uncle Josh and the children.

'Well, Josh is away for a few days; his mother's been taken ill. And I know he had no choice but to go and see her, but I'm really missing him. He's so good with the children, especially Robin. But, once he's back, you should come down for a cup of tea and try one of my *barm* cakes.'

'Yes, that would be lovely,' she called as Alice walked on with her basket.

As she pushed off and pedalled towards the bridge, she was already concerned at the news of Uncle Josh being away from Ingleside. It would probably be alright given Alice and the children were now here and not isolated at Fell Farm. But she was easily triggered back to the threat Vic Taylor posed to her and his family and she carried those thoughts with her as she pedalled out to the country lanes. And, as her breath steamed in the cold air and the stillness that usually eased her was broken by the mournful cry of a curlew, she needed to push hard against her pedals to feel the calm she always had out here on the country lanes.

22

The Fleece was smoke-filled and packed out on Saturday night but, even though she was squashed in next to Marion on a bench at the side, barely able to hear above the hubbub of noise, she was glad that Angus had rallied them for a trip to the Dorchester. The dark evenings and colder days sat heavy at times and to some extent the light and warmth of the pub felt like compensation for that. And it was easier to go out in the village now that she knew more of the locals, and she'd got used to a glass of froth-topped ale rather than sipping a port and lemon. As she clinked glasses with Angus, then with Marion, she enjoyed the lively cheers.

Glancing to the bar, she saw Ada hard at work serving pint after pint and marvelled at how she managed to keep up with pulling the pumps, calculating money paid, change given. Then, seeing Ed Cronshaw at the bar swaying a little, she hoped he hadn't had too much given how he could be when he was drunk.

Marion nudged her arm then. 'You alright?'

'Yes, it feels good to be out,' she breathed, relishing the

warmth of the pub fire stacked with logs as it crackled and spat in the grate.

Then, as Marion offered her a cigarette, Lara took it instantly. It made her cough a little, but in those few moments as she drew in the smoke, it linked her back to Liverpool and the nights out she'd had there with her nurse friends.

'Is Leo coming tonight?' Marion asked Angus.

'Nah, I saw him earlier, but he said he needed to go up to Ingleside Hall to check one of the Arabian horses Lord Harrington has just purchased – it's gone lame or something.' Angus grinned then. 'Well, at least that's what he said he was doing. But he's often there and, between you and me, I think lovely Pip Harrington has everything to do with that.'

'Really,' Marion gushed, 'tell us more.'

And as Angus shrugged and said he didn't know more, Lara felt her heart clench at the thought of Leo with that woman.

The moment moved on as Marion got more drinks and Angus began to talk of his time at boarding school and some of the capers he'd got up to. It was nice to hear him speaking of his past and what struck her was how isolated he must have been in the big house and on his grandfather's estate in Scotland. And she knew from her own experience how claustrophobic a life at boarding school could be. She admired him for breaking away and coming to work in Ingleside. And, given his privileged background, it felt strange how easily he fitted in as part of the team.

Later, as she walked back to the surgery, linking Marion's arm, she glanced down to the Old Oak just as the pub door burst open, and a loud group of men tumbled out laughing and shouting. It was lively and it felt good, but Lara was always at her easiest in the village when she was called out to a visit in the early hours, just before dawn. She loved the deserted streets with nothing more than the ripple of the brook or the hoot of an owl.

Marion seemed tired and distracted when they arrived back to the surgery, so they both went straight to their beds. Lara slept well, and she even managed a Sunday morning lie-in. But, even so, she was still first down to the kitchen while her colleagues slept on. And, as Mrs Hewitt mixed a large fruit cake in her earthenware bowl, Lara sat quietly at the table with her cup of strong tea and bowl of porridge. Glad to be in the warm kitchen, she felt comforted by the spit of the Aga and the sweet, spicy aroma of Mrs Hewitt's cake. And, after the final stirring of the mixture had been done, the housekeeper shushed Tiddles the cat away from the Aga so she could slide the baking tin into the oven. With the heavy clunk of the stove door, the housekeeper sighed, then wiped her hands on a blue and white striped tea towel. Then she came to the table, sat down in Marion's place and poured her own cup of tea.

Just as she took her first sip, Bingham came into the kitchen. 'Morning,' he called brightly, almost with a smile.

They exchanged a wide-eyed glance – the senior doctor always ate his breakfast in his room, and his lively greeting was very unusual.

Settling himself into his chair at the head of the table, he leaned forward on his elbows. 'It's good to see you two up bright and early as always.'

'Yes, thank you,' Mrs Hewitt stumbled, shooting an alarmed glance across the table to Lara.

But Bingham was still beaming, and it made Lara smile.

'Cup of tea, Dr Bingham?' Mrs H asked, gesturing to the pot.

'Oh, that's alright, I can pour it myself.' He grinned, standing up to pull the teapot towards him.

Lara had to press her lips together now to stop herself from laughing and she daren't even glance to Mrs Hewitt because she could sense how amused she was by Bingham's out of character behaviour.

Mrs Hewitt seemed to rally then. 'Did you have an enjoyable visit to Ridgetown last night?' she called to him.

'Yes, indeed. A very enjoyable time. And, as you know, I was seeing on old acquaintance.'

'Well, it looks like it did you the world of good.'

He blew out a breath. 'Yes, it most certainly did.'

Lara saw the slight twist of Mrs Hewitt's mouth and knew there was more information to be had here regarding Bingham's trip to Ridgetown.

The doctor's face slowly brightened then, and he drank the rest of his tea, down in one, then exited the kitchen humming a tune.

Mrs Hewitt leaned across the table then and whispered, 'He's full of himself this morning, good to see him so cheery. I've not known him like this since the last time he was seeing someone.'

'What do you mean?'

'A woman. Seeing a woman. Must be someone in Ridgetown... because that's where he was last night.'

'Oh, I see,' she said, mildly shocked by the revelation. Then they were both giggling like two schoolgirls.

The rest of the morning passed quietly, with Angus and Marion lying in until late and Lara back to her room to read *Pride and Prejudice*. It felt good to sprawl on her bed as a slice of pale sunlight peeped in through the sash window and the church bell tolled to call the church goers to morning service. She looked forward to hearing them emerge chatting and laughing and, often on a Sunday morning, she heard Reverend Hartley calling a goodbye to each of them. She'd heard on the grapevine that Miss Dunderdale had begun to attend services again after an absence of many years, and it pleased her to know that her patient was becoming part of the community.

She was just about to turn another page of her book when she heard the telephone ring. She listened out, heard the tap of Mrs Hewitt's feet on the tiled corridor, and tried to gauge the tone of her voice as she answered. It was about a patient, most definitely, and she readied herself to be summoned. But, when Mrs Hewitt tapped on her door, it felt like a tentative request rather than an emergency.

'It's up to you what you want to do with this, but that was a call from Nora Hurst – that good neighbour of the Lennoxes. She's had young Michael down there this morning to report his younger brother and sister have a fever and his mother is very worried.'

Lara drew a slow breath. 'Well, there are lots of fevers around at this time of year, it's probably nothing to worry about. But Mrs Lennox is struggling at present, so yes, of course I'll go out to her.'

Mrs Hewitt nodded. 'I've still got Nora on the line, I'll let her know.'

As Lara cycled out of the village and down towards the sawmill, it felt quiet on the lane with the factory closed for Sunday. It was a day off for everyone – she smiled wryly to herself then – not the nurses and doctors, of course, there always had to be someone on call. As she got down to the mill, she noted a newly constructed wooden hut close to the factory gate and guessed it was for the night watchman. She wondered who they'd get for the job… she wouldn't like to sit out there all alone at night, aware of every tiny sound. Then, after she'd passed by the mill building, she was soon alongside the mill pond. Daniel Makepeace had told her there used to be swans on the water here and villagers came out regularly to view the graceful creatures. She hoped one day the swans would come back... she'd once seen them on a lake in a Liverpool park and she'd been entranced. Slowing now to peer over the stone wall and gaze out over the flat expanse of water to the trees and bushes beyond, she noted a shiver of pale sunlight on the dark water. And then a deer emerged from the shadow of the trees as if in greeting. The beautiful animal raised its head and gazed directly at her as if in acknowledgement. Then, in the blink of an eye, it was gone, back into the shadows, and she wondered if she'd imagined it. But, no, she still felt the prickle of hairs at the base of her neck and knew it had been there.

Pedalling faster now, she was soon dismounting and leaning her bicycle against the wall of Foxglove Cottage. And even as she pulled her medical bag from the basket, she heard the wail of a sickly child from within and knew it had to be Freddy or little Ava. She stood and knocked, then waited. Michael opened the door, slightly out of breath, his eyes round. 'Come in,' he called, 'I'm not sure what to do with these little ones.'

Lara walked straight through to see him wrestling with a pink-faced, fractious Freddy, while Ava slept on the truckle bed. Already she felt troubled by Lydia's absence, surely she should be managing the sickly children and not leaving it to Michael. Assuming their mother was in the bedroom, she told Michael she'd only be a moment, and she tapped on the bedroom door. When there was no response, she clicked open the door to see Lydia lying on her side, her eyes wide open, staring into space while baby Jamie slept quietly in his crib.

'Mrs Lennox,' she called gently, and the woman roused instantly and sat up. 'Oh, there you are, Nurse Flynn. Sorry to bring you out all this way on a Sunday, but we're struggling with the little ones.'

Sensing the woman's fragility, she kept her voice steady. 'That's alright, I'm happy to attend,' she said, glancing around the room, knowing instinctively that something wasn't right here.

Lydia thrust her legs out of bed, sat up and, as she slowly rose to standing, Lara saw how pale she was, how much weight she'd lost. 'How are you doing?' she asked gently, reaching out a hand to her.

'Oh fine, just fine,' Lydia said, offering the rictus of a smile.

'Shall we go through, see what we can do for the two little ones?' Lara asked gently, holding out an arm to her. Lydia smiled, and took her arm as if they were about to set out on an afternoon stroll.

Michael seemed to have settled his younger brother now, but Freddy's cheeks were fiery red with what looked like a raging fever. 'I'll just take Freddy's temperature,' Lara said.

'Yes of course,' Lydia replied with a wan smile and a wave of her hand as she slumped onto a chair at the table.

Freddy's temperature was high and, when she took Ava's, it was the same. They were both burning up and the heat from the stove was making things worse. 'We need to get some of these woollens off the little ones,' she said to Michael, 'and maybe open the windows a bit just to try and bring their fever down.'

'Righto,' Michael said, taking the information in very quickly. She admired this boy so much it almost brought tears to her eyes.

'Aren't you going to offer Nurse Flynn a cup to tea, Michael?' Mrs Lennox smiled in his direction.

He glanced to Lara then, uncertain.

'No, thank you, that's alright. We'll get on and sort these two little ones.'

Michael nodded then, all business.

Freddy and Ava were soon much more comfortable and, after Lara had given each of them a small dose of crushed aspirin in honey, there was a definite improvement. But, when the baby began to cry in the bedroom, Michael was up on his feet again while his mother still sat at the table, gazing out of the window. Lara knew then there was something badly wrong here and she was already forming a plan for next steps.

Once the poorly children were settled and the baby had been fed at the breast, Lydia seemed to rally, and Lara wondered if earlier she'd just been groggy after waking from sleep. But, before she returned to the surgery, she'd pay a visit to Nora at the farm to ask her opinion on how things were for the family.

Then, as she prepared to leave, her decision to speak to Nora felt less appropriate because the little ones were even more settled now, and Lydia had rallied enough to be busy at the stove making porridge. But that's when Lara's training kicked in and she recognised the importance of never ignoring a gut feeling even if it turned out to be something and nothing. So, after saying her goodbyes, she was out through the door and cycling down to the farm.

'Nurse Flynn?' Nora called with a brisk smile as she opened the door. 'Is everything alright with Lydia and the children?'

'I'm not sure, is the honest answer... Can I come in for a quick chat?'

'Yes, of course,' Nora replied, frowning a little as she pulled back the heavy front door and beckoned for her to enter.

'Sorry, Nurse Flynn, we're a bit upside down here at present,' Nora called over her shoulder as she led her through to a cluttered sitting room. 'I should have realised when I married a farmer that he'd care more about how tidy his shippon was than anything inside the farmhouse.'

Lara smiled. 'That's alright. I've not been working here long, but I've already got to know the ways of some of the farmers around here.'

Once Lara was in an armchair and Nora felt satisfied that she was comfortable, the farmer's wife perched at the end of a sofa packed up with what looked like bags of animal feed and asked, 'Right, what do you want to know?'

'Well, it's just a niggle I've been having and with the two little ones being unwell today it felt stronger. I'm just interested to know if you've had any concerns regarding how Mrs Lennox is coping since Jamie was born?'

'Well, it's hard, isn't it? I had four of my own and they were close in age and, thinking back now, I probably wasn't in my right mind. But I had my mother come to stay for a while after my youngest son was born and then my husband Jim was bobbing in and out as well. So, yes, I do feel concerned about Lydia. Without Michael, she'd really struggle and I do worry about him. He's such a lovely lad, the way he is with those little ones. But he should be in school, not looking after his brother and sister.'

Lara sighed out a breath. 'Yes, I agree. But I suppose, with her husband working away, there's not much chance at present.'

Nora nodded, turning her mouth down at the corners. 'I mean, some days when I go there, I'm only seeing Michael and he tells me his mother's sleeping. I suppose that's fair enough and at least she seems to be doing a good job of looking after the new baby. I mean, there's no question that little Jamie is thriving. But I'm wondering about the other children – Freddy is so cute, but he can be a handful at times, and Ava, with her blonde curls, sometimes it feels as if she's the little girl I always wanted... Four boys, that was me. I'd have loved to have had a daughter, but I certainly wasn't going to keep trying and end up with another lad.

'Sorry, Nurse Flynn, I'm going off the subject... so, regarding Lydia, I think she's probably doing the best she possibly can in the circumstances, but I do worry about her. Out here all alone with the children and cut off from her family in Yorkshire. The poor woman. I wish I had more time to help her, but we're full on with the farm.'

'You're doing such good work with your daily visits, so don't be worrying about that.'

Nora sighed then. 'Let's hope her husband gets work around here soon. He's a nice chap is Steven, always cheerful and so good with the children. She must miss him terribly.'

Leaving Nora waving a cheery goodbye at the door of the farmhouse, she set off back, passing the cottage as daylight was just beginning to fade. It looked all cosy inside with the oil lamps lit. It was quiet as well, so all seemed settled. But she still had those niggles, and she'd make sure to report them to the whole team this evening. She'd be surprised if Dr Bingham didn't advise daily visits for the time being, at least until the two little ones had recovered from their fever.

All were present at the kitchen table bar Angus. 'He's gone off for the afternoon with Leo, who knows what they'll be getting up to,' Mrs Hewitt announced as she brought a platter of cold cuts from the Sunday roast and placed it down on the table next to fresh bread from Alice's bakery, pickled beetroot and thick slices of creamy Lancashire cheese.

'Don't you worry, Mrs H,' Marion grinned, 'I only saw them coming out of two pubs in the village.'

'Hah,' Bingham spat, 'given there are only two pubs then they've got all bases covered. And, yes, it's alright me sitting here going on about it... but in my younger days I'd have been out there with them.'

Mrs Hewitt twisted her mouth. 'Yes, true. But, when were

your younger days? Just remind me... Was that when Queen Victoria was on the throne?'

'Oh no, Mrs H, more like the days of Henry the eighth,' he quipped good-naturedly. Then, directing his gaze to Lara, 'So what was it you wanted to discuss regarding the Lennox family?'

After she'd explained the issue, he reached with his fork for another slice of cold lamb, then used a silver spoon to get more pickle. Then he leaned back in his chair. 'Right. So, it sounds like we need daily visits, especially with Freddy and Ava sick with fever. Mrs Lennox is overwhelmed, like many mothers of four children, but it's also possible that she's suffering from melancholia. Do we know where her husband works? If not, let's find out and I'll give him a call.'

Lara felt heartened by Dr Bingham's response but, given the urgency of the situation, she knew she wouldn't rest easy until she'd been back to the cottage to reassess. Sensing her disquiet, Marion mouthed, 'You alright?' across the table.

'Yes,' she replied. 'You know how it is when a family gets under your skin, and you can't settle until you've got everything sorted.'

'I know exactly what you mean. But, you'll be back there in the morning to reassess and, if required, you can strengthen your response.'

Lara wished she could go back out there right now, tonight. But it was dark, and hopefully the children would be sleeping. So, she'd probably only unsettle things further. There was no choice but to wait until morning, and she'd be there first thing. A shiver ran through her then and there was no explanation for it apart from spiralling thoughts of the Lennox family. *Tomorrow, I'll be there tomorrow.*

23

After being woken regularly during the night by rain lashing at her window, Lara was out of bed early and straight down to the kitchen for her porridge and a cup of strong, sweet tea. With her brain already ticking over the Lennox family issue, she startled when the telephone rang loudly in the hall. Mrs Hewitt was straight there, and she was calling down the hallway in moments. 'It's an emergency, Nurse Flynn. Be ready to go.'

By the time Mrs Hewitt had replaced the receiver and returned to the kitchen, Lara was all set to go in her macintosh and rain hood, clutching her medical bag.

'That was Ingleside Hall, the gamekeeper – Robert Thompson – he's been found delirious and unwell by one of the estate gardeners this morning. He sounds poorly, so he'll need an urgent visit. Given Marion and Angus aren't even up yet, and our senior doctor is always slow first thing, it's probably best if you take the call and we send Dr Bingham to the Lennox family. You can be off on your bicycle and up at the hall before any of the others have woken up properly.'

Lara felt disappointed she wouldn't be able to do her

planned follow-up with the Lennoxes but, of course, the housekeeper's plan made sense. Mrs Hewitt pulled a pen from her apron pocket, quickly amended Lara's list of visits, then passed it to her. 'There you go. If it hadn't rained so hard last night, I'd be telling you to take the little blue Austin. But it chugs and stalls through every deepish puddle, so best you take your bicycle. Take care, though, please take care, there's a lot of flood water out there this morning.'

'Will do, Mrs H,' she called, already heading to the back door to retrieve her bicycle from the shed. She was soon freewheeling down towards the bridge to see the river swollen with rainwater, so churned up and brown it sent a shiver through her. Pedalling out to the country lanes with flowing streams of rainwater at either side, she pushed hard to pick up her speed as water gushed and sprayed and the bare, leafless hedges revealed vast areas of standing water in the fields.

Out of breath as she reached the turning to Ingleside Hall, it was heavy going up the loose surface of the drive, with gouts of water coming at her. But, the harder she pushed at the pedals, the more determined to get to her patient she became, and she was soon wheeling her bicycle across the gravelled area in front of the hall. She barely glanced to the impressive façade; all her attention focused on reaching her patient in the gamekeeper's cottage.

Leaping off her bicycle, she pushed it against the cottage wall, pulled her leather bag from the basket. Striding to the door, she knocked then entered and in the small, enclosed space she easily detected the sweet sickly smell of a suppurating wound. Robert was slumped back in his battered armchair, his brown hair greasy and dishevelled, stuck out at all angles. His leg was raised on the worn leather footstool, and he appeared to be soundly sleeping. Right then, it struck her as odd that the wound had begun to fester at this stage, but she'd found the bandage grubby a few times and had suspected the fella had probably been pottering around outside when he'd been told to stay indoors. But, a man used to being in the open air could easily go crazy confined to a tiny cottage. There'd also been some tension with Lord Harrington over sick pay and it angered her to know Robert had been put under extra pressure. She noted the empty whisky bottle by his chair then and it felt testament to the stress he'd been going through.

'Robert,' she called, needing to rouse him.

'What? Have you come about the foxes?' he croaked, clearly disorientated, trying to sit up but then slumping back, shouting and swearing with pain.

'Robert,' she insisted, giving him a gentle shake, 'it's Nurse Flynn. I'm here to treat your wound so I need you to lie back and keep still. It might hurt when I remove the dressing.'

'I don't care,' he croaked. 'Cut the bloody leg off if you want. It's no good to me now that I'm out of a job.'

'What?' she called. He didn't reply, and she understood that what he'd just said might be part of his delirium. But she felt a stab of anger even at the possibility of him being fired. Right now, though, she needed to hone her response to this urgent situation.

'Robert, your foot is a mess. I'm going to fill that bucket we use with plenty of hot water and salt and soak your leg in it. It'll sting like mad but, the more it hurts, the better it'll be doing.'

'Don't bother, just cut it off,' he wailed.

'Listen to me,' she said firmly, taking his arm now, giving it a gentle shake. 'Your foot is badly infected but, with the right treatment, we can save it. And, believe me, you'll be grateful for it once it's healed.'

He slurred out a jumbled response then laughed. 'I'm in your hands, Lord Harrington. Do what you need to do.'

She placed the back of her hand against his forehead, she'd check with her thermometer later, but he wasn't burning up so his delirium might be down to the amount of whisky he'd drunk. She set to then, and as she unravelled the sticky bandage and saw the swollen red suppurating flesh of his foot, she felt some relief at least that, although the infection had developed rapidly and bitten in hard, there was no sign of it tracking up his leg. There was everything to play for here, so, as she poured hot water from the kettle to mix with cold in the bucket, she added some big handfuls of salt then grasped his leg and slowly lowered it in.

'Bloody hell fire. That stings,' he growled, but she kept on lowering until his foot hit the bottom of the bucket. He groaned and scrunched his face in agony, but she held on to him firmly.

When he sighed and rested back, she knew the worst of the stinging was over, but she was already heating the kettle for the next bout. It was good to see him more relaxed but, then, when she took his temperature, he'd spiked a mild fever. So it was still possible he'd need urgent hospital admission. He seemed to have relaxed back so much now he was almost asleep. But, when the door flew open and a startled looking fella in a scruffy jacket patched at the elbows rushed in, closely followed by a grey-haired well-dressed gentleman in a deerstalker hat, she almost jumped out of her skin.

'What the heck?' Robert gasped with shock and lurched in his chair, almost upsetting the bucket.

'Whatever do you think you're doing?' she cried and the man in the patched jacket shook his head, unable to speak.

The man behind removed his hat and she recognised Sir

Charles Harrington. 'I'm just doing a routine visit, that's all,' he said, his voice clipped.

'Well, could you come back when I've finished treating this man's wound?'

He narrowed his eyes, pursed his lips.

'And you are?'

'Nurse Lara Flynn, a district nurse and midwife from Ingleside surgery.'

'Ah, yes, the new nurse. I've heard about you.'

'All good things, I hope. But I need to get on with treating my patient, so if you could come back in fifteen minutes or so...'

'My time is very precious this morning, Nurse Flynn.'

She cleared her throat, spoke firmly. 'Not as precious as my time right now. I'm trying to save this man's foot.'

Lord Harrington pursed his mouth then harrumphed and said, 'Come to the hall when you've finished, Nurse Flynn, and I'll speak to you there.'

'Alright, but I need to get on. So, if you could...'

She waved her hand to dismiss him and, as he retreated, the scruffy fella in the patched jacket winked at her, then followed Lord Harrington out of the cottage.

'I told you, Nurse Flynn... he's going to get rid of me is Harrington.'

'Not on my watch,' she said firmly. 'Now let's get on and treat this mangled foot of yours.'

He offered a bleary smile. 'I'm putty in your hands, nurse. Putty in your hands.'

Later, after more soaking in salt water, lashings of iodine to the wound, and a clean dressing and firm toe-to-knee bandage had been applied, she left Robert lying back in his chair with his leg elevated on the leather footstool. She'd impressed on him the need to follow orders and keep the wound clean and he'd promised he'd pass the information on to his mate Len, the fella in the patched jacket who'd been with Lord Harrington. And, as she stood at the door of the hall and rang the bell, she felt ready to say her piece in support of the gamekeeper.

As soon as the door was opened by the uniformed housekeeper, she was ushered through to Lord Harrington's study. He stood up from his leather chair as she entered and asked the housekeeper for a pot of tea.

'I need to get on to my other visits, Lord Harrington. So, I'm afraid I won't be able to take tea.'

He shrugged, twisted his mouth, but still didn't say anything.

It didn't daunt her; she drew on the experience she'd had with haughty consultants and officious ward sisters at the Liverpool Royal.

He glanced her up and down, but still didn't speak. Then he pulled a pack of expensive-looking cigarettes from his pocket, the same brand Patrick had smoked, and offered one.

'No, thank you,' she said politely, 'but, if you don't mind, please can you say what you need to say because I have patients waiting to be seen.'

'You are a very spirited young woman.' He smiled, flicking a silver lighter to his cigarette, then taking his first drag.

'I apologise in advance if I sound rude, Lord Harrington. But I'm not really interested in what you think of me. I just need to discuss Robert Thompson's case and then I'll be on my way.'

He shook his head, then glanced down to the thick Persian carpet. She didn't react, but she startled when a knock came to the door and a maid carrying a silver tray entered.

'Thank you, Margaret,' he called, then, with a kindly smile, added, 'Please, Nurse Flynn, sit down so we can speak properly.'

She agreed, but still refused the tea.

'So, how is our Mr Thompson doing? I was rather shocked this morning to learn he'd taken a turn for the worse.'

'This can happen, but I think we've caught it in time. We're not looking at a hospital admission yet, but, if things don't improve, that might be required.'

'I see, so right now he's holding his own,' he said as he breathed out a lungful of smoke.

'Yes, he is. But there is one thing, Sir Charles, and I hope you can help me with this. Mr Thompson has been very stressed about the security of his post here at the hall, and I believe you've cut back his wages?'

'Well, the man isn't working.'

'Yes, I'm aware of that, but, by the sound of it, he's provided good service all these years and often chosen not to take his full holiday allowance. So, I'm just wondering what the next steps will be for him. He's afraid you'll cut his pay completely, turn him out of the cottage.'

'Well, in these cases... when a man isn't fit to work, then it might just be one of those things.'

She left a beat before she spoke again. 'Come on, Lord Harrington, it's never just one of those things when you have sole control of everything here. Robert Thompson has worked for you since he was a lad, and I don't know the first thing about gamekeeping, but I'm sure he's good at his job or he wouldn't be here. I mean, if you were to replace him, how long would it take to train someone else to that standard?'

'Well... we could always—'

She stood up from her seat abruptly. 'It's not good enough, Lord Harrington. Robert Thompson deserves to be treated fairly and, if that happens, I feel certain he'll be a loyal employee for the rest of his days.'

Sir Charles's eyes flashed then; he shook his head. For a

second, she thought she'd gone too far. But, when he stood up from his leather chair, he began to smile and reached to shake her hand. 'You have bowled me over, Nurse Flynn. My daughter told me how strong you were at the scene of that terrible accident. But I always judge for myself. You've put your case well and, given how you helped Philippa and her injured friend, I'm going to do as you say. I'll keep Robert on – half pay, mind – but I'll keep him on and in the cottage until he's ready to go back to work.'

Lara thanked him then and, as she turned to leave, she said, 'So, please can you go back to inform him of that. And, he needs a careful eye and regular checks, so if you could make sure to give his colleague, Len, the opportunity to do that, then all will be well. And I or my colleague, Nurse Wright, will be back to redress the wound in the morning. But, if there are any concerns before then, you must call the surgery.'

He raised both eyebrows, looked mildly shocked to be spoken to so directly. But he smiled then and said, 'Yes, I will see to all of that personally... Oh, and please... let me get Mrs Stewart, the housekeeper, to show you out.'

'No need, I'm already on my way,' Lara called as she pulled open the heavy door.

As she mounted her bicycle, she felt a buzz of satisfaction at the good thing she'd done for a hardworking man like Robert Thompson. And, as she freewheeled gently to the bottom of the drive, she smiled all the way. Then, after pausing for a few moments to admire the red berries on a holly tree, she cycled on to the rest of her visits, splashing through puddles, all the while buoyed up by her management of the case. And, by the time she was heading back to the surgery for lunch, the sun had begun to glint through the clouds, reflecting off the waterlogged fields and casting shimmering rainbow light through the wet hedges.

24

As soon as Lara arrived back to Ingleside for lunch, she was anxious for news of Lydia and the children. But, Dr Bingham was running late due to the house call he'd had to make to the Lennox family, so he was still seeing patients in surgery.

'Don't fret, Nurse Flynn,' Mrs Hewitt called as she bustled from the pantry with a tray of sandwiches, 'he didn't seem overly concerned when he got back, until he went into clinic to find Dr Fitzwilliam way behind with the patients. Not the young doctor's fault, though, he's still learning and, one thing about Angus, he likes to go into every detail with his patients, so of course it takes time. And, no doubt, in due course, he'll speed up, but currently he's falling way short of the mark for time management. So, Dr Bingham is currently working his way through a backlog.'

'I understand,' she sighed, 'it's just that I'm frustrated because I wasn't able to reassess the situation with the Lennox family myself.'

'I know. But you'll be able to speak to him soon and talk things through.'

'Yes, of course,' she breathed, 'and I'm sorry if I seem agitated, but sometimes, when a case is all consuming, I get impatient if there isn't any information.'

'Of course you do. And that's what makes you an excellent nurse. And you always seem so calm... but I suppose it's all going on under the surface... like they say about a swan, all serene on top but underneath those legs are going like the clappers just to stay afloat.'

'Hah, a good way of putting it. Except I'm more like a duck darting about from one thing to another.'

'No, Nurse Flynn, you are most definitely a swan.'

'What's this about swans?' Angus called as he lurched through the kitchen door. 'They make a lovely roast dinner. Have you ever eaten one, Mrs H?'

'Most certainly not, Dr Fitzwilliam. How could I? They're such beautiful creatures. I can't even eat pheasant or grouse.'

'You should try, Mrs H. Gamebirds are delicious.'

Lara groaned out loud. 'No, that's not right, they're wild birds. Would you eat a thrush, a blackbird or a robin?'

He turned his mouth down at the corners for a second. 'Yes, probably, I'd eat one. But there wouldn't be much meat on the smaller birds.'

Mrs Hewitt spluttered. 'That's horrible, Dr Fitzwilliam. Stop that talk right now, or there won't be any lunch for you the rest of the week.'

He glanced to Lara, then raised his eyebrows. 'Don't worry, I'm only teasing, I wouldn't eat any of the wild birds. But, you know that big lazy cat that lies in front of the Aga...' He smacked his lips theatrically. 'Yum, yum.'

'No, stop that right now,' Lara groaned.

'Stop what?' Dr Bingham asked as he strode in.

'Nothing,' Lara insisted as Angus opened his mouth to speak, 'it's just Angus teasing me, that's all.'

'Ah, I see.' He sighed as he took his seat at the head of the table. 'Well, maybe Dr Fitzwilliam, you could tease me a little by giving me a clue as to where you hid my best stethoscope when you were in clinic this morning.'

'Ahh,' he offered sheepishly, 'it's in my bag, I slipped it in there by mistake. Didn't see it until I got to my first house call. Sorry about that.'

Bingham was shaking his head, but good humouredly.

Lara spoke then, not able to contain herself any longer. 'Dr Bingham, please can you tell me how things were in the Lennox household this morning?'

He pressed his mouth together, frowning. 'Well, it's strange, isn't it? There was nothing I could put my finger on... Mrs Lennox was up at the table with the baby on her knee. The two young ones – Freddy and his baby sister, Ava, still had a mild fever, but they seemed to be recovering. Michael, as ever, was making sure everyone was looked after. But, you're right about Lydia, she looks thin, pale and exhausted and there was a certain faraway look in her eyes. But, when she spoke, she sounded lively enough, talking so fast at one point she jumbled her words.'

'Sounds very much what I observed, apart from the rapid speech. It's niggling, though, because we're sensing something's not right but can't put our finger on it.'

'Exactly,' Bingham said, reaching to the plate of sandwiches Mrs Hewitt had just placed on the table.

'I'd still keep her under close surveillance, though,' Angus added between bites of his first ham sandwich. 'It's just that there was a tragic incident at the hospital where I did my obstetrics training. A young mother – quiet, pale, that faraway look in her eyes. It turned out she was struggling with puerperal psychosis. She killed her baby and then herself.'

'Oh my goodness,' Mrs Hewitt murmured.

'That's just awful,' Lara said, feeling her heart contract painfully tight.

Dr Bingham didn't speak, but he placed his half-eaten sandwich down. 'You might be onto something there, Dr Fitzwilliam. These cases are so rare that few doctors or nurses have seen them... But, over the years, I've read about some and what you've just said has jogged my brain.'

Instantly, Lara felt a clammy sweat gathering at the back of her neck. 'I need to get back to the Lennoxes' right now,' she said, rising from her chair, placing her half-eaten sandwich down on her plate.

Bingham nodded firmly. 'Yes, of course, Nurse Flynn. You know the case better than anyone, so you're in a strong position to assess. Oh, and take the little Austin, it'll be much quicker.'

Swiftly, she took a swig of her tea, then she was picking up her bag, pulling on her coat and hat and running to the car. A painful tension building in her lungs as she reversed down the side of the surgery, then turned and headed out towards the sawmill. She drove fast and, as she zoomed down the hill, the screech of the big saw set her teeth on edge. It was tight to manoeuvre over the bridge and the water in the mill race was so high and fast it increased her agitation. 'Come on, you little beauty,' she called out loud to the car, and she was about to shoot off up past the mill pond when Inspector Stirling stepped out almost in front of her and raised a hand.

Quickly, she wound down her window. 'I'm sorry, detective, I'm en route to an urgent case. Can I see you on the way back?'

'Just a quick question then. Those two nights you saw the fires, did you see anything that might resemble a lit cigarette in the darkness? It's just this stub's been found and it's an expensive brand, nothing the men have ever seen, never mind smoked.'

She glanced quickly to his hand and a shiver ran through her. She had definitely seen a stub just like that with its tiny gold crest. It had been Patrick's favourite brand and she'd recently seen it being smoked by Lord Harrington.

'I might have some information for you later,' she called to him. 'But I need to get off right now to my emergency.' She was already revving the car and, as she pulled away, she wound down the window and shouted, 'I'll see you later at the surgery or phone me.'

'Righto,' he called as she raced away.

After another hold up, where she had to reverse into a gateway to let a shire horse pulling a heavily laden farm cart pass, she felt certain her head was going to explode with agitation. She sucked in a breath, told herself she was simply checking a hunch, that's all. But, the more time ticked by with her waiting by the side of road as the cheery red-faced farmer raised his hand and the slow cart trundled by, the more she needed to scream with frustration.

She had a straight run to the cottage now, so she put her foot down. Skidding to a halt, she jumped out of the car, her medical back clutched in one hand. A voice screamed in her head, *you're checking, just checking*. No need for alarm. But, the moment she saw the door to the cottage ajar, she knew something was badly wrong. It had never been left open, not with a toddler in the house. A feeling of dread tightened her chest as she walked through and called out for Mrs Lennox, then for Michael. But the kitchen was silent and empty and right away she knew something was very wrong.

She swallowed the bile rising in her throat, calling out again for Mrs Lennox.

Still nothing.

A chair was overturned on the floor by the kitchen table, but all else was tidy. Something odd, though, there were four bowls of porridge placed neatly on the rickety table – all untouched. It was an odd time of day for eating porridge, but perhaps this had been a late breakfast or Dr Bingham's visit had upset the usual routine. Quickly, she felt at the bowls, they were stone cold. Turning then, she saw beside the stove the tin of rat poison – lid off, some spilled on the counter. Dread clutched at her heart. The building blocks, the toy truck and Ava's rag doll were on the truckle bed, and she knew by the silence that the children were gone or fast asleep. The clock ticked loudly in the deserted cottage and there was complete silence from the bedroom. Her breath tight with dread, she didn't want to have to open that door. But she was here now, and the welfare of a mother and her children was at stake. So, she had no choice, she had to check the bedroom.

She sucked in a breath.

Just do it. Do it now.

She made herself walk, called out for Lydia and then her hand gripped the latch, and her thumb depressed it, and she was in. The blue and white checked curtains were closed but light leaked in around the edges, and baby Jamie was silent in his crib. The shape of Lydia on the bed, fully dressed and on top of the covers, was completely still. It felt as if there wasn't a breath of sound in the room.

She shuddered. There was a bitter taste at the back of her throat and her heart was hammering so hard in her chest it was painful. She drew a deep, shaky breath.

Lydia looked dead, but she needed to confirm, so she made

herself walk around to the other side of the bed. That's when she saw a bottle of laudanum, spilled on the bedside table. 'Lydia,' she called, shaking the woman's shoulder. The woman's face appeared white in the gloom. And Lara was just reaching to check her carotid pulse when the woman groaned and tried to open her eyes. 'Lydia,' she called, giving her a firm shake, needing to rouse her.

'What is it?' the woman called blearily. 'Is it the children? Is something wrong?'

'Yes, they're gone, Lydia.'

The woman tried to struggle up, but instantly she slumped back down. 'They've probably gone out for a walk in the park...' she whispered before she fell back into a deep sleep.

Lara walked to the crib, her breath catching on a sob when she saw baby Jamie, white-faced, so vulnerable. And, for a second, she felt sure the infant she'd delivered only weeks ago was dead. She reached out to feel his tiny cheek... he was warm, thank God, he was warm. Then he snuffled, blinked open his eyes, and her heart soared. Lydia groaned then and Lara glanced to her on the bed... but, once more, she'd slipped straight back to sleep. A cold shiver ran through her then at the thought of the laudanum and the baby also having been dosed. She bent down, sniffed at the infant's mouth... there was no trace of the distinctive smell. But she just needed to check, so she roused him, turned him onto his back to waken him. He blinked open his eyes and thrust out his little arms. He wasn't floppy, he could move his arms and legs, and she felt sure he hadn't been dosed. But, clearly, she needed to get him away to a place of safety. This was a very precarious situation – anxious about leaving Lydia for too long and with no telephone in the house, she'd have to take Jamie to Nora. As she quickly swaddled him in a knitted shawl, she prayed she'd find his brothers and little sister safe at the farm.

Swiftly, she balanced Jamie in the crook of her arm. Then, as she walked through the kitchen, she collected some spare nappies, a feeding bottle and shoved them under her arm before walking briskly to the car. Thankfully, the baby had gone back to sleep, so she laid him on the passenger seat, placed her medical bag in the footwell, and set off at a steady speed down towards the farm.

In five minutes, she was knocking on Nora's door with the baby and the bare essentials for his care cradled in her arm. As she stood, she strained her ears for any sound of the children inside. There was nothing.

She knocked again. Then, thankfully, she heard brisk footsteps in the hallway.

When Nora opened the door, her mouth dropped open. 'What? Is that baby Jamie?'

'Yes,' Lara replied, then she spoke urgently. 'Are the other children here?'

Nora frowned. 'No,' she said, then with her voice rising in panic, 'what's happened to the children? Where are they?'

Lara sucked in a breath. 'If they're not here with you, I don't know.'

'Come in,' Nora said, opening the door wide, walking through to the farmhouse kitchen.

Nora motioned for Lara to sit, but she couldn't, she needed to get back to the cottage. So, rapidly, she explained what she'd found and, once she was done, Nora stood silently for a few moments, supporting herself with one hand on the kitchen table. Then she gestured urgently for Lara to hand over the baby. 'Give Jamie to me, I'll look after him. You need to make some calls, then get back to the cottage. Those children will be running scared. And Michael is such a good, careful older brother, he must have sensed the threat and taken them into hiding.'

Nora swiped tears from her eyes, then pulled the baby close. And, when she spoke again, her voice broke on the edge of a sob. 'Those children need to be found before it goes dark. I can't bear the thought of them being out there all alone.'

'Have you any idea where they might be?'

Nora shook her head. 'None, they've barely been out for a walk since the baby was born… But, I'll speak to my husband, get him to search all of our outbuildings and cabins.'

'Yes, that's good. And call the surgery if he finds anything at all.'

'I will,' Nora said as Lara walked to the hallway to report what she'd found to the surgery.

Mrs Hewitt could barely speak and, when she put Dr Bingham on, his voice was tight with emotion. 'Those poor children, they probably got scared and ran off to hide.' Then he listened carefully to the detail and, when he spoke again, his tone was measured. 'Right, so, this is the plan. I'll call an ambulance right away to attend Lydia – it sounds like she'll need a spell in hospital. Then I'll contact the police and report the children missing. When you get back to the cottage, have a quick scout around the immediate vicinity, just in case they're hiding close by.'

'Yes, will do,' she replied, knowing she'd follow his instruction, but already her gut instinct told her the children had gone way further than that.

With her mind whirling, Lara walked briskly back to the kitchen to report to Nora. As the woman listened, she was folding blankets one-handedly into a wooden drawer that would serve as a temporary crib, with Jamie expertly balanced in the crook of her arm. And she'd pulled out the tin of powdered milk and the glass feeding bottle she kept for when her youngest grandchild visited. 'Me and Jamie will be fine, Nurse Flynn. You need to get off.'

In minutes, Lara was walking back into the cold, empty kitchen at Foxglove Cottage. She shivered. The room felt freezing, the stove had burned out and the cottage door must have been open for ages. After a quick check on Lydia – still sleeping soundly – she went back to the kitchen and leaned with both hands on the table. Her brain was trying to process everything, but her thoughts were racing. She gritted her teeth, forced herself to think logically – so, first, as Bingham had suggested, she needed to check if Michael and the little ones were hiding close by. Out through the door, she walked all the way around the cottage calling their names, then made a thorough check across the road and in the field behind. Nothing.

By the time she was going back into the cottage, she heard a car approaching at speed and hoped it was Dr Bingham. No, it was Inspector Stirling. He screeched to a halt, jumped out of the car. 'Dr Bingham called to say there are missing children. Can I have the detail?' She walked straight to him, and began telling the whole story. He listened carefully, all the while scribbling notes on his pad.

Once all his questions were answered, he reached out to her, gave her arm a squeeze. 'You've done well this morning, Nurse Flynn. And a search party for the children is being mustered as we speak. Now, if you could take me in to see Mrs Lennox... and, just so you're aware, we've informed the father, Steven, at his place of work, so he should be here in due course.'

Once she stepped back into the cold, silent kitchen, her throat constricted painfully tight, and she felt as if the walls were closing in on her. She tapped at the bedroom door and, when there was no response, she called out to Lydia as she pushed open the door, then walked in ahead of Inspector Stirling. Lydia was still sleeping soundly. 'I can try to rouse her if you want,' she said. But, still scribbling on his pad, he glanced to the spilt laudanum drops on the bedside table and shook his head. 'Let's wait until she comes round, it's best to keep her settled and quiet until we get her to the hospital.' He glanced to the empty cot then, and she couldn't be certain, but she was sure she heard his breath catch on a sob. He cleared his throat, made some more notes, then quickly strode back through to the kitchen.

In the same way Lara had been troubled by the spilt rat poison, Inspector Stirling narrowed his eyes, then tapped his pencil on the pad. He glanced to the bowls of porridge on the table. 'Do you think her state of mind was such that she might have tried to poison her children?'

Lara drew a slow breath. 'Seeing this now... Yes, I think it's very possible. But, thankfully, the porridge hasn't been touched. And we don't have an official diagnosis yet, but medically speaking we think Mrs Lennox is probably suffering from puerperal psychosis, therefore she has very little control over her actions.'

He drew a slow breath. 'Even to the point of poisoning her own children?'

'Yes,' Lara said. 'It's rare, but apparently there are case histories of tragedies like this.'

The inspector drew another breath. 'It doesn't bear thinking what might have happened here if the children hadn't left the house... Let's hope they're safe, hiding out somewhere.'

Then he just stood in the kitchen for a few moments, staring at the rat poison, glancing to the bowls of porridge. He seemed at a loss for words. Then he gathered himself. 'So, what can you tell me about the three missing children – Michael, Freddy and Ava?'

Lara gave a physical description of each child and explained how caring Michael was and how well he looked after his siblings. 'Freddy is almost four and he can be a handful, but little Ava, with her blonde curls, she has the face of an angel. Michael adores them both.'

'Sounds like Michael is a special wee lad,' the inspector said, glancing up from his notes.

'Oh, yes. Definitely.'

'So, the husband, Steven, works away. But are there any regular visitors here, any close contacts you know of?'

'Just Nora Hurst, the farmer's wife I told you about, who is looking after the baby. She's here most days with milk and eggs for the family.'

He nodded, scribbling some more. 'And, finally, do you have any idea at all where the children might be?'

'No. They're a close family. They've always been here in the cottage every time I've visited.'

In the next second, she heard the tinkle of an ambulance bell. 'I need to get out there, flag them down.'

The ambulance was pulling up as she stepped out and, as the back doors opened, Dr Bingham stepped down. 'I'll be accompanying Mrs Lennox to the hospital,' he said. 'So, has there been any change in her condition since we spoke on the phone? And is there any news on the missing children?'

'No change in Lydia's condition and unfortunately no sign of the children.'

He swallowed hard, shook his head. 'We need to get the search party out as soon as possible. And I want you to join in with that, Nurse Flynn. Those children may well need medical attention when they're found.'

'Righto,' she said, as she walked beside him, back into the cottage where he solemnly greeted Inspector Stirling.

'We meet again, Dr Bingham,' Stirling said, reaching out to shake his hand. 'I just wish it was under different circumstances.'

'Yes, me too,' Bingham replied.

Then, as the ambulance men moved through the cottage with their stretcher, Lara and Dr Bingham followed to supervise the moving of their patient.

Lydia was still very drowsy as they transferred her to the stretcher. 'No, I can't go with you, I'm going out to a dance,' she called slurrily, then, 'What about the children?'

'Don't you be worrying. Everything will be taken care of,' one of the ambulance men told her gently.

Once Lydia had been loaded into the back of the ambulance and Dr Bingham had checked her vital signs, the vehicle bumped slowly away. Inspector Stirling, intent on organising a search for the children as quickly as possible, was in his car, using the radio. And, as Lara walked back into the silent cottage, she fought to hold back tears. She wanted to be out there, searching the fields, farms and outbuildings. Then, glancing to the back of the kitchen door, she noted an important detail... the children's coats and knitted hats were gone, so that meant Michael had taken charge of the situation, and the youngsters had a much better chance of staying warm. Reading between the lines, she felt sure he must have seen Lydia with the poison, and he'd feared for the safety of his siblings. The little ones were too young to understand, but Michael must have been terrified. She was sure now he'd taken them into hiding and it couldn't be that far away. She told herself, right then, she'd stay out all night, if need be, to find Michael, Freddy and sweet little Ava.

25

After an urgent, murmured conversation with the policemen who'd arrived to support him, Inspector Stirling was directing operations from the kitchen. 'We have a large group of local people heading this way to help with the search for the missing children. In fact, the sawmill has closed for the afternoon so the workers can help. The children's father – Steven Lennox – has been informed and he'll be here soon. So, before he arrives, we need photographs of the kitchen, including the bowls of porridge and spilt poison. Then, everything needs to be boxed up and taken to Preston Police Station for analysis.'

Lara sensed the heightened emotion of the police officers, and it rippled even stronger when she heard the sharp, metallic clatter of clogs on the road as the men from the sawmill marched towards the cottage. As soon as she saw their sombre, determined faces, her heart swelled. 'Don't you worry, Nurse Lara, we'll find those children,' Ed called from the head of the group, and she saw Danny right there beside him.

'I'm coming with you,' she shouted, walking to join the rapidly expanding group of volunteers as more locals joined from behind. A grey-haired policeman took charge, shouting out a search plan. As they were broken up into groups with designated areas, Lara tagged along with Ed and Danny. And, right at the last minute, a voice called, 'Wait, I'm coming too!' and it was Leo, his hair wild, his eyes bright.

The police officer despatched the groups one at a time, telling them to head back as soon as the children were found, so a policeman could be sent to the sawmill to order the sounding of the emergency siren. It seemed a good plan and, when their turn came, her group were given a section of the fields and open country that led up to the fells.

'Follow me, I know this area,' Ed called, already leading the way.

The group shouted for the children as they walked, scrambling up grassy banks to peer over drystone walls, gazing out over scrubby fields. Lara was glad she was wearing her leather boots and thick overcoat. And Leo had brought a haversack, so she pushed her macintosh and essentials from her medical bag in there alongside Leo's torch and flask of brandy. Initially her focus was razor sharp but, as time stretched on and a light mist drifted over the tufts of dead grass and dried rushes dotting the fields, she felt a slow seep of despair at their lack of a result. 'Maybe we should shout less and listen more,' she offered.

'Good thinking,' Ed said, slipping on mud then, and falling into a ditch.

'I'm alright,' he called as he heaved himself up and limped away.

They kept going, shouting each of the children's names in turn, 'Michael... Freddy... Ava!' And, as time stretched on and all they had in return was the bleating of sheep and the rough cries of the black crows that fluttered overhead, Lara fought to control her despair. They were close to the base of the fells now and the landscape was barren. Open, scrubby moorland with tumble-down drystone walls and isolated barns. They searched every barn, glad of her flashlight and the one Leo had brought. The musty smell of hay and the sinister rustle of living creatures in the recesses of the tumbledown structures was all they found. But, they had a pact – they would keep searching until they were physically prevented from doing so.

At one point when they'd checked three barns in succession, Ed stopped abruptly, slumped forward with his hands on his knees. 'I can't bear it. That little lass, Ava, she's a similar age to my Sue.' He groaned loudly. 'It's like torture, not knowing where they are. And it won't be long before we lose the light and they'll be out here all alone.'

Lara placed a firm hand on his back. 'We'll find them, someone will find them. Even if we need to come back at first light.'

'But they'll be out here in the dark,' Ed croaked, and she felt the heave of his shoulders. It triggered something Daniel Makepeace had told her about Ed as a boy. His father had come back from the war physically wounded and badly shell-shocked and he'd treated Ed cruelly – sometimes turning him out of the house at night. So, she understood where his desperation was coming from – he had a young child himself, but Ed was that little boy again, alone and afraid of the dark.

'Michael is very capable, and he'll look after his brother and sister. I know he will.'

Ed sucked in air, straightened up.

Leo called to Ed then, his voice so gentle it almost brought tears to her eyes. 'Come on, mate, let's keep going.'

'I was going to ask if it'd help for me to sing a song.' Danny grinned. 'But if I start caterwauling, there'll be no chance of us hearing the bairns.'

'Too bloody true,' Ed coughed, 'I've heard you in the Fleece when Ada starts playing the piano. I'm amazed you don't set the dogs howling.'

Danny chuckled then and Ed patted him on the back. They were good mates, those two, and it was heartening to see.

Sensing Leo was beginning to struggle with the frustration of not finding any trace of the children, Lara dropped back to walk beside him. 'Are you alright?' she asked.

'Not really,' he said, shaking his head, 'but I will be when those children are found. It's just... it gets very cold out here at night. They might be wearing their coats, but with no walls around them, no fire to keep them warm... they're not going to be able to maintain body temperature, especially the little girl.'

Lara swallowed hard. 'I hear what you're saying. And all I have to offer is that the older brother, Michael, is a clever, remarkable boy and he will do everything in his power to keep his siblings safe.'

'Thank you for those reassuring words,' Leo breathed. And, as he linked her arm, then pulled her close to the side of his body, it didn't feel odd. In fact, she liked the feel of him next to her.

But, as the light began to fade further and she realised they would soon need to abandon the search and rest up for an early start tomorrow morning, she hardly believed her own optimism. Her group kept going, though, shouting each name in turn, shining their torches through the gathering gloom. Thankfully the mist had cleared, so they now had the moonlight to guide them. But, once cloud began to drift in and they were plunged into pitch dark, barely penetrated by the thin beams of their torches, they had no choice but to make their way back to the cottage. Fully disorientated, she had no way of knowing which way to turn but Ed strode ahead confidently. 'Come on, this way.

I'm not going to tell you how I know these roads like the back of my hand in the dark but, put it this way, Lord Harrington was missing quite a few pheasants and grouse from his stock when I was in my teenage years.'

Danny chuckled and, in the light of her torch, she glimpsed Leo's smile.

'We'll be back tomorrow, first thing,' Leo said, as if reassuring himself more than anything. 'Are you all in?'

'Yes,' they called together.

It felt forlorn to be back to the cottage and see the groups of exhausted searchers huddled in subdued conversation or sitting with slumped shoulders. And, as others set out to do what they could overnight, all of those returning vowed to be back at first light.

It felt heartening to find Alice Taylor in the cottage kitchen, brewing tea on the stove, handing out sandwiches and slices of cake that had been donated by villagers and farmers' wives.

'Ah, there you are at last, Lara,' Alice called from the stove. 'I need to tell you this right away – Nora gave me strict instructions when she came up here with her husband to collect the cot and all the baby's things. She's going to take care of baby Jamie for as long as required. She said tell Nurse Flynn there's absolutely no problem at all with that.'

'Ah, that's good to know... I was thinking I might need to take Jamie back with me to the surgery. Is there any news on Steven, the children's father?'

'He's in there, resting up,' Alice said quietly, pointing to the bedroom door. 'He was so distraught when he got here, I thought we'd have to call Doc Bingham to give him a shot of something. But, then Nora arrived, and she managed to calm him down, told him he was doing the right thing staying here and waiting, because the children might come back to the cottage, and they'd need to see him straight away.'

'Good thinking, Nora.' Lara sighed, her eyes snagging on the discarded toys on the truckle bed. It took her back to all those times she'd visited when Michael had taken the little ones in hand to play quietly. And that visit with Dr Bingham when they'd sat around the table drinking tea and eating cake. She thought of Freddy and Ava with chocolate round their mouths and needed to fight back tears.

'Are you alright?' Alice asked gently.

Lara cleared her throat. 'I will be when the children are found... It's just I can't bear to think of them out there in the cold.'

Alice nodded. 'Everyone is saying how good the eldest is, how he'll look after them. And I'm thinking he's very much like my two... they're stronger than you think, children. Especially those who've endured difficult circumstances at home.'

Lara nodded. 'Yes, of course. And, after what you went through up at the farm, I trust you on that.'

Alice reached into her apron pocket, pulled out a silver flask. When she spoke again, her voice was firm. 'Right, I need you to sit down at the table. You're having a cup of sweet tea with a good shot of whisky from this flask.'

Given the tone of Alice's voice, Lara knew she had no choice, and the hot drink came with a hefty slice of fruit cake. 'Eat,' Alice ordered.

When Leo came in through the cottage door and strode towards her, the ongoing disjointedness of everything struck her afresh. 'Do you want to help me finish this cake?' she asked him quietly, so Alice wouldn't hear.

'I'm more than happy to assist,' Leo said with a smile, taking the remains of the piece and eating it hungrily as Lara finished her cup of tea.

'I'm heading back to the village now with Ed and Danny, so we'll see you in the morning bright and early. Do you want a lift? I can pick you up from the surgery if you want.'

'Yes, that would be good. Then we'll all be here at the same time, and we can get out there straight away.'

He glanced down for a few seconds and, when he looked up, his eyes were shiny with tears. 'We'll find them, we have to find them tomorrow.'

Lara knew her voice might break if she spoke, so she reached out to give his arm a squeeze.

He offered a single nod. 'Right, I'll see you in the morning.' And the raw emotion in his voice made her want to stand up from the table and hug him.

Most of the searchers had dispersed by the time she emerged from the cottage and, as she gazed up to the night sky, the clouds parted and the moon appeared. 'You make sure to keep those children safe,' she whispered into the night air as the clouds closed in again and the moon was gone.

She was straight to the Austin and soon heading down towards the mill. It felt as if time had shrunk or expanded, her brain was far too weary to work it out exactly, but she felt disorientated. It was hard to believe it wasn't much longer than half a day since she'd set out from the surgery to check on Lydia. And, as she drove by the sawmill, she realised she hadn't even thought about the fires that had been set, or that incriminating cigarette stub Inspector Stirling had shown her earlier. None of it seemed to matter anymore, it had all been overshadowed by the missing children.

Dr Bingham's car was parked out front at the surgery, which

was highly unusual. And, when she walked through to the kitchen, she found him alone at the table quietly drinking a glass of whisky, the bottle at his elbow. He glanced up, his eyes heavy, bloodshot, and when he spoke his voice sounded weary. 'I haven't heard the mill siren go off, so I'm assuming there weren't any last-minute breakthroughs regarding the whereabouts of the children.'

'No, nothing yet. But, we'll be back out tomorrow.'

He sighed heavily, slowly shook his head. 'This is terrible, I can't bear the thought of those little ones out there alone. What if they haven't found shelter? The girl is tiny, she won't do well in those conditions.'

For the first time since she'd arrived at the surgery, Lara saw Bingham's vulnerability on full display and instinctively she walked to the head of the table and placed a hand on his shoulder. 'My gut instinct is that they are alright. I know Michael, he's an old soul and a sensible lad... he'll make sure the little ones are safe.'

Bingham emitted a low groan. 'I hope to God you're right, Nurse Flynn.' Then he took hold of the whisky bottle, glanced to her. 'Fancy a tot of single malt?'

'No, thank you, I've already had a shot in my tea at the cottage...' She waited while he poured himself another measure, then she asked, 'So what's the news on Lydia?'

He was slowly shaking his head. 'It isn't good, I'm afraid. There's already talk of her going to an asylum.'

Lara's heart jolted; she'd briefly visited the female wing of a large mental hospital in Liverpool as part of her training. It had left an unfavourable lasting impression of unkempt patients roaming the corridors and bloodcurdling screams from behind closed doors as horrendous treatments were carried out. Despite having concerns about Lydia's safety as a mother, she dreaded the thought of her ending up somewhere like that.

'Are they sure that's what she needs? Before what happened today, she seemed like a mother who was struggling with her mood and maybe just needed more support.'

Bingham heaved a sigh. 'Well, given there's evidence to suggest she was on the verge of poisoning her children, there's probably no question that's where she'll end up. And all I can do is try to swing the decision towards her being admitted to a smaller hospital, close to home, like the one just beyond Ridgetown.'

Lara was nodding now. 'That makes sense, and it'll be easier for Steven to visit.'

Bingham sucked in a sharp breath. 'Well, almost certainly she will receive a diagnosis of puerperal psychosis, so she will be fully isolated without any family visiting.'

Lara gasped. 'Really?'

'Yes, I'm afraid so. And, in addition, they'll administer a cocktail of drugs, subject her to cold baths and goodness knows what else. So it's going to be a long haul for Lydia.'

Lara couldn't form a response for a few moments, she hadn't imagined the consequences of the diagnosis would be so drastic.

At the rumble of feet on the stairs, then brisk steps in the tiled hallway, Marion appeared. 'Any news about the children?'

Lara slowly shook her head. 'Sorry. But, we're going back out at first light. Leo's picking me up in the van with Ed and Danny.'

'Aaargh,' Marion groaned with exasperation, 'I wish I could join you... if I had a strong enough flashlight I'd be out there now.'

Bingham called from the head of the table. 'Most of the village and surrounding district will be out there tomorrow.

And, I know it's hard not to be able to join in, but we still have our other patients to look after.'

'Yes, I know that, and you're right.' Marion sighed.

Bingham glanced to Lara then. 'Do you have any concerns you want to express? After all, Lydia Lennox is your case.'

'Yes, I think there are a few things, but top of the list for me right now is that I can't help but feel responsible. Lydia was my patient, and my gut feeling told me she wasn't doing well. I should have clicked much sooner she was heading towards a breakdown. I wish now I'd flagged up my concerns earlier and much more strongly.'

'Stop right there,' Bingham said firmly, 'I'm the senior physician and you reported all your concerns in a timely fashion. The buck stops with me, end of story.'

'Yes, but I should have shouted louder.'

'No,' he said simply, 'and if you burden yourself with this, Nurse Flynn, I just might lose my own mind.'

Lara pressed her lips together, glanced to Marion.

'Dr Bingham's right, Lara. He's in charge and all you or I can do is report back to him and flag our concerns.'

Bingham topped up his whisky. 'Listen to your colleague, Nurse Flynn... and don't you dare even think of taking any of this on yourself. If there's blame to bear, I will bear it. You still have a great deal of work to do with that family and when those children are found, they will be your patients because you're the one who knows them best. I've worked here for more decades than I care to remember, and I'm devastated by what's happened. But, as head of the team, it's my duty to take full responsibility and, if there is a police enquiry, I'll meet it head on. The nature of our work is ever evolving, we must move forward. If you stay with us at this surgery, there are bound to be other troubling incidents we'll have to deal with. So, we need to stay strong, Nurse Flynn, and we'll all work together as a team.'

He reached for his whisky then, and took a good slug.

When he spoke again his voice was thick with emotion. 'We show our dedication in the way we hold fast and judiciously apply our medical knowledge. We show our love by the manner in which we care for our patients.'

He drained his glass, placed it on the table with a firm clunk. Then he stood up and looked Lara in the eye. 'Take heed, Nurse Flynn. And leave the weight of this with me... I've lived through many triumphs and disasters; I was made to carry responsibility.'

Lara felt drained of every scrap of energy now and, when her voice came, it was barely above a whisper. 'Thank you, Doctor Bingham.'

Mrs Hewitt walked in through the door then, and as soon as she saw Lara she pulled a white handkerchief from her pocket and started dabbing at her eyes. 'I've had so many calls from folk asking if they can help to find the children or bringing food to the door for the search party. It's all been a bit overwhelming. But it just goes to show what close ties we have in the village.' She walked to the kitchen cupboard then, pulled out the sherry bottle and a large glass.

She glanced up the table to Lara, where she still stood next to Bingham, then down to Marion. 'Either of you want to join me?'

'Yes, please, Mrs H,' Marion said.

'Not for me,' Lara replied, 'I think it would knock me out completely.'

'I'll have a glass,' Angus called as he bustled in through the kitchen door. 'It's been quite something in the pub tonight with the strength of feeling over those missing children. I've witnessed grown men, real tough guys, crying into their beer.'

'You're right, Angus. It is quite something,' Mrs Hewitt said, her hand wobbling as she poured her sherry. Then, even before she took her first mouthful, she began to sob and Angus walked around the table to put an arm around her shoulders.

26

Riding up front in Leo's van, squashed up against a pile of leather halters smelling of cow dung, Lara felt the urgency of their mission. All she could focus on was getting back to the cottage and being able to continue the search. Ed and Danny had both fallen silent after their initial jocular response to the mess of veterinary equipment and smelly pile of blankets covered in animal hair in the back of the van.

'You alright, Nurse Flynn? Are you sitting comfortably amid the stink of animals and manure?' Leo said with a wry smile, a flash of his usual self that lifted her spirits.

'Yes, just a bit tired, like the rest of us,' she replied, noting the grey smudges of exhaustion beneath his dark eyes.

She'd tossed and turned last night, unable to settle and with the voices out on the street in the early hours and the opening and closing of cottage doors, she'd realised that half the village had been the same. Late last night, just before her and Marion had headed to bed, there'd been a knock at the door. It had been Miss Frobisher, the retired schoolmistress, in tears about the missing children. They'd brought her inside, shivering in her nightie beneath a thick overcoat and fur hat. 'I won't keep you long,' she'd said, 'but I just wanted to see you especially, Nurse Flynn, to wish you luck with the search tomorrow. I don't know the children, I believe the eldest, Michael, should have been in school but he was needed at home. But I just wanted to tell you about the child we had go missing thirty years ago... a bonny little girl with blonde hair, full of personality. We found her after two days huddled in a barn... she'd run away because she feared sitting the summer test at school. We had the search party out, just like now, and we were at the point of thinking we weren't going to find her when we did.'

'Phew, I'm glad she was found,' Marion had said, then she'd put an arm around Miss Frobisher's shoulders, thanked her for the encouraging story, but gently insisted she go straight back home to bed.

'I don't think I'll sleep at all until the children are found, but I have a comfy chair next to the fire and I'll be dozing off with the cat on my knee.'

Exhausted as she was, Lara had smiled, thanked Miss Frobisher and then Marion had offered to escort the elderly schoolmistress back to her cottage.

Leo's van lurched into a deep pothole and shook Lara back to the present. She felt groggy, as if she'd been startled awake.

'Steady on there, Nurse Flynn. I feel like I'm transporting a feisty thoroughbred horse,' Leo offered, scraping the gears as the van lurched and bumped along.

Despite her anxiety, his analogy made her smile and when Ed called from the back, 'Does that make me and Dan a couple of carthorses?'

Leo threw back to them, 'Yeah, a couple of broken down knackered old carthorses at best.'

The two men in the back were chuckling and punching each

other and it felt as if they enjoyed a moment of respite before they fell silent again. Then, once they were driving up past the mill pond, a shiver ran through her, knowing they were almost at the cottage. Less than twenty-four hours had gone by since she'd driven up here to find Lydia and the baby alone in the house and it still felt raw. Sensing her disquiet, Leo reached out and gave her arm a gentle squeeze. 'It's going to be alright; we'll find them today.'

She drew a shaky breath. 'Yes, we have to stay positive.'

As soon as Leo pulled up near the cottage, she jumped out to join the huddle of local people waiting to continue the search. It felt heartening to have a clear sky, but the weather could change rapidly out here, so she'd made sure to wear woollen trousers and a thick knitted jumper and she had a woolly scarf and macintosh in the haversack containing her medical supplies. She hoped she'd have enough stamina to search all day if need be and, even though she hadn't felt hungry at breakfast, Mrs Hewitt had made her eat the biggest breakfast ever and she'd pushed some biscuits and a bag of sweets into her pockets. So, with the practicalities taken care of, she was itching to get going. And, as she glanced around the search party, she sensed that edge, that ripple of nervous energy matching her own. When a police officer stood up to offer a short address, she felt her breath catch with anticipation and then they were ready to go. And, briefly, just before the groups were about to move away, Steven appeared at the cottage door, his face ashen. 'I'm coming out with you today,' he said, then staggered, and a young policeman grabbed hold to steady him. 'I just want to thank you all so much... for helping me search for my children.'

Ed released a held breath and Danny had tears shining in his eyes, as fathers they clearly understood the horror Steven was going through. Leo cleared his throat. 'Right, you lot. We've got a full day ahead of us and that should be more than enough time for us to cover the ground we missed yesterday and maybe go back over some key places. So, Ed, you lead the way, and we'll follow.'

Ed pressed his lips in a firm line, and they got back to their task. It felt good to be moving, standing still was far too agitating for Lara as her mind constantly flashed back over snapshots of the children – Michael with little Ava on his knee and Freddy laughing, full of mischief. She groaned out loud then and Leo shot her a concerned glance. 'Sorry,' she said, 'I can't get the Lennox children out of my head.'

He reached out then, pulling her close as they walked on. 'We'll find them today, I promise we will. Right.'

'Right,' she croaked.

Then he changed the subject. 'You're a good walker, Nurse Flynn, so I'm thinking that one day when the better weather comes you could come with me up to the fells. It gives a sense of perspective looking down from on high and the view from up there is incredible. What do you think?'

'I think that would be an excellent idea... Just let me know when you're going, and I'll see how I'm fixed.'

'Excellent,' he said, unlinking her arm then and dropping back to walk with Ed and Danny.

For some reason, thoughts of fell walking freed her up and in moments her head was whirring with something so obvious she felt astonished she hadn't realised it earlier. She stopped dead in her tracks, turning to the three men. 'I need to say out loud some thoughts I've just been having... I know these children and I'm aware of how careful and caring the eldest boy, Michael, is. So, I've been trying to think like he would. For a start, he wouldn't take his younger siblings out into open country where they'd be exposed to the elements. And, given he'd have to carry little Ava most of the way because she's a toddler, and there's Freddy who's only three, he will have carefully chosen somewhere to hide, and it will be a sheltered place not too far from the cottage. All the obvious barns and outbuildings will have already been searched, but if there's some other place in reasonable walking distance that's well hidden, I think there's a good chance that's where they'll be.'

'Good thinking, Nurse Flynn,' Ed called, while Leo and Danny were still mulling over what she'd just said. But then Ed sighed. 'I just wish I could say, yes, I know the exact spot. But nothing comes to mind. I'll keep going over it, though, something might trigger.'

As they clambered in turn over a wooden stile, Lara's eyes scanned the patchwork of fields divided by drystone walls and wire netting. There was nothing to see beyond a few scraggy sheep, an expanse of dried-up grass and some stunted trees with gnarled branches. At this time of year, the landscape was inhospitable, and it made her chest tighten with more anxiety. Then a blackbird began to chatter in a holly bush, and it gave her enough of a boost to feel hope and urged her on. 'There must be a shelter of some kind out here, maybe we need to walk closer to the fells.'

'Aye, let's do that,' Ed called back to her, 'come on, I know the way.'

They trudged for what felt like miles, and they were walking over new ground now, but it was taking them back closer to the Lennoxes' cottage. When her boot slipped into a boggy rut, she felt her ankle twist and she fell to the ground.

'You alright?' Leo called, already hauling her up.

She stamped her foot, waggled her ankle. 'Ouch, it's a bit tender, but nothing broken. So, I can crack on. No need for us to stop.'

He tipped his head to one side. 'Well, it makes sense to take a break anyway. We've been walking for hours, and it'll perk us up if we have a bite to eat and a nip of brandy from my flask.'

'Alright, but no more than ten minutes,' she urged, glancing to a pile of loose stone in the corner of the field. 'Let's go and sit over there.'

'Yep,' he said, then shouted to Ed and Danny and gestured to the stones. 'Just a short break, lads. Over here.'

As they passed the brandy flask around, she shared Mrs Hewitt's biscuits and sweets. And, as Ed and Leo sprawled out on the stones smoking cigarettes, Danny just sat and stared up to sky. At the distinctive cry of a lapwing, she glanced to the next field to see a group of the birds rising and swirling in the air. That's when her eye caught what looked like more stones and she stood up and laughingly said, 'Well, now we've had our rest, we should at least be able to make it over there to the next pile of stones.'

Ed lifted his head, glanced, then grinned. 'Might be a step too far for me until I've had another ciggy.'

Then he cried out, shot bolt upright, and he was on his feet. 'What the…! I know what those stones are, why the heck didn't I remember it before?'

'What?' she asked urgently, but he was still peering into the near distance.

He turned to her then, his eyes wide. 'I heard of this place back in the day… It's a shepherd's hut and it's well hidden in a dip so, unless you know it's there, you miss it. If I was hiding out, that's exactly the place I'd choose.'

Lara felt her stomach clench. 'Come on, let's go,' she called, up on her feet, already running.

With her heart hammering against her ribs, she crossed the field then scrambled over a drystone wall, with the men following. As they neared the hut, she noted the low roof was further obscured by gorse bushes. She raised a hand to bring the group to a halt. 'If the children are in there, I think it's best if I approach alone. They're bound to be frightened given they're hiding out, but it will probably help that they know me.'

'Most definitely,' Leo offered, and the other two nodded.

So, as Ed struck a match to light up a smoke, she walked quietly over the remaining distance then down into the dip. The door to the hut was firmly closed and there was just one tiny window to the side. She steadied her breath, thought through the best approach, then she called, 'Michael, this is Nurse Flynn. Are you in there?'

There was nothing to hear bar the cry of the lapwings as they circled overhead. But, somehow, the silence felt different, and she could sense the children were in the hut.

She walked closer, calling to them again. 'There's no need to be afraid. You've done nothing wrong. It's just that I promised your dad I'd find you.'

Still nothing.

Then she caught the tiniest noise, not much more than a squeak, but it made her heart jump. In seconds, the noise blossomed into the full-blown angry cry of a small child.

Then the door shot open.

And in a split second of pure joy, Freddy ran through the door, straight towards her. His face was grubby, his nose was running, but he threw himself at her with some energy.

'Hello there,' she cried, holding back tears as she gathered him against her. Feeling how cold he was as he sobbed and snuffled and tried to speak.

Leo, Ed and Danny were straight there, and she passed Freddy over to Ed then walked to the hut door.

'It's alright, Michael, it's Nurse Flynn and I'm here to help you. You're not in any trouble.'

She heard a ragged sob then and her heart twisted as Michael emerged from the hut in his knitted hat and gloves with little Ava in his arms. 'She's not moving, Nurse Flynn. She can't open her eyes.'

Lara forced a smile, but her heart had already twisted painfully tight. 'Alright then, give her to me, please, Michael. I'll be able to take care of her.'

He gulped, nodding, as she took Ava's limp body.

Gesturing then for Leo to take charge of Michael, she whipped off the toddler's thick coat and knelt with her on the damp grass. Ava's tiny body felt limp as she laid the little girl across her knee. Her face was white, her lips tinged with dark blue. The little girl had stopped breathing. Immediately, Lara bent forward, gave a gentle kiss of life. Still nothing. She steeled herself, tried one breath after another in quick succession. Then, with shaking hands, she felt for a carotid pulse in the girl's neck. 'She has a pulse, but it's weak!' she shouted.

Then she tried another kiss of life and felt despair at the coldness and pallor of the child's skin. She sat her up, rubbing her back as if she were a newborn struggling to breathe. Leo was there with her now as Ed and Danny took charge of Michael and Freddy and began to walk them away.

'She looks like a newborn lamb that's struggling to breathe. Give her to me,' Leo urged. He stood up with the child then, laid her across his arm and rubbed her back. Lara had her coat off now, laid out on the ground. He placed the child down, blew a couple of breaths mouth to mouth then rubbed at her again and turned her onto her side.

'Come on, Ava, come on,' Lara growled, fighting to hold back a spiral of despair. Then she placed two fingers against the child's neck again. 'She still has a pulse, let's just keep going.' She turned the little girl onto her back, tipped her head back and tried another kiss of life. Making sure she saw the rise and fall of her tiny chest.

Time seemed to stretch out and her heart tightened with despair. Then, in the split second before she tried another breath, Ava coughed quietly, then spluttered. Lara scooped her up from the ground, cradled her, rubbed her back, then spoke gently to her. Leo had stripped off his woolly jumper and it was still warm, so she swaddled the child in it. 'We need to get her back to the cottage and down to the surgery as fast as we can,' she called to Ed.

'I know the way over the fields,' he shouted. 'It's not as far as you'd think.'

They set off at a rapid pace. Ed and Danny almost running, taking turns to carry Freddy. Leo following with Ava cradled against his body as Lara ran at the rear, holding Michael's hand. The older boy was silent, wide-eyed with shock. 'Don't worry, Ava's going to be fine,' she told him, but he didn't seem able to take it in.

Then he asked, 'Are Mum and Jamie dead?' and the enormity of that question struck right through.

'No, Jamie is safe with Nora at the farm and your mum has been taken to be looked after at the hospital.'

He gasped out a breath, muttered, 'Good, that's good.'

As soon as they reached the cottage, Ed burst in through the door with Freddy, then Leo went straight to the truckle bed with Ava. Two young police officers were there, wide-eyed and visibly moved. 'Their father's still out with the search party; shall we try and find him?'

Lara took control. 'No, it might take ages to do that... one of you go down to the mill and ask them to sound the siren, so everyone, including Steven, will know that the children have been found. And the other put the kettle on, so we can have a bowl of warm water. And milk, warm some milk and put sugar in it. Oh, and we need someone to radio in and pass on a message to Ingleside surgery – tell them the children are found, they're safe, and will be arriving with Nurse Flynn and their father soon.'

The police officers set to as she sat cradling Ava, glad of the gentle rasp of the child's breath and the squirm of her body. Ed and Danny had taken charge of the two boys, but Michael still looked stricken and he hovered close to his baby sister as Lara sponged her face with warm water. Then she began to spoon some sweetened milk into her, and the little girl took it greedily. 'You take her now, Michael,' she said gently, needing him to physically feel his baby sister was rousing and knowing it would help Ava to know her older brother was there.

It wasn't long before they heard the noise of the siren at the sawmill and in due course the search parties began to return. The young police officer had been instructed to keep the returning locals at bay, until Steven had been reunited with the children. And, when he staggered in through the door, the reunion of the father with his children was one of those moments Lara had experienced only a few times during her nursing career. Steven clutched his chest then sank to his knees to pull the boys close, one in each arm. 'Is Ava going to be alright?' he croaked, swiping tears from his eyes as he gazed up to Lara as she rocked the little girl side to side.

'Yes. She was very cold when we found her, and she needed sweetened milk. But she's rallying now and, as soon as we get to Ingleside surgery, we'll have her checked over by Dr Bingham.'

'Righto.' Steven gulped as he struggled up to standing with

Freddy clinging to his leg while Michael stood quietly to the side.

Lara stepped towards him then and handed Ava over. 'Speak to her, Steven, she'll rally once she hears your voice.'

As Steven murmured Ava's name, his voice broke, and he began to cry as he stood rocking his little girl. Ava blinked open her eyes, reaching up a tiny hand to his face. 'Dada,' she said.

Instantly Michael called out, 'Dada, she said Dada. That's the first time.'

Steven gulped. 'Yes, Ava, I'm here.' Tears streaming down his cheeks.

Ed, Danny and then Leo came to pat Steven on the back and each of them stroked Ava's chubby cheeks and said a few words.

Leo came to Lara then. 'We'll be off now,' he said, swiping at his eyes with the heel of his hand. 'And we'll probably be straight to the Fleece for a pint.'

'That's alright, you go,' she said with a smile. Then, without even thinking, she pulled him into an embrace and murmured a thank you. He smelt of clean sweat and tobacco, she could feel his warm breath, and right then she felt something shift, vibrating between them like a plucked string. She heard his breath catch and the way he looked at her when she stepped back made her skin prickle. Given all the heightened tension of the last two days, she tried to brush it off as something ordinary, but she knew, deep down, it was more than that. She broke his gaze then, glanced to the other two men, hugged them as well and said thank you.

Ed and Danny nodded, then they were walking towards the door as Leo still stood gazing at her. Then he cleared his throat, said his goodbyes and he was catching up to Ed and Danny as they went out of the door together.

The room felt quiet and empty once her team had gone and

she had to make an effort to think through what she needed to do next.

'I'll take you down to Ingleside surgery in the police car,' the young constable offered, indicating for her and Steven and the children to exit.

'Right, yes. Good thinking,' she replied, a little too loudly as she began to walk towards the door. She realised then with a punch to the gut that the two youngest children didn't know their mother had been admitted to hospital. She'd speak to Steven quietly about how to break the news when the time came.

Quickly she exited the cottage and clambered into the front seat of the police car. Steven was in the back with Ava on his knee and his arm around Freddy, while Michael, still ashen faced, sat quietly at Steven's other side, gazing out of the window. As the police officer slipped nimbly into the driver's seat and offered a wide-eyed glance to his precious passengers in the back, she sensed his glow of satisfaction as he skilfully reversed, turned, then began the journey to Ingleside.

And, as they passed by the sawmill, the men who'd joined the search were standing in line in their work clothes, clapping and cheering as the police car drove slowly by. It felt blissful, but it also made her cry, and she knew she'd remember this moment forever.

27

Mrs Hewitt was right there, waiting at the surgery door, and the instant the police car pulled up she was helping Steven to clamber out with little Ava cradled against him, then Freddy came next as Michael pushed open the car door at his side and scrambled out. Michael stood ashen-faced, a deep frown between his brows, and Lara felt her heart squeeze painfully tight as she recognised the enormity of the decision he'd had to make to flee with the little ones. What he must have gone through in the moment he'd realised his mother was about to poison the whole family was unthinkable. He'd done the right thing, but it had been a drastic decision, especially for a child. She could only imagine how it must have felt during the night in that dark, cold shepherd's hut as he tried to console the little ones. And then, the next day, seeing Ava so poorly. She wondered why he hadn't gone straight down to Nora at the farm, but maybe he was too scared his mother would run after them, and of course there would be fear and shame knowing what Lydia had attempted. There was a great deal to unpack and, of course, the police would be involved, so right now the focus had to be on getting the children warm and fed and checked over by Dr Bingham. This was a complex situation – and she was glad the two little ones were too young to understand, but for Michael this was potentially earth-shattering.

The young police officer came to her then. 'I'll get off now, but if you need anything else at all, just ring Ridgetown police station.'

'We will, thank you. You've done good work here today.'

He offered a smile then slipped back into his car and drove away.

Lara felt as if she were coming back down to earth and wasn't quite sure what to do with herself. But, the moment she saw Michael gazing to her with a grief-stricken expression, she walked straight to him, put an arm around his shoulders and pulled him close. 'You did what you had to do, Michael. You couldn't have left the little ones in the cottage, it wasn't safe.'

He gazed up to her then, fresh tears shining in his eyes and, when he spoke, his voice broke on a sob. 'I had to protect them. I didn't want them to die like my other sister and brother did when I was little.'

'No, of course you didn't... and that's so sad what happened to your siblings.'

He swallowed hard, nodded, and she pulled him close to her then with both arms, holding onto the big-hearted, brave little boy who'd had to grow up way too fast.

She felt him relax a little then, but, when Dr Bingham came out of the surgery and walked towards them, she felt the boy shudder. She whispered to him, 'I know the doctor looks fierce, but I can assure you he is one of the kindest men in the world.' And, in moments, the senior doctor was right there, speaking gently to the boy, holding out a hand to him. 'Come on, young fella. Let's get you a hot drink and a piece of cake.'

Michael glanced to her, and she nodded. Then, as Bingham led the boy away, he shot a glance over his shoulder that was so full of compassion it brought tears to her eyes.

Mrs Hewitt was fully organised in the kitchen, and she'd stoked up the Aga to make it very cosy. Already Steven and little Freddy were looking comfortable and even Michael had relaxed a little as he sat squeezed in at the head of the table beside Dr Bingham. She had to fight to hold back tears of relief as she lowered herself onto a stool at the end of the table. Then, as Marion bustled into the kitchen between clinic patients, she could barely speak at seeing Steven and the children. And when her gaze snagged on Ava, who was now sitting on Mrs Hewitt's knee being fed small pieces of jam sponge, Lara saw Marion's face blanch and she drew back, her voice choked with emotion as she said, 'It's wonderful to see you all here safe and sound...' Then all too quickly she was gone, out of the kitchen and back to the clinic.

At the jangle of the telephone, Mrs Hewitt handed Ava over to Dr Bingham and squeezed around the table to answer it. Lara kept half an ear tuned to the housekeeper's voice, readying herself to go out on an emergency call if need be, but there seemed more surprise in her tone than anything. She heard a clunk as the telephone receiver was placed down on the hall table, then Mrs Hewitt appeared at the kitchen door to call across the table to Steven. 'I've got Celia Dunderdale from Brook House on the telephone. I don't know if you've heard of her at all, but she's a kindly, elderly spinster. Well, she's aware you're here at the surgery with the children and she's offered you the use of her house until you're ready to return to Foxglove Cottage or find new accommodation. How do you feel about that?'

Steven blanched a little, tried to speak, but the words wouldn't come. He looked shocked, and it felt as if he'd only just realised the cottage was potentially a crime scene and Michael had left there in fear for his own and his siblings' lives. Lara saw his turmoil and the depth of his exhaustion, and she rose from her seat to put an arm around his shoulders. 'It's a lovely house, there'll be plenty of space for you and the children until you get yourselves sorted.'

He gulped, nodded, then he croaked, 'It's just so kind, isn't it...? After the way this all happened...'

'We look after each other here, Steven,' Mrs Hewitt called to him. 'And you might be relatively new, but, after what's happened, we'll put a protective arm around you and your children.'

He cleared his throat, nodded. But he looked broken.

'I think it's a good idea to move to another house,' Michael piped up quietly from the head of the table.

'Yes, Michael, I agree,' Dr Bingham offered.

Steven cleared his throat, nodded, and Mrs Hewitt went back to the telephone to give Miss Dunderdale the news.

Later, after the children had been checked over by Dr Bingham and passed as fit enough not to need hospital admission, Mrs Hewitt had telephoned Miss Dunderdale numerous times regarding arrangements for the family. That's when other villagers began to arrive with gifts of food, toys and children's clothing. Miss Frobisher was the first to come and she handed Steven a cash donation. And, when she spoke to the children, Lara had never heard the gentle tone of voice she used or seen her smile so warmly. Mrs Hewitt kept many other villagers at bay, otherwise it would have been too overwhelming for Steven and the children, but the scale of generosity was life-affirming. And when Alice Taylor bustled in through the back door with Lucy and Robin in tow and a basket full of freshly baked bread over her arm, she was full of emotion as she saw the Lennox children surrounded by teddy bears and building blocks.

'We like it here, we're moving to your village,' Freddy said out loud, and it seemed incredible to Lara to see how quickly the little lad had adjusted. Hopefully Ava wouldn't remember any of this, but Michael would bear the brunt of it, and she'd keep a special eye on him because of that.

It felt too quiet in the kitchen once the family had left in Bingham's car and, as she helped Mrs Hewitt clear the table and put the chairs in their usual order, she felt exhaustion hit her.

'It'll just be sandwiches for tea,' the housekeeper said. 'But we've got Alice's fresh bread and plenty of meat and cheese. And I've got a big rice pudding in the oven as well, your favourite, Lara.'

'Yes indeed, the best in the world, Mrs H.'

Lara helped reset the table and, as soon as Angus and Marion were back in the kitchen, Mrs Hewitt laid out the sandwiches. 'There's no point waiting for Dr Bingham, we've no idea how long he'll be at Brook House. Oh, and I saw Betty Cronshaw, Ed's mother, getting into the car with him – she's a generous soul and a good organiser and she's volunteered to help with the children. But, my goodness can she talk... so it might be midnight before Dr Bingham's home.'

'Ah, yes, Betty Cronshaw,' Angus mused. 'She was one of the first patients I saw in clinic. She'd only come in with something minor, can't remember what it was, but she ended up talking through at least three other potential diagnoses. I was miles behind with the appointments by the time I got her out through the door. But she was so pleasant, such a good sort.'

'Yes, she is, for sure,' Mrs Hewitt added. 'And I know they say it's not good to speak ill of the dead, but that husband of hers, he was a right so and so.'

Angus twisted his mouth. 'From what I've heard, you're spot on there, Mrs H.'

The housekeeper sighed then. 'It's such a shame when a kind soul like Betty ends up with someone like him.'

As Lara opened her mouth to comment, Marion glanced down to the floor and her face blanched sheet white.

'Whatever is it?' Lara called across the table.

Marion tried to speak but a broken sob escaped from her chest, then she stooped down to pick something up from the floor.

Lara jumped up, went straight there, to find her with a child's toy in her hand. It was a cloth rabbit with a pink button nose and floppy ears that must have been left behind by the Lennoxes.

Marion was staring at the toy.

'Whatever is it?' Lara asked gently.

Still holding the cloth rabbit, Marion gazed to Lara with unseeing eyes, and began to emit a deep, gut-wrenching groan.

'Please, Marion, you must tell us what it is!' Mrs Hewitt shouted.

Then Angus scraped back his chair, ran to grab hold of Marion and put an arm around her shoulders. 'What is it, are you in pain?'

'No, not physical pain,' Marion sobbed, then she began to wail. 'I'm broken, my heart is broken.'

Lara spoke gently but firmly. 'Come on, Marion, let's get you up from this chair and into the sitting room.'

Marion gulped in air, the toy rabbit still clutched in her hand, as Lara took one side and Mrs Hewitt the other. They guided her, still sobbing, through to the front room.

Once they had her down on a chair, she sat staring into space, her right hand still clutching the toy rabbit.

'I'll bring you both a glass of sherry,' Mrs Hewitt offered gently, then she was gone.

Lara lowered herself into the armchair next to Marion's and sat quietly, waiting for her friend to start talking. She'd known there was something with Marion from her first week at the surgery when she'd seen her crying. And there'd been other things that had hinted at a past trauma that needed to be spoken out loud. It felt as if all of that had come to a head. And, once Mrs Hewitt had bobbed back with two big glasses of sherry and put them on a small table between the two chairs, she retreated to leave Lara and Marion alone.

Lara picked up her glass, took a good swig and it warmed her, made her feel more at ease.

Marion mirrored her then and took a big gulp of sherry. She began to cough and, as Lara got up to take the glass from her, her friend was crying again. Lara held on to her, knowing this was the beginning of a loosening up, a time for important things to be said out loud.

Seeing the toy still clutched in her friend's hand, she asked gently, 'What is it, Marion? With you and this bunny rabbit?'

Marion uttered a cross between a groan and a desperate laugh. 'Well, not exactly this rabbit, but one very much like it. We go back a long way,' she hiccupped, then pressed the toy against her cheek.

Lara slowed her breathing right down, then she took another sip of sherry. She didn't want to press her friend too hard, but if she didn't start talking soon, she'd be asking questions.

Then, after Marion had taken another slug of her drink, she placed the glass down with a firm clunk, cleared her throat and began to talk, quietly at first, her voice husky. 'So, Lara, you are the first person to hear this story, but I knew from those first few weeks of us working together that, if I was going to tell anyone, ever, it would be you... As you know, I trained in Edinburgh as a nurse, worked in the hospital, then got my District Nursing certificate. I headed back home then and came to work here. Your predecessor, Nancy Beecham, she was strict but straightforward and I learned a lot from her, and, once I had enough experience, I went back to Scotland. I'd fallen in love with the Highlands when I'd had a holiday there with some nurse friends, so I applied for a post in a town called Kingussie. I absolutely loved it, especially after I learned to ride a motorcycle. There was such freedom out there close to the mountains and I felt on top of the world. So, when I met a fine-looking fella, a gamekeeper who worked on one of the big estates, I was head over heels. The relationship was intense, and it romped along. We spent hours together in the cottage he tenanted, and it felt like heaven. Then, and I'm sure you've already guessed this... I got pregnant with his child. It didn't throw me; I wanted to have this man's baby but, when I gave him the news, he was horrified... And that's when he told me he already had a wife and three children in Glasgow...'

'Oh, Marion, I'm so sorry,' Lara breathed, reaching out to her.

Marion's mouth twisted when she tried to speak, and Lara gave her hand a squeeze. After a few moments, she emitted a low growl. 'I still can't believe how badly that man behaved. We'd never argued before, but he was blazing mad, and he started shouting and throwing things, he overturned the table with all the crockery on it. Naively, I thought it was just an initial reaction, and he'd come round. But he didn't and he cut me out of his life from that day on.'

Lara was shaking her head. 'I'm so sorry, that was so cruel.'

Marion dropped her head and, when she looked up, her eyes were bright, blazing. 'All the feelings I'd had for him vanished. It felt shocking how quickly it happened. I mean, who wants a mealy-mouthed excuse for a man anyway... But, of course, that left me with a baby on the way... I didn't want the child, so I exerted myself physically, drove like crazy on my motorbike, hoping I'd miscarry. Of course, it didn't happen, so once I got to a stage where I could no longer hide my belly, I had to leave the Highlands, move back to Edinburgh to a nursing home and use all my savings to pay for it. I didn't want the child, and I'd already decided to put him or her up for adoption. It was a horribly painful labour, and my baby girl was delivered with the cord wrapped twice around her neck. The midwife did her best, but the baby's shoulders got stuck and, by the time she was delivered, she was navy blue...' Marion's voice broke then. Lara squeezed her hand, waiting for her to continue. 'The midwife tried everything, but she couldn't revive my baby girl... I held her briefly, then she was taken away and I never saw her again.'

Marion sobbed and covered her face with both hands.

Lara stood up from her chair, murmuring a jumble of words as she tried to soothe her.

She gulped, then gazed up to Lara with tears streaming down her face. 'She was my daughter, my baby girl, and I didn't even give her a name.' Marion emitted a strange laugh then. 'She haunts me in dreams... she even haunts me in broad daylight – that day I had my accident on the motorcycle, it was her birthday. And, the more I tried to push her out of my head, the harder she came back at me... then bang, the world went blissfully black.'

Lara felt a dull throb of sadness thicken her throat and, when she spoke, her voice almost broke. 'Oh, Marion... I'm so sorry you've been struggling alone with this for such a long time.'

Marion gulped, began to shake her head. 'I feel so much lighter already.'

'Good, that's good... and you know what... It's not too late to give your baby girl a name. It doesn't matter how much time has gone by.'

Marion swallowed hard, nodding. 'Yes, you're right. I'll think it over and let you know. And she was beautiful... my baby girl, with her dark hair, and a tiny rosebud mouth...'

'Keep talking, Marion, tell me more.'

And, as she talked on, she continued to clutch the cloth rabbit as it all poured out.

When Marion was done, and Lara was able to leave her exhausted and resting in the armchair, she stepped out of the room and stood quietly for a moment in the corridor. All Marion had confided had put meat on the bones of what Lara had already imagined. And saying it out loud had been a huge milestone for her friend. It hadn't been easy to hear the story of the baby girl who had died, and seeing Marion in such turmoil had been hard to bear. The intimacy they shared made what was a routine part of her work with a patient a much more demanding experience, requiring her to hold back the deep sorrow she felt for her colleague. Out of the room now, she gulped back a sob, then pressed her lips together, determined to stay strong for Marion.

As she took her first steps down the tiled corridor, Mrs Hewitt bobbed out of the kitchen. 'Well?' she asked, both eyebrows raised.

Lara offered a wobbly smile. 'It's done, she's given me the whole story, but she'll probably need to speak again later when we're round the table together.'

Mrs Hewitt sighed out a breath. 'Good work, Nurse Flynn... Now let's get you a strong cup of tea with plenty of sugar.'

Later, when the three women were together at the kitchen table and Marion had told her story to Mrs Hewitt, Marion gazed across to Lara and said, 'You know what you mentioned earlier about it never being too late to name my baby girl? I've decided I want to call her Isla. It's a lovely Scottish name and I think it's derived from an island off the west coast... I'll go there one day, I'll ride up there on my motorbike.'

'What a lovely name.' Lara smiled. 'So now, when Isla's birthday comes around in the summer, let's set some time aside, maybe go out together on Gloria, mark the occasion in some way.'

'Yes, and not by crashing into a tree this time.'

'Exactly,' Lara breathed.

Then Mrs Hewitt dabbed at her eyes, topped up the sherry and raised her glass in a toast. 'Here's to Isla.'

'To Isla,' the three women called, clinking their glasses.

28

Time moved on quickly for Lara and, as she kept busy with her visits, a spell of cold, frosty weather arrived and there was talk of preparing for Christmas. And, one day, as she rode out to Ingleside Hall for her ongoing visits to Robert Thompson, she saw Philippa in the grounds riding her black horse. The young woman raised a hand in greeting and trotted over, the horse's breath steaming in the icy air. Leaning down from the saddle, she said, 'I just want you to know we've sorted that issue with the tenancy for Miss Alston. It took a while, but given Grace is doing such a fine job at the farm, it made absolute sense. I put the case very strongly to my father. He dug in his heels at first, until I pointed out that I'm the woman who is next in line to take over Ingleside Hall... So, why not give the farm tenancy to Grace?'

'Exactly,' Lara echoed, making herself smile. The result was what mattered, not the way it'd been brought about. But what Philippa had just said had come directly from the conversation with Dr Bingham at the surgery.

'Does Grace know?'

'Yes, I've just come from there. She seems very pleased.'

'Oh, that's good... And can I just ask after your friend who was injured in the accident, Mr Bowley. How is he doing? I know you said he was going for convalescence, but is he home yet?'

'Yes, did I not say...? He's making an excellent recovery. Still weepy at times over Quentin and he won't go anywhere near a motor car. But he's doing as well as he possibly can be.'

'Ah, that's so good to hear,' Lara breathed.

Philippa pulled on her reins and turned as if to trot away, but then halted, calling over her shoulder. 'Oh, and one more thing. I've just remembered I invited you and your nurse friend for afternoon tea at the hall. I'm just wondering if you should come for dinner one evening instead. It would be lovely to see you out of your uniforms and I'll also invite Leo, he's been doing such sterling work for me recently with the horses.'

'Yes, thank you,' Lara called after her, a little bemused by the invitation, especially with the mention of Leo, but at least it had seemed friendly. Maybe she had judged Miss Harrington too harshly.

Then, as she wheeled her bicycle over the remaining distance to the gamekeeper's cottage, she had to push heightened thoughts of Leo and Philippa out of her head as she focused on her next case. Knocking and entering the cottage, she found her patient on fine form. The cottage was clean and tidy and Robert's mate, Len, was in there supping a brew of tea. 'Did you see Miss Harrington on her horse?' Len asked with a wry smile.

'Yes, I did,' Lara offered as she began to unravel Robert's bandage and take down the dressing.

'I hope she didn't look down her nose at you like she does with me.'

'No, as a matter of fact, she was very pleasant.'

Len pursed his lips. 'Even so, Nurse Flynn, I'd steer clear of that one if I were you. She's a tricky mix of things, our Miss Harrington. She can be nice as pie one minute, then she'll nearly snap your head off. And that young vet needs to watch out as well or she'll eat him alive.' Len swigged the rest of his tea then and, with a grunt, he was up from his chair and washing the dregs down the sink.

'See you later, mate,' he called to Robert. 'And you as well, Nurse Flynn... We yokels are grateful for your good works out here.'

'Thank you very much,' she called after him, but she was still pondering what he'd said about Philippa.

'You alright, nurse?' Robert asked.

'Yes... just assessing the wound...' but as she was doing so, her brain was still ticking over what Len had said.

Then, even before she'd finished reapplying the bandage, her patient dropped his voice to speak confidentially. 'I'd take heed of what Len told you about Miss Harrington if I were you... because I don't trust her either. His lordship's a piece of sweet apple pie compared to that young lady and her mother.'

'I'll remember what you've said,' she said, tapping her forehead to show it had sunk in.

And, as she closed the door to the cottage behind her and walked to her bicycle, she began to wonder if she should have accepted Philippa's invitation to dinner after all. But then she thought of how excited Marion would be and knew she had no choice but to attend. Releasing a held breath as she wheeled her bicycle across the gravel drive, she felt the watery sun on her face and began to relax. Noting two stubborn autumn leaves still clinging to a branch, followed by a mass of red holly berries in the hedge, her thoughts turned to Christmas – her first one away from Liverpool. And, quite unexpectedly, she felt a little homesick for the city she'd grown up in and the close group of nurse friends she went carol singing with each year.

That feeling of 'missing' stayed with her as she worked through her morning list, and she needed to find a distraction. So, once she'd completed her visits, she called by Brook House to see Steven and the children. It felt glorious but rather strange to be tapping at the door knowing she'd be met by three excited children running straight at her. There would probably be no sign of Steven, he was often tucked away in the sitting room – still quietly working his way through things. He hadn't yet been granted permission by the asylum to visit Lydia. But the good news was that he'd been offered a job as a joiner at the sawmill – they needed his skills now the chair making side of the business was beginning to take off. And, in the new year, one of the worker's cottages in the same row as Danny Ryan's would become free and Steven and the children were first on the list for taking it.

As Lara tapped on Miss Dunderdale's door again and received no reply, she pushed it open and entered. Clearly no one had heard her because, as she walked down the corridor, she glanced through the door of the dining room to see Michael sitting quietly at the polished oak table strewn with paper, pencils and wax crayons. His brow furrowed as he worked on a drawing. Ava and Freddy were down on the carpet, amid many toys, including the wooden building blocks that had been brought from the cottage.

'Nurse Flynn,' Miss Dunderdale called as she pushed open the kitchen door. Still a little breathless, but remarkably her heart failure had improved since the family had moved in. Michael and Freddy ran out to her then, with little Ava toddling behind carrying a jingling cloth ball. 'Throw,' the little girl said, as Freddy excitedly chattered, and Michael quietly showed Lara the drawing of Brook House he was working on. Then he said,

'Guess what, Nurse Flynn? I'm going to start school after Christmas.'

Lara felt a bloom of pleasure deep in her chest and, as Michael stood there grinning, she felt so proud of him. 'That's such good news... and, from what I've heard, the new headmaster, Mr Armistead, is excellent.'

'Come on, children,' Miss Dunderdale called, clapping her hands. 'We need to let Nurse Flynn catch her breath and get a cup of tea.' Then, as Miss Dunderdale led the children back to the dining room, she called over her shoulder to Lara, 'Betty Cronshaw's in the kitchen, she'll provide you with tea and biscuits.'

Before Lara made it that far, the door to the small parlour up the corridor clicked open and Steven walked out with a newspaper in his hand. Instantly, he smiled and called down to her.

'How are you doing? Are you alright?' she asked.

He began to walk towards her. 'Yes, we're doing as well as we can be... and, as you can see, there's never a dull moment with the children.' He grinned then as Freddy came running at him. And, in one easy move, Steven picked up the little boy and began to tickle him. Freddy squealed with delight, then Steven mock-growled. 'And, as for you, little Freddy... I think we're going to put you in the cupboard under the stairs.'

'No!' Freddy giggled, and it felt as if this house had waited far too long to hear children at play.

Lara pushed open the kitchen door to find Betty washing up at the sink. She turned with a beaming smile. 'Hello there, Nurse Flynn... I've just brewed a pot of tea, and I've brought some ginger biscuits today – a new recipe – so I'll be with you in a second, just need to finish up here.'

Betty was soon sitting down at the Formica-topped table

and, as Lara poured the tea, the older woman leaned in to speak quietly. 'Have you heard the latest from the sawmill?'

'No, what?'

'Well, Ed told me they might have found out who set those fires you reported.'

'Go on,' she urged, 'what are they saying?'

'Well, as we all expected, Vic Taylor seems to have had a hand in it. But there's talk of another fella, one who drives a flashy red car who's been seen with Vic. Then again, there's some who're saying it's that prize-fighting uncle of Alice Taylor's. Apparently, he was in Preston prison in his younger days.'

Lara's chest tightened at the mention of Patrick and Vic, and she recalled the cigarette stub, Patrick's favourite brand, that Inspector Stirling had picked up at the mill. But then, Lord Harrington also smoked the same... and she couldn't imagine he would be involved. And Patrick, for all his faults, worked as a solicitor, so being a potential suspect in an arson attack at a sawmill miles away from Liverpool didn't make sense. Anyway, it had all gone quiet now apart from the occasional grumbling rumour among local folk, so Inspector Stirling hadn't been back to her about the cigarette stubs. And the idea that Uncle Josh might be involved also seemed ludicrous. Alright, maybe he'd got a bit carried away in a street fight many years ago and he'd served a short prison sentence. But, since that first day she'd met him at Marion's homecoming, she'd known he was a gentle giant. And, only the other day, she'd heard that there'd been a string of thefts and assaults in Ridgetown by a gang coming up from Preston, so maybe, if the police began looking into the fires again, they should bear that in mind.

'You alright, lovey?' Betty asked gently. 'Sorry, I didn't want to trouble you with gossip about the mill. And I shouldn't have mentioned that Vic Taylor after what he did to you.'

'Oh, well, it feels like water under the bridge now. And he's never bothered me again, not since he's been away from the village.'

Betty nodded. 'A good thing too... But it must still be hard for you, out here with us lot, miles away from where you were brought up.'

'Yes, sometimes it is. But I like it here,' she breathed, feeling her body relax.

She reached for one of Betty's ginger biscuits then and took a bite. 'Mmm, these are delicious,' she said, through a mouthful of crumbs.

It took ages to get out through the door of Brook House with saying her goodbyes to Betty, Miss Dunderdale and Steven. Then she had to hug and say a few words to each of the children in turn. Michael stood back at first, still quiet from his ordeal. He was showing signs of his old self, but the light hadn't fully come back into his eyes yet and his smiles were few and far between. Lara saw enough in him now, though, to feel sure he was recovering.

Once she'd clicked the door shut behind her, it felt quiet and peaceful out on the lane. And, as she set off back to the surgery, she cycled slowly so she could breathe the air, gaze out over the fields, and enjoy the ever-changing play of light and shade. She remembered then the fell walk Leo had promised her when they'd been out searching for the children. And when the better weather came in the spring, she'd remind him of it. She recalled something then that Leo had told her when they'd been close to the fells. He'd made a remark about how everyone should climb up high at least once a year so they could gaze down to where they'd come from and see the place differently. He claimed it was a good way of keeping perspective, making sure you stayed aware of the important things in life. She could see where he'd been coming from with that, and she still felt surprised at the unexpected philosophical side of the young vet.

She startled then at the loud chatter of birds from an open, muddy expanse of field as a group of lapwings took flight. Noisy and joyous they rose up to the sky. It had surprised her, but she felt boosted by the wonder of it all and, as she turned her face to the pale sun, she knew it would take a drastic happening to keep her from this place.

And, as she covered the rest of the distance to the surgery for lunch, she thought of the warm kitchen with Tiddles the cat stretched out in front of the Aga and all her team in their places around the table. Maybe Dr Bingham would be grumpy, Angus lively and mischievous, or quiet and focused, depending on his mood. Marion, of course, even at the worst of times, often had a delightful playfulness as she leaned across the table for a chat. And, as the twisting kaleidoscope of daily life at the surgery fell into place, Mrs Hewitt would catch Lara's eye, and they'd share a smile. And right then she'd feel the peace and love that was now hers to keep if she chose to do so.

* * *

MORE FROM KATE EASTHAM

The next book in this heartwarming saga series is available to order now here:

https://mybook.to/CountryNurse3BackAd

ACKNOWLEDGEMENTS

In this second book of the Country Nurse series I used a tragic story told many times by my grandmother, a farmer's wife, of a local mother in the village of Inglewhite who poisoned her children by mixing rat poison into the porridge. She often recited this while standing at the Rayburn, stirring the porridge pan, and then, once it was served into our bowls, she relaxed back in her chair with a cigarette, while we gingerly took our first spoonfuls. As part of my research, I checked out this harrowing account and found it had occurred in the 19th century. I was surprised, my grandmother's telling had felt so recent... but then, she was a good storyteller. So, I used the detail of the poisoning, set it alongside the single case of puerperal psychosis I encountered as a midwife in the 1980s, and Lydia Lennox's story was born.

Less daunting recollections took me back to autumn preparations for Guy Fawkes night at the farm, when the weather had turned much colder, the nights darker, and we excitedly collected wood for our annual bonfire. The firewood was often too wet and usually it was raining, so it was hard to light. But once the first flames caught, our joy surged.

Memories still warm my heart and make the writing of these books even more special. And given this Country Nurse series also draws on my early experiences of nursing in the days of Nightingale wards and starched caps and aprons, the spirit of the work and the nurses I worked with, also buoys me up. It feels good to write it out and channel my experience into Nurse Flynn's adventures.

Now, as I press on with the third book in the series, I'd like to thank my agent, Judith Murdoch, for her ongoing advice and support. And of course my lovely editor – Francesca Best – and the team at Boldwood for all that they do.

And, as ever, I want to say a special thank you to my family for their love and continuing support.

ABOUT THE AUTHOR

Kate Eastham is the author of heartbreaking wartime historical fiction. Before this, she was a trained nurse and midwife, and spent 20 years working in palliative care. During this time she had the privilege of listening to stories from patients of all ages and backgrounds, many of whom were veterans of the world wars.

Sign up to Kate Eastham's mailing list for news, competitions and updates on future books.

Follow Kate on social media:

𝕏 x.com/eastham_kate

ALSO BY KATE EASTHAM

Diary of a Country Nurse

A Fresh Start for the Country Nurse

Changing Seasons for the Country Nurse

Sixpence Stories

Introducing Sixpence Stories!

Discover page-turning historical novels from your favourite authors, meet new friends and be transported back in time.

Join our book club Facebook group

https://bit.ly/SixpenceGroup

Sign up to our newsletter

https://bit.ly/SixpenceNews

Boldwood

Boldwood Books is an award-winning fiction publishing company seeking out the best stories from around the world.

Find out more at www.boldwoodbooks.com

Join our reader community for brilliant books, competitions and offers!

Follow us
@BoldwoodBooks
@TheBoldBookClub

Sign up to our weekly deals newsletter

https://bit.ly/BoldwoodBNewsletter